LETHAL
NIGHTSHADE

THE NIGHTSHADE SAGA: BOOK THREE

LETHAL NIGHTSHADE

EVELYN
LEDERMAN

Paperback: ISBN-13: 978-0692746035
Paperback: ISBN-10: 069274603X

eBook: ISBN-13: 978-0996629874
eBook: ISBN-10: 0996629874

All characters and events in this book are fictitious. Any resemblance to actual persons living or dead is strictly coincidental.

Cover Design by Fiona Jayde Media
Interior Design by The Deliberate Page
Editing by Tina's Editing Services and Lori Garside Editing

TITLES BY EVELYN LEDERMAN

Worlds Apart Series

The Chameleon Soul Mate: Book One
The Crystal Telepath: Book Two
The Warrior Woman: Book Three
The Mind Control Telepath: Book Four

Nightshade Saga

Nightshade: Book One
Feral Nightshade: Book Two
Lethal Nightshade: Book Three

Zaratan Trilogy (Young Adult)

Selected

Magic, New Mexico Kindle World Novella

A Touch of Patience

ACKNOWLEDGEMENTS

Thanks to my content/line editor Tina for an outstanding content edit. This being the third book in the series, she kept me honest. She has a better memory than I do. I always respect her recommendations and feel I provide a better product for all my readers to enjoy.

Thanks to Lori and Tamara for getting the book ready to publish. Grammar and formatting are not my forte. I figure I am a great story-teller, but need help getting the words cleaned up and formatted. For those that know me, I am not the most patient person on this planet or any dimension.

My books would not be complete without an outstanding Fiona Jayde cover. She never ceases to amaze and delight me.

CHAPTER 1

THE NIGHTSHADE UNIVERSE

Cries of the hopeless woke Miranda from a fitful sleep. Another harvest was upon them. The creatures always came in the dead of night, a fact that was not surprising considering they were vampires.

The door to her bedroom opened and Miranda temporarily shielded her eyes from the light. Beatrice, her half-sister, ran into Miranda's open arms. Her sister was granted the ability to visit Miranda whenever she desired. They normally spent harvests huddled together; taking what little comfort they could get from each other, both of them exempt from the terror happening around them. Even knowing they were safe did not lessen their paralyzing fear.

"They just had a harvest," Beatrice cried. "We all should have been safe until the summer solstice."

Miranda could feel her sister tremble. There was nothing she could do to stop the outside horror from touching them, except hold Beatrice tighter.

Human breeding farms were plundered quarterly. Humans were raised to fulfill the needs of starving vampires in a world overpopulated by the creatures. This particular farm belonged to the Venture Hive and was reported to be the largest of its kind in this dimension.

People were either born and raised here, or fell from inter-dimensional portals and brought to the farm. Everyone's sole purpose was to reproduce and ultimately die feeding a vampire. Humans were good for little else in a vampire's eyes.

"It will be over soon," Miranda cooed. No other words came to her which would comfort the younger girl. They both had been through too many harvests to spin a hopeful tale of rescue by some fairy-tale hero.

"One day, I will be one of the poor souls they will be taking," Beatrice sobbed.

Both Miranda and Beatrice were safe from being selected to feed the voracious appetites of the Venture Hive's vampires. In Miranda's case, it was because she carried the gene abnormality that would allow her to breed with a vampire. She had a very different fate ahead of her. Miranda would ultimately be forced to mate with Yorik, the Venture Hive's master vampire. Miranda expected the vampire to claim her when she turned eighteen several months ago. Even with the horror taking place outside, the thought of Yorik touching her caused a chill to run down her spine.

Beatrice would be sixteen in two months, at which time her sister would be placed in the breeding program. She would be taken from the complex where the children were housed and moved into the women's quarters. Each month, when Beatrice was fertile, she would be forced to lie with a man. Males were rewarded based on how many children they sired. The females were forced to bear children with a doomed future and then separated from their offspring soon after the babies were weaned.

The vampire scientists logged every paring and birth. A male was viable as long as he did not impregnate too many women. Vampires were cautious not to allow close family members to reproduce, afraid it would impact the quality of the blood. Hemophilia was not uncommon if cousins bred. If a bleeder was born, both parents would be ripe for the next harvest. A female was safe from the harvests as long as she remained fertile. Each human in the complex wore a bracelet containing their genetic makeup.

"We will get you out before that happens." Miranda repeated the promise she made her half-sister on her fifteenth birthday. Beatrice's changing body was a constant reminder of what was in store for the girl if she stayed. Miranda had to act soon, or Beatrice would be taken and harmed physically and psychologically.

They planned to sneak out during the confusion of the next harvest and make their way to a settlement rumored to protect humans. Miranda had heard the lab technicians talking about a vampire named Lorenz and the environment he created for humans. Lorenz had entered into an arrangement with Yorik to protect his keep from vampire aggressors. She was not sure where the settlement was, but she was determined they would find it…somehow. Miranda hoped the unplanned harvest would not ruin her plans to slip Beatrice out before she turned sixteen.

Miranda looked around the sterile environment of her bedroom, searching for words to comfort her sister. The gene she carried had been identified when she was a baby. Upon its discovery, she was moved into the laboratory, both for her protection and to be studied. The children born of humans and vampires were half-lings. It was believed these children held the answer to vampires being able to once again walk in the light of day.

Rather than growing up with the other human children, she grew up in the lab. When she was older, she was given a room adjacent to the laboratory. The vampires taught her how to read and write to occupy her time. Through her education, she learned Beatrice was her half-sister. Miranda also learned her mother died giving birth to Beatrice. Curiosity also brought her the knowledge of when her biological father was harvested.

"The vampires always perform harvests on each solstice and equinox, even if they have off-scheduled collections," Miranda assured her. "Nothing will stop our plan to escape. The new lab technician enjoys telling stories about everything he has seen and done. I will keep milking him for information about Lorenz's settlement."

"One of the guards said they might move me early," Beatrice choked, "since they are below their quota of births. I do not like the way he looks at me and the terrible things he says. We may not be able to escape before a man forces himself on me. I do not want one of those men touching me. I cannot give birth to a child who will live and die for the sole purpose of providing a vampire blood."

Selected human males guarded the farm during daylight hours. They received their choice of women, the best food, and were safe from harvests. She also noticed the looks some of the guards gave Beatrice.

Miranda pushed back her sister's brown, wavy, long hair out of her face. It was so different from her straight, blond tresses. She had no memory of her mother and her father was just a number on a page. Where did she get her blue eyes? Beatrice's were brown.

The two women froze when they heard footsteps coming down the hall. Miranda gazed at the door and was relieved when she saw it was the new vampire lab technician. He always chatted with her. During normal harvests, the vampires who kept the genetic records told the collectors which humans to take. Miranda's heart raced at his presence. Was he here for Beatrice?

"You both need to leave this place," he said. "It is only a matter of time before Yorik claims you, and your sister forced into mating. I will help you escape to the settlement I told you about. Lorenz will welcome you both into his community."

Miranda was surprised by his presence. He talked with her all the time, but had never bothered to tell her his name. She never thought they developed the type of relationship where he would care enough about her to rescue them. The chaos of the unscheduled harvest would provide better cover for their escape than a routine one, but something did not feel right.

The vampire before her resembled the rest of his kind. Rotting flesh covered his skeleton. His cheeks were shallow, a reflection of his starvation. He wore a robe to cover most of his partially decomposed body.

It was as if time stood still as thoughts bombarded Miranda's mind. She was literally frozen in place, overwhelmed with the options her brain mulled over. In her short life, it was rare she had a decision to make. Certainly, not one of this magnitude.

"We should go," Beatrice whispered. Vampires had superb hearing, very little escaped their sensitive ears.

The vampire seemed agitated, concerned about time. He went into the hall to see if he was followed. Miranda knew her options and time were limited. A decision had to be made and fast.

"There is still time to escape on our own," Miranda responded. She spoke in a low voice, hoping the vampire nearby would not hear.

"I have run out of time," Beatrice whimpered. "With this harvest, there will be more pressure to produce offspring. They may even come for me tonight, after the collection has been completed."

Her sister was right. If they did not leave now, Beatrice's life could change dramatically for the worse. Miranda could not let that happen. She jumped out of bed and started to dress. All humans in the facility wore the same outfits. Miranda threw a white top and pair of pants at Beatrice, indicating she should put them on. The girls were both five-foot-five and roughly the same weight. They were both skinny because of the little food afforded to them.

Miranda had not considered taking a compassionate vampire with her, if such a creature existed. Assuredly, they stood a better chance making it to safety if they had a vampire to protect them outside the farm. It could take days, if not weeks, before they reached their final destination.

"Thank you for helping us," Miranda said, when the vampire returned. "I do not even know your name."

"I am called Tomas," the technician answered. "My mission is to rescue you. I am part of a society dedicated to preventing half-lings from being born by saving women like you. Lorenz will shelter you and make sure no other vampire ever touches you. He joined with a half-ling and understands such children should not suffer what his mate went through. Lorenz will protect you from Yorik."

Tomas's words about his mission did not ring true, but he had spent so much time talking to her about Lorenz and his settlement. This vampire had been the one who planted the idea in her head to seek sanctuary within the unique being's community when they finally escaped.

Once she left the safety of her rooms, there would be no going back. As far as Miranda could see, she had no other options before it was too late for Beatrice. She needed to have faith that Tomas was exactly what he said. Otherwise, she would be directly responsible for her and her sister's deaths. Miranda tore off the bracelet she had been forced to wear and followed Tomas out of the complex.

Sammuel's preternatural hearing picked up the cries of the harvest occurring at the human farm to the west. He had planned to go directly to his blood brother's settlement and not make any detours along the way. As it was, he was days late in responding to the call for assistance.

"Something must have happened," Patrice said. "It is weeks before the summer solstice. There must have been a great battle requiring the replacement of blood."

Patrice was one of the two women who traveled with him, both vampires. He had turned his one surviving daughter and his sister-in-law shortly after he was changed. As far as he knew, these two women were the only female vampires in existence. Women were not converted because of their ability to give birth to vessels that would feed their species.

She sat tall in the saddle. Her long black hair tamed by a band she wore around her head. Patrice always wore black leather tops, pants, and boots. His daughter wore a hat with a wide brim to keep the night bugs out of her eyes.

It was unusual for a vampire to wear a hat, since they never ventured into direct sunlight during the day. Any exposure to the sun's rays killed a vampire. Settlements had purple filters protecting them, but vampires were still weakened by the filtered rays. Occasionally, he left the confines of the structure he dwelled in to breathe fresh air. Sammuel would take the time and gaze at what appeared to be a purple firmament. How he longed to see the blue skies once again.

"We should continue on our way and not be distracted by what we cannot change," Sammuel said. "My brothers fight a monster, and I have pledged my aid and support. The Venture Hive's farm is too large for the three of us to engage."

"There may be babies we can liberate," his sister-in-law, Tanya, said. "Security around the nursery will be nonexistent during a harvest. We cannot pass up such an opportunity. We are on our way to the safe haven created by your blood brother, so it will not be necessary to take the babies to our home."

Like Patrice, Tanya had long black hair. Tanya was shorter than Patrice and his late wife. The resemblance she bore to her sister kept his wife alive in his mind after all these centuries, yet her actual image had faded with time. However, he would always remember her sky blue eyes. Tanya's were blue-gray.

The two women had but one purpose in their immortal lives. They existed to save the lives of human babies doomed to feed the vampires of the Nightshade universe. Their home was nestled in the mountains on the edge of the continent, a two-week journey from their current location. Humans were safe within the haven they created. Unlike Lorenz's settlement, their mountain home did not contain any other vampires. There was a single passage into the mountain valley they called home. Shifters who fell through the inter-dimensional portal not far from their settlement prowled the area at night, attacking the random vampire who dared enter their territory.

"Besides, I am hungry," Patrice complained.

Unlike other vampires, they did not drink the blood of humans. From the very beginning of their unnatural existence, they drank only vampire blood. On a regular basis, they hit smaller human farms, liberating the humans, rescuing the babies, and drinking the vampire guards dry. The Ventura Hive's farm was larger than the facilities they usually attacked.

"We need to be at full-strength if we are going to aid your blood brother," Tanya said. The two women often thought with one mind. "I can keep coming up with reasons why we should take action now if you require more."

Sammuel looked into Tanya's determined eyes. For a fraction of an instant, he thought his late wife was before him. The two women looked so similar, he often sought out aspects of his wife in the woman who was before him. Patrice had inherited his coloring and features. Unlike Patrice, Tanya wore a long flowing dress and overcoat.

"Very well," Sammuel said wryly. "It appears I have been out voted."

The women generally followed his lead. He did not have the heart to deny them their occasional request. In two moments of weakness, he had sentenced the surviving women in his family to a horrific immortality. He would be lying to himself if he believed he would not have done the same had he the ability to change things. He truly would have been alone in his misery without them.

They steered their horses in the direction of the screams and the mayhem that would soon become visible. Humans impacted by the harvest generally handled the collection in one of two ways. A few willingly went along with the collectors, accepting the fate they were destined to meet from the day they were born. Others fought with what little strength they had. These poor souls were no match for the more powerful vampires, regardless how dilapidated these creatures were.

When possible, the trio freed the fighting humans. They would ultimately be recaptured or fall victim to a rogue vampire. Regardless, for a period of time they were free for the first time in their lives. It was only the babies they would take to the safety of their fortress.

The farm was now before them. It had been enlarged since the last time Sammuel had seen it. The Venture Hive must have become stronger and needed more humans to support its burgeoning size. Aside from his overwhelming desire for human blood, Yorik had always been power hungry. The monster did not merely drink, he enjoyed terrorizing his victims. There was a reason he spent little time in vampire hives, unlike his blood brother, Drake.

Several vampires led a group of humans through the front gate. Patrice went after the guard to the far right. She struck him down and drained him before any of the other vampires were able to react. Patrice was claiming her second victim as Sammuel got off his horse. Tanya released the humans, instructing them to run. He joined the feeding frenzy his daughter started.

What minute amount of blood he was able to liberate from the malnourished vampires fed his hungry cells. He needed little blood to sustain him, requiring only a victim twice a week. Starvation over the years had changed his metabolism and that of his female companions. This feast would last them at least two weeks. They would be in tremendous shape when they reached his blood brother's settlement.

They left a trail of bodies as they made their way underground to the nursery. There were only four babies in a room capable of holding ten times that number. For a facility this large, the lack of infants surprised him.

Sammuel picked up an alluring scent as they approached the nursery. He doubled back to investigate what created the lovely bouquet, but lost the scent before discovering its origin.

"We should get some of the women who recently delivered children to accompany us to feed the little ones," Tanya suggested.

His sister-in-law's voice brought his attention back to the rescued infants. Each woman held two babies in their arms. The children slept, ignorant of the horror taking place around them.

There was sadness in her voice. Sammuel imagined she was thinking of the time she had her own babies to suckle at her breast. It had been another world, another time, another life. They had all lost so much in the last days they were human.

A rival clan had sent a small force to kill everyone in their village while the men battled elsewhere. It was a terrible breach of war etiquette. Men died in war, not women and children. When he returned home, he discovered his wife and sons slaughtered like animals. Patrice was not among the dead or wounded. She had been taken by the enemy to be sold into slavery. The sixteen-year-old was stunning and would be worth a king's ransom to the victor.

He stalked the army, deranged with grief. Sammuel made a pledge to himself to kill every one of the horde who had destroyed his life. For days he traveled, barely eating or sleeping. All he found was more destruction at the hands of the men he hunted. His only hope was that Patrice was still with them and untouched. A virgin would capture a greater price once she was finally sold.

In his travels to seek revenge, he came across two strange beings. These creatures fed off the blood of men. Rather than claiming him as a victim, the one who called himself The Creator, offered him immortality. Crazed, he accepted the offer, believing the additional strength would allow him to exact his revenge.

The Creator and the other creature, Drake, aided him in his mission. Sammuel enjoyed hearing their victims' terrified cries as the two creatures fed off his enemies. He made sure to tell his new friends to drain them slowly, and savor their taste. Vampires had the ability to make their feeding enjoyable. He asked them to make it as horrific a death as possible. Sammuel grasped his wife's wedding band with her killers' screams echoing in his head.

It was Drake and his other blood brother, Lorenz, he would soon join. The other two brothers had been called as well. Soon, all five brothers would be reunited for the first time in centuries. No good ever came about when they were all together and Sammuel doubted this time would be any different.

They left the farm, continuing their journey to meet up with his blood brothers. With the babies safe, Patrice and Tanya would be content, and not insist on rendering additional aid to the doomed humans. There was nothing that would further delay reaching Lorenz's settlement.

Sammuel sensed something he could not identify. He pulled back on his horse's reins and directed the animal to a path north of where he originally set as their route. A force was driving him. Ahead was a clearing where a vampire and two human women were stopped. There was something about the blonde that captivated him.

CHAPTER 2

"**T**ime to die, abomination," the vampire in the clearing sneered.

Sammuel could not fathom why the vampire was toying with the two human women. The vampire could have attacked the female he addressed and fed on her in less time it took to taunt her. These creatures rarely addressed their victims, they just simply fed. Both women had their backs to him. Sammuel was not sure if the vampire had been referring to the blonde or the brunette.

"I do not understand the charade," the blonde said. Her voice was steady, which surprised Sammuel due to the danger she was in. "Why would you help us escape, only to kill us here?"

They must have been residents of the farm. Rather than harvesting the females, the vampire led them to believe he was saving them. Sammuel waged an internal battle. Should he save them or continue on his way? He already had four infants and two human women slowing him down, yet there was something about the blonde that intrigued him. Feelings he had never experienced as a vampire coursed through his body.

"It was never my intention to do anything other than end your pathetic lives. You certainly made it easier for me, falling into my hands. I cannot stand the cloying stink of you any longer," the vampire admitted. "There is a reason why humans like you need to be destroyed as soon as you are discovered."

The blonde must carry the genetic marker. Vampires can identify such women by scent. While Sammuel was too far away to smell the sweet aroma, he recalled the scent he picked up near the nursery. What he smelled at the farm was not produced by the mutated gene. Something had him glued to the spot, and it was not the possibility he could lay with her. In the three thousand years he had existed, he had been faithful to the memory of his dead wife.

Although he could not see the blonde's face, an inexplicable force drew him to her. He wanted to touch her and drive into her, breaking an oath he made to another woman so long ago. A painful erection made it almost impossible to think. Balling his hands into fists, Sammuel tried to get his body under control while battling the emotions crippling his ability to function.

"You will die with the knowledge that I will enjoy your sister for some time before I feed on her last drop of blood," the vampire claimed. "The League will reward me greatly for your corpse."

He struck before Sammuel had time to react. He was disgusted with himself. Standing around considering his feelings, instead of eliminating the danger before him. With speed that surprised him, Sammuel pried the vampire from the blonde's neck and tossed him in the direction of Patrice, who followed behind him. An emotion close to panic consumed him. He must save this woman.

Sammuel took the girl into his arms and licked her gashed throat. His saliva had the healing agent, which all vampires possessed. Her blood was unlike anything he had tasted before. He convinced himself it was because she was human, but he doubted that was the case. The attraction he had for this woman was what made her blood special. It energized him like nothing had in the past three thousand years.

With newfound strength, Sammuel tightened his hold on her, careful not to hurt the delicate human. After centuries of starvation and feeding off vampires, he never before felt such power surge through his body. He could live off this energy for years. Although his life force surged, he could feel the girl's fade.

He bit into his wrist and placed it against the woman's mouth. His glance went from her neck to her mouth, not truly registering her looks. He knew the mingling of their blood was the only hope he had of saving her life.

"What are you doing?" Patrice cried out.

His daughter's voice penetrated the obsessive focus he had on the woman. Never did he have more clarity than in this moment. He knew exactly what he was doing. If the only way to save her was to convert her to a vampire, so be it. Sammuel could not lose her.

"Stop, before it is too late," Patrice begged him. "You are doing the poor thing no favor bringing her over. She will heal or die as a human. Please, Father."

Patrice rarely called him by that term. She had never forgiven him for turning her into a vampire. Her pleas caused him to withdraw his wrist from the girl's mouth. Another selfish act almost doomed another female to a life of darkness.

For the first time, he saw the face of the woman in his arms with no obstructions blocking his view. Hers was a delicate face, crowned with honey blond hair. She had a flawless, ivory complexion. He immediately regretted stopping the conversion process. This was a face that should be preserved.

She lay motionless in his arms. Her breathing was barely detectable. There was far too little flesh on her bones. His blood should be repairing the internal damage and energizing her cells and muscles. She would be unusually strong for a human until her heart pumped out enough blood to dilute his.

"Miranda?" a voice beside him whispered.

The younger woman who accompanied the blonde stepped forward. The lovely creature in his arms was named Miranda. Sammuel reluctantly released his hold on the captivating female. He gently moved her into the arms of the girl who had cried out her name.

"She will be all right," Sammuel reassured the girl. "What are you called?"

The girl looked up at him. Her warm brown eyes were full of tears. Sammuel wondered if Miranda would have the same colored irises. He had always been partial to blue eyes, like his late wife's. Katelyn's eyes always sparkled with laughter, but she had been in her grave for just under three thousand years.

"My name is Beatrice," the girl answered.

He saw the fear in her eyes. She was visibly shaking, terrified of everything around her. Beatrice held on to Miranda as if her life was dependent on the other woman.

Sammuel knew humans born to be bred and ultimately drained did not have last names and had no family. He wondered what linked the two girls. Beatrice could not be more than sixteen years of age. Miranda appeared to be a little older.

"We should be going," Tanya said. "These babies should be out of the cold night's air and we need to find a place to spend the day. You saved the two women. Leave them to their own devices. There are only three horse and I will not leave the nursing women behind for these two. Our women hold value, these girls do not."

Tanya was right, but he refused to leave the blonde in her condition. Sammuel needed her to awaken before he considered what his next move should be. He longed to gaze into her eyes and taste her lips.

"Take the horses and head for the day shelter we saw on the map," Sammuel instructed. "I will join you before the sun starts to rise."

"Do not be ridiculous," Patrice groused. "The babies are our top priority."

"Go," Sammuel shouted. He had never raised his voice to his child.

Patrice stalked off. Part of him wanted to go after her and apologize, but he could not leave Miranda's side. She was like an appendage he had not known he was missing. Sammuel knew he would be incomplete without her by his side. Nothing concerning this woman made sense, yet he was powerless to stop his inexplicable emotions.

When Sammuel was human, he thought of sex most of the time. As a vampire, although he was functional in that regard, he never desired intercourse with any women in the vampire harems. Suddenly, his mind was clouded with images of ravaging the woman before him. His body ached for her.

"You will stay and protect us?" Beatrice asked, once again distracting him from his sensual daydreams. The girl's eyes pleaded for his aid. "Why has she not awakened yet?"

As if responding to Beatrice's words, Miranda's eyes flew open. Her beautiful blue eyes grew enormous with fear when she looked upon him. Before he could say anything, Miranda screamed.

Terror consumed her. She remembered the vampire's teeth ripping at her throat. Miranda could still smell his foul stench. What her mind replayed and the man before her were not the same. She was in someone's soft embrace and the most handsome creature she had ever seen was before her. He was not human, nor was he a vampire…she was not sure *what* he was. All Miranda knew was she needed to be with him.

"It is all right, Miranda," she heard Beatrice say.

She believed her sister. They escaped the farm with Tomas. He had attacked her, but now they were safe. Something happened in between she was unaware of. Beatrice's calm voice assured her they were out of danger...for now. Although she was ignorant of what transpired, Miranda knew this man – the one she could not take her eyes off of – was responsible.

The male before her was huge. His brown hair was cut short, leaving his thick neck exposed. She longed to run her tongue along the taut muscles of his throat. Her thoughts confused her and the man's presence disturbed her physically.

Amber eyes stared back at her. They were brown with flecks of yellow making them appear amber. She had never seen eyes that color before. They seemed to lighten the longer he gazed upon her. Miranda struggled to pull her glance from his.

"Who are you?" she asked. Her heart beat so loudly she could hardly hear herself speak.

"Sammuel," he rumbled, his voice so deep she could feel it in her very bones. It fit the large man before her.

Miranda's body heated at the sound of his voice. She needed to pull herself from her lust induced haze and gain control of the situation. Beatrice depended on her.

"What happened?" Miranda asked. "The last thing I remember, Tomas attacked me. He said he was part of a group dedicated to protecting women like me from having to bear vampire children. I knew, deep down, he was lying to me, but thought he was our only chance to escape the farm."

"Part of what he said was true," Sammuel commented. "He was a member of The League. Their mission is to destroy women who carry the genetic marker. It is an outlawed group, but that only makes them desperate and more deadly. He needed your body for a bounty paid by one of The League's leaders. We cannot stay here. I can take you to a place you will be safe. My blood brother, Lorenz, runs a settlement where humans and vampires live in harmony. Humans willingly give blood and they are treated extremely well."

This man was offering her the same bait Tomas had. Yes, he had saved her, but could he be trusted? He certainly was different from any other men she had come across at the farm. Her limited experience handicapped her ability to make a proper decision.

"I heard rumors of such a place," Miranda admitted. "We would be most grateful if you could escort us there."

"She needs to be able to stand. It is only a matter of time before vampires come after us."

Miranda heard words in her mind. She rubbed her forehead, confused about what was happening. Those were not her thoughts.

"Listen, we need to get out of here before they realize you are gone," Sammuel said. "I assume you hold value to the Venture Hive since you were protected from The League within the farm's walls."

How had she read his thoughts? She did a quick survey of how she felt physically, as mentally there was something obviously wrong. Considering everything she had been through, she felt great. Miranda noticed a strange metallic, salty taste in her mouth.

Sammuel seemed entranced, staring at her mouth as she ran her tongue over her teeth and lips. She looked up and caught him staring at her. Miranda became warm from the heat in his eyes. She was used to vampires looking at her as if she were a specimen and human males as if she were a pariah. His look was totally different. If she was not mistaken, it was stark...need.

"Her lips look so kissable. I'm getting hard just thinking about them. We need to get moving so I can focus on something else."

"We need to go," Sammuel said.

"Something is terribly wrong," Miranda admitted. "For some reason, I can hear your thoughts. I have never heard of such a thing. I know vampires can compel, but did not think they could push their thoughts into a human's mind. This makes no sense."

She took several deep breaths and tried to relax. Miranda would not be able to think clearly if she panicked. Whatever the creature was before her, he was disturbing her in ways she had never experienced.

Sammuel seemed troubled by her confession and a frown crossed his handsome face. At least he was not dismissing her. The vampires in the labs only listened to what she said when they asked her a direct question.

Miranda continued to stare at him while he considered her words. The black shirt he wore brought out the gold flecks in his eyes. His chest was broad and powerful. Her fingers itched to touch him. Sammuel did not resemble the human males from the farm, not even the well-fed guards.

"I gave you my blood," Sammuel said. "Actually, quite a bit of it. My blood's concentration in your body must allow you to read my thoughts. I have never heard of such instances in the past, but that does not mean it is not possible."

Miranda placed her hand on her neck where Tomas had sunk in his fangs. The area was sensitive, but there was no open wound. Sammuel's blood healed her and left behind unusual, and hopefully, temporary consequences. It should have repelled her that she drank his blood, but it did not. If anything, she craved more of it. Her mouth was dry and only his life force would quench her thirst.

Suddenly, his thoughts about her lips came rushing back to her. She unconsciously touched the pad of her index finger to her lower lip. Miranda longed to feel the pressure of his lips on hers. Never had she reacted to another living soul in this manner. She had never even been kissed.

"What are you?" Miranda asked. She did not want to insult him, but she needed to know what he was. There had to be a reason for her strange attraction to him.

"I am a vampire," Sammuel admitted, "but different from the ones you are used to. I was made by The Creator himself."

"The Creator?" Beatrice asked.

Her sister's words reminded Miranda of Beatrice's presence. She had been so enamored by the being in front of her, she had totally forgotten about her sister. Miranda placed her hand around Beatrice's forearm and directed her attention back to Sammuel. Although he claimed to be a vampire, he looked more human than monster.

"We do not have time for this," Sammuel answered. "Just know I am different and I mean you no harm. You will be recaptured if you do not follow my orders."

Miranda knew he spoke the truth, just as she knew Tomas had lied to her. They did not have the luxury of debating what to do next. Sammuel was correct, the vampires from the farm would come after her. Miranda might be safe from punishment, but they would not hesitate to torture Beatrice in order to teach her obedience, something they had done once in the past. For her welfare, as well as her sister's, Miranda had to trust this man. Although he said he was a vampire, she did not see him as one. She did, however, hope he had a vampire's strength.

She lifted her hand to Sammuel, who took it and helped her to stand. Her eyes fell to their entwined hands and her mind flashed to an image of their naked bodies entangled together. Miranda stumbled, but Sammuel was quick to steady her. When he removed his hands from her, Miranda felt a great sense of loss.

Horns sounded in the background. The vampires must have discovered their prize had left the farm. Their fates would be sealed if they stood in the clearing any longer.

"We must get to the day shelter," Sammuel said. "The vampires will be unable to travel during the day. You drank from me, Miranda. For the time being, you will be faster, stronger, and more agile than you have ever been in your life. Follow me and do not stop for anything."

Sammuel reached down for Beatrice and picked her up as if she were a baby. He started to run and Miranda did exactly as he commanded, she followed him. She hurdled fallen tree trunks as if they were mere twigs. The forest passed before her eyes in a blur due to her incredible speed. Miranda managed to keep up with Sammuel. Occasionally, he would slow and turn his head to assure himself she was still behind him.

She had never felt more alive. But that was not saying much, considering what her life had been like to this point. Her first taste of freedom was overwhelming. Miranda's body continued to traverse the forest at an alarming speed. She was one with her body. She did not give the vampires pursuing her another thought. They had run for miles, yet she was not winded. Miranda felt invincible.

There was a river with a waterfall before them. The water roared as it cascaded down the rock formation. The moon illuminated the view before her. She never knew such a lovely sight could exist. Miranda was finally going to experience life outside the farm. Sammuel had stopped and Beatrice drank from the cool, sparkling stream.

"Drink from the water falling over the rocks," Sammuel said. "It will be the cleanest."

Miranda took him at his word and knelt next to Beatrice, cupping the water into the palms of her hands. She drank greedily, never tasting water so delicious. After quenching a thirst she was unaware she had, Miranda washed her face with the refreshing liquid.

"How much further?" Miranda asked.

Sammuel looked at her with a critical eye. "Just a little further. You have done well keeping up. The blood you consumed has transformed you."

Miranda had no idea what he was referring to. She wanted to run, not stand around and talk. As long as his blood was in her system, she wanted to enjoy the power it gave her frail body. She dreaded returning to her previous condition.

CHAPTER 3

They arrived at an isolated cabin just as the eastern sky started to lighten. The sun would shortly start its ascension in the sky. Miranda could continue running and increase the distance between herself and her pursuers. She even felt powerful enough to carry Beatrice. All she needed was the location of Lorenz's settlement.

Miranda followed Sammuel into the weathered cabin. Various planks of wood were missing and others were rotting away. The scent of damp, earthy, rotting soil assailed her nose. She could not imagine how this dilapidated structure would protect Sammuel from the sun. Before she had the opportunity to tell Sammuel she and her sister would not be staying, he pulled back a piece of wood hiding a stairwell.

"Come," Sammuel said. "We will spend several days below. There are ample food stores below for humans. My blood brother, Drake, uses this day shelter from time to time to entertain his donors. The vampires will believe they lost your trail and return to the farm. There are probably enough corpses of escaped humans killed by rogue vampires to make those trying to recapture you believe you perished."

The wooden stairs were lit by torches leading to the bottom. Sammuel had mentioned they were meeting up with women who had continued their journey while she recovered from Tomas's attack. Miranda did not like the sound of unaffiliated vampires scouring the forest to feast on escaped humans. In addition, there was no telling how long Sammuel's blood would remain active in her system. As she was not sure how many nights it would take to reach Lorenz's settlement, prudence dictated she remain with him.

The boards creaked as she took her first step. Her eyes teared, first from being temporarily blinded by the brightness of the torch and then from the smoke it produced. Miranda blinked to clear her vision. Fortunately, there was a railing she held on to with her left hand as she continued to walk down.

Miranda heard female voices when she neared the bottom. If she was not mistaken, she heard laughter. Humans rarely laughed in the farm facility. Only the children who were ignorant of what their future held ever made such carefree sounds. She ran down the last several steps to see who made such an infectious sound.

Miranda entered a well lit room populated by four women each holding a babe in their arms. She recognized two of the women from the farm and assumed the other two were Sammuel's traveling companions. They were pale, but still appeared human. All conversation ended when they spotted her. Beatrice was right behind her and continued walking until she stood next to the table where the women sat.

The humans at the farm had always easily accepted her sister, even when the parental link they shared was discovered. Miranda had always been the outsider. Once again, she felt the chill of not belonging.

"May I hold one of the babies?" Beatrice asked.

Her sister enjoyed going to the nursery and looking at the newborns. Every baby spent the first week of its life in a room off the laboratory so the technicians could determine the child's health. Sickly babies were cared for until they were strong enough to be moved to the building housing infants and children. Any child's death was unacceptable because it lowered the chance of future offspring and the harvesting of their blood.

This room was large and contained a table, chairs, and several small beds. Torches were lit in each corner, spilling light throughout the space. Several lanterns were strategically placed to provide additional light. Miranda stood frozen in place, unsure where to go.

Sammuel came up from behind and placed a hand on her shoulder. "Come, you will want to change. You are close to Tanya's size. Her clothing should fit you."

Miranda imagined he was referring to the smaller of the two women. She was seated, so Miranda could not judge how tall the woman was. She was significantly heavier than Miranda, considering she had very little meat on her bones.

Regardless, she followed Sammuel to a chamber at the back of the room. The women at the table did not give her another thought as she left their company. Sammuel's women were not pleased he had requested they leave him and continue with the babies on their own. Beatrice had relayed all sorts of information earlier, while they drank beside the river.

The clothing she wore had been soaked by her own blood. Miranda could not wait to change out of the human farm uniform she was forced to wear.

As soon as the door closed, Sammuel forced her against the wooden structure and placed his lips on hers. She gasped in surprise when Sammuel's tongue invaded her mouth. Instinctively, her tongue met his and began a swirling, erotic dance. He had a woodsy, spicy taste. She cried out when his hand caressed one of her breasts. Sammuel deepened their kiss.

She had never before been kissed, so she had nothing to compare this all-consuming experience to. If all contact between men and women was this intense, she could not understand why females were forced to mate. Miranda placed her hands on his shoulders in an attempt to steady herself. Her newly powerful legs struggled to keep her erect.

Sammuel grabbed a handful of her shirt and ripped the fabric. The tearing sound excited her. He stepped back to remove the ruined top and brought his mouth to her exposed breast. When he started to suck on her hardened nipple, Miranda moaned in pleasure. Her hands grabbed his head, steadying herself once again. He continued to suck, while his hands made quick work of removing her pants.

Everything he was doing to her generated sensations she never experienced. There was a rightness in what she felt, as if she was born for this purpose. To be with this man. The more he touched her, the more she wanted.

"I smell your need," Sammuel communicated to her through their blood connection.

Miranda had run through the forest and never became winded. Now, with just one kiss, she was breathing erratically. This man over-powered her mentally and physically. Her brain stopped working while her body reacted to the wonder of his touch. Miranda somehow knew she would not be complete until Sammuel was inside her.

Sammuel removed his mouth from her breast. Her body mourned his departure. Miranda knew babies sucked at a woman's breast to feed, but she never imagined a man doing the same thing would create the need for something…more. The dampness between her legs had not gone unnoticed by either of them.

Her neck was now Sammuel's obsession and he kissed along her long, narrow throat. He scattered kisses and ran his tongue along her carotid artery. Miranda's world fractured when he bit into her neck. Euphoria overcame her as Sammuel fed.

Rather than feeling depleted, Miranda became energized the longer he drank. It was almost as if she was feeding, not the other way around. Her body became warmer with each draw of his lips.

An ache deep within her core cried out for this man. She would not be satisfied until they were one. Miranda knew she would not be complete until he entered her.

Sammuel released her neck and pushed away from her. He left her standing nearly naked, exposed to the chill of the room. Miranda arranged her arms to cover her breasts. When she looked up at Sammuel, she was surprised by the expression on his face.

Disgust. There was no other word to describe what she saw reflected in Sammuel's gaze. His warm amber eyes had turned cold. What had she done wrong?

"There are garments in the chest," Sammuel growled and pointed to a large red wooden box. "Put something on and join us in the other room."

Sammuel exited the room, leaving her alone with her shame. Miranda had allowed a vampire to take liberties with her and, heaven help her, she enjoyed his touch. This time she could not blame her tears on the smoke.

Miranda was consumed with shame. She hurried to the chest to find something to cover herself. A reflection caught her eyes as she passed a mirror.

Miranda stopped dead in her tracks and stared at the person in front of her. Sammuel's blood had not only given her strength, but muscle mass. Her small breasts were now full. She could not believe what she saw before her. Even her fine blond hair was thicker and fuller.

For the first time she took in her surroundings. The room was elaborate and had a large bed that dominated the space. Sammuel did mention his blood brother brought women here. The lothario had created an environment for seduction. Rich vibrant shades of red, blue, and yellow decorated the floors and walls, bringing a different type of warmth to the room. All primary colors, like the primal needs that would be fulfilled here.

The brightness of the room did not lift her spirits. Everything they had done felt right. She did not understand Sammuel's reaction and abandonment, and her body still cried out for his touch.

A number of chests were placed to the right of the bed. Sammuel and his women must have visited this day shelter enough for each woman to have additional clothing stored here. Tanya's garments were in the red chest. Miranda opened the top and was surprised by the sheer volume of clothes she found. She selected a dress in royal blue.

Rather than hanging on her, the dress showed off her new curves. The long flowing gown made her appear taller than she really was. Miranda released her hair and ran the brush she had found nearby through her thicker locks. Everything about her was different.

Sammuel requested she join him after she dressed. Miranda stood frozen before the door. What if he looked upon her with the same disgust as he had earlier? With everything that had occurred today, she was on the cusp of falling apart. She was stronger physically, but emotionally, she was a mess. It was not the vampires who hunted her who made her weary, but the man who stole her breath.

Sammuel glared at the closed door, waiting for Miranda to join them. His stare so penetrating, he half expected it to burst into flames fueled by the conflagration within him. He had never reacted to a living soul the way he had with the woman in the other room, not even his beloved wife. Sammuel struggled with the extreme need he felt for Miranda and guilt at betraying his dead wife.

He was still overflowing with the power generated by their kiss. How was such a thing possible? She drew him to her like a moth to a flame. Rather than catching fire, he burned in a different way. It had taken every ounce of willpower he possessed to walk away from her. Her sweet taste was still in his mouth, overpowering the taste of her blood.

Perhaps concentrating on something else would ease the heat rising within him. Focusing on a routine task, Sammuel pulled out his sword and placed it on a block of wood sitting on the side table. Using a file from his saddlebag, he carefully stroked the blade. For an instant, he imagined stroking Miranda between her feminine folds. He shook his head and returned his attention to his work. Alternating turning the sword or file over, he continued the process until the blade showed no nicks. It needed to easily sever a vampire's head from its body.

Sammuel grabbed the whetstone from his bag, as well as the oil. He applied a thin film of the liquid to the whetstone and proceeded to sharpen and polish the sword. His father had taught him the proper way to maintain a weapon before he ever had the strength to pick one up. He ran the sword up and down the whetstone. Satisfied with the sharpness, he placed it back in its sheath.

Wanting to continue to distract himself, Sammuel proceeded to sharpen both Patrice and Tanya's swords. He was disciplined enough to give the task his full attention. Sharpening a sword was an art he took very seriously. He could not obsess over whatever Miranda was doing in the other room, while he worked with the file and the whetstone,

She was perfect. His hands fit over her breasts as if they were created to hold them. He had not realized the fullness of her breasts when he first saw her. His initial impressions were quickly corrected when his eyes feasted on her after removing her shirt. His cock grew harder in his leather pants.

The door to the other room opened and a vision walked through the entryway. Miranda was in a deep blue gown that accentuated her blue eyes and her cream colored breasts nearly spilled out from the top of the bodice. His fingers longed to pull them from their confinement. His mouth watered, ready to share a kiss. Sammuel's lips had not forgotten how incredibly soft her lips were.

"Miranda," Beatrice whispered in awe, "you are beautiful!"

The beauty's eyes had been transfixed on his until the girl uttered those words. He discovered he did not like her attention on anyone other than him. An irrational feeling of jealousy consumed him. Sammuel had to find a way to separate himself from the group of women surrounding him. Unfortunately, the sun had risen and they were all prisoners within the day shelter until the golden orb set.

"Yes, she looks lovely in my dress," Tanya commented. "It suits you. Although I will find you something to travel in, you must keep the gown. Gifting you the garment gives me cause to buy another one. After all these centuries, I still enjoy shopping."

Sammuel relished spoiling his women. Numerous dress purchases over the years seemed insignificant to the sentence he passed on to

Patrice and Tanya. Tanya would never bear another child and Patrice would forever be sixteen, the age he converted her to a vampire. They were all over three thousand years old, but it still bothered him knowing his little girl had sexual relations with the occasional human male.

Whenever they entered a village or keep, the three separated for a number of days. He was ignorant of what Patrice did and was grateful when she did not share her sexual escapades. On the rare occasion they ran across his blood brother, Jace. Sammuel knew his daughter hooked up with the youthful looking vampire. Jace had been eighteen when The Creator converted him. It would have been done much earlier, but Drake requested the boy be allowed to mature. He wished Drake had asked the same of him when it came to Patrice. Sammuel never questioned his daughter's relationship with Jace.

They were still a five-day's ride from Lorenz's settlement. He could not risk taking the tram that ran underground and connected various hives and settlements. Traveling with the babies required the utmost caution. Vampires primarily rode the trams and too many questions would be asked.

Patrice rose and collected her sword. She had been quiet since he arrived with Miranda and Beatrice. It seemed Patrice liked Beatrice, but he had not failed to notice she never once looked in Miranda's direction. Sammuel assumed Patrice had heard Miranda's cries of passion. When he re-entered the room after abandoning Miranda, Patrice shot him a look fierce enough to kill most men in their tracks.

"Thank you," Miranda said. "Are there clothes Beatrice can change into?"

"Beatrice, let us try to find you something to wear. Some of my clothes may fit you." It was not lost on Sammuel that Patrice ignored Miranda by directing her response to the girl close to the age she was before her conversion. "I hope you do not mind pants. They are all I wear."

Beatrice was far too short to wear any of Patrice's clothing. Sammuel figured his daughter would make it work just to spite him. It was obvious to all that Patrice did not like Miranda being among them.

Patrice grabbed Beatrice's hand and went into the bedroom, with Tanya and the two other women following closely behind. The babies slept in makeshift cribs made from a number of dresser drawers. Miranda stayed behind, no doubt feeling Patrice's disdain.

Sammuel could feel Miranda's discomfort. He took the guilt he felt over his attraction to her and redirected it at the innocent before him. It was more than the physical need he felt for her. When he was in her company, he did not think about his dead wife or the promise he once made. But when Katelyn drifted back into his mind after he drank from Miranda, he became distraught.

How was he going to control his need for her over the three or four days they needed to stay hidden? He could not sacrifice the babies' lives by leaving prematurely. Sammuel would have to find a way to coexist with Miranda until he was free of his prison and could drop her off at Lorenz's. He would need to find an excuse to leave shortly after arriving and to fulfill the promise he made to his blood brother.

CHAPTER 4

The last two days had been a living nightmare for Sammuel. He was trapped with a woman who was beyond tempting. His body's craving for Miranda had nearly driven him mad with need. Tanya and Patrice patrolled the area outside the day shelter and reported the forest still crawled with vampires searching for the escaped humans. They would have to continue seeking refuge from both the sun and the creatures seeking the ones under their protection.

By the third night, Sammuel was climbing the walls. He needed to escape his confines and hunt. There were plenty of vampires prowling the woods to feast upon. Sammuel did not need their blood, just the distraction. Miranda's blood still coursed through his veins, further fueling his desire.

The first vampire Sammuel came across was a living skeleton. His decomposition so advanced, he offered no nourishment. Sammuel ran from his hidden position and onto the path the vampire patrolled. Before the creature could turn and see who stalked him, Sammuel lifted his sword and decapitated him. There was little sport in destroying the mere husk of what was once a human being.

Sammuel glanced at the pile of bones and rags and continued on his campaign to kill every vampire he encountered. He traveled several miles before finding another target. This one was feeding off an escaped human. It was too late to save the unfortunate soul, but his attacker would not live long enough to digests the blood he consumed.

His last kill offered no challenge, but this one he would take with his bare hands. Sammuel hoped his opponent would put up a fight and prove to be a worthy adversary. An easy battle never excited him. A routine beheading would not help purge Miranda from his mind for even a second of relief.

"Are you so thirsty, you would drink blood from a dead man?" Sammuel asked, hoping to provoke the vampire. There was no greater insult a vampire could receive. He hoped his words would enrage the creature.

The vampire cast his victim from his embrace and slowly rose to his feet. His glowing red eyes glared at him. Only blood-lusting vampires had eyes that glowed. Sammuel could not help the smile that crossed his face. An inhuman growl came from the vampire. Sammuel did not sense any of The Creator's blood in him. The vampire would not provide the challenge he sought.

"I am strong from his blood," his enemy said. "After I have destroyed you for what you dared utter, I will drink your dead blood. Let us fight without weapons, but match our true strength against each other."

His opponent did not realize he was fighting one of the five blood brothers converted by The Creator. It was clear he thought he was about to fight a human. Sammuel was royalty among vampires. He was a creature who did not decompose. A vampire with pure blood not contaminated by death.

"Nothing would give me greater pleasure than ripping your limbs off your decrepit body and drinking what is left of your life force before I wrench your head from your shoulders," Sammuel said. "How long did you taunt the poor human before you feasted?"

The human at the vampire's feet was covered with bites. His was not a fast, merciful death. Many vampires liked to play with their food while they dined. Sammuel would make sure the vampire would get a taste of what he put the dead man through.

His opponent used his preternatural speed to make the first strike. Sammuel easily defected the blow and wrenched his opponent's hand behind his back. Holding his victim in his arms, Sammuel bit into his neck for the first of many bites he would leave on the vampire.

The foul taste of rancid blood entered his mouth. Sammuel pushed his victim forward and spit out the tainted blood. While Sammuel was still reacting to what he swallowed, the vampire came at him again. His opponent landed a blow and knocked Sammuel off his feet, but was too slow to escape him after remaining close and admiring his handiwork. Sammuel reached out and grabbed the vampire's knees, bringing him to the ground. He was too disturbed by his reaction to the vampire's blood to toy with him any longer. He dragged himself up his opponent's body until he had his hands around the vampire's neck, his body mass preventing his victim from fighting back. Sammuel used his full strength and snapped the vampire's neck, severing his spinal cord.

Once back on his feet, he reached for his sword and decapitated the vampire. Sammuel sniffed the blood running from his victim's neck...it did not smell tainted. The human's blood was also free of contaminants. He was close enough to the corpse to smell any irregularities the dead man may have possessed.

Sammuel had originally planned to return to the day shelter after his second kill, but he had to know if all vampire blood was now off limits to him. His craving and reaction to Miranda's blood had troubled him, but now he was truly alarmed. Would he only be able to feed from her in the future?

Sammuel ran through the forest like a crazed animal. When he picked up the scent of another vampire, he did not stop until he overpowered his prey and dug his teeth into his jugular. He staked the vampire as soon as he drew his first sip of blood into his mouth. As with the vampire before, Sammuel found the blood repellent. There was no sense in seeking a third victim. Sammuel had his answer.

A myriad of thoughts circulated through his brain while he made his way back to the day shelter. When he fed, both he and Miranda were energized by the interchange. His blood fueled not only her body, but produced a physical transformation. In the three days he had been feeding off her, the girl had gained weight, added muscle mass, and even her hair's texture had changed.

It appeared he could now only tolerate her blood. He did not bother to try to find a human to feed from. Sammuel knew without trying, he would not be able to digest it. Miranda not only attracted him physically, but it appeared only her blood would provide him sustenance from here on out.

Upon his return, Sammuel hesitated going down to the sanctuary of the day shelter. What was he going to say to her to make Miranda stay? In the little space available to her, the girl kept her distance from him and Patrice. Patrice must have sensed the bond growing between him and the mortal woman.

"You have returned," Tanya said.

His sister-in-law carried a satchel full of apples picked from a nearby tree. Although they had dried food in the day shelter, Tanya made sure the women ate fresh fruit. She was particularly concerned for the well being of the women who nursed the four infants.

"Can you visit with me for a short time before heading back?" Sammuel asked his sister-in-law. "Something has happened that I need to discuss with you."

"There is so much to do to care for the babies and the four human women," Tanya said. She started to head for the entrance of the shelter and stopped. "The girl has Katelyn's eyes. My sister has been gone so long, I can barely remember her face. When I think of her, I believe I have given her image more of my features than the ones she possessed. When I look at Miranda, I remember her beautiful crystal blue eyes. It must be the same with you. She is mortal, do not grow closer to her than you already are. You will only be hurt in the end."

He had been concerned how Tanya would react to his obsession for a woman other than her sister. Sammuel was not sure what he expected. Patrice had already shown her understandable anger, yet Tanya seemed neutral on the subject. It was obvious she saw his attraction to Miranda based strictly on the minor resemblance she bore to his dead wife. Nothing could be further from the truth.

"Her blood restores me like nothing I have experienced before," Sammuel admitted.

A strange look crossed Tanya's face, but was gone before he could name the expression. Her face was once again wearing the placid countenance she often presented to the world. The longer he looked at her, the more be doubted he had seen any other reaction than one of mild contentment. He was glad he had only mentioned his growing dependence on her blood, not the other emotions he was feeling concerning the girl.

"I have noticed she is also revived after donating blood," Tanya commented. "In all these centuries I have never seen anything like it. She has transformed before our eyes. We have never run across one of her kind before. It must be the genetic marker she carries."

Sammuel knew what was happening between him and Miranda was not related to the genetic marker she bore. Although he had not run across such a woman before, stories would have arisen about the blood dependence and the physical changes to the carrier if the gene was truly responsible. But then again, Sammuel was not like other vampires.

What he had with Miranda was more than just feeding. The blood he took was secondary. He would want to touch Miranda even if he did not get nutrition from the exchange. Whatever was between them was not totally obvious to those around them. For the time being, he would keep his own counsel regarding how he truly felt for her.

Sammuel massaged his temples. He did not have a headache, those stopped when he became a vampire. It was pure frustration that brought about the human response.

"Miranda grows stronger every day," Tanya said. "Teach her how to protect herself in case we get attacked. It would be to our advantage to have another fighter among us. When you eventually leave her, Miranda will be better suited for life in this dimension."

It was futile to further discuss his emotional bonds to Miranda with her. His former sister-in-law saw Miranda as a temporary distraction in their immortal lives. Tanya was right about one thing, though. He needed to teach Miranda how to defend herself. The mortal woman's life was targeted by The League and Yorik had claimed her as soon as the genetic marker was discovered.

Miranda's eyes lifted to the room's entry when she heard a man's footfalls on the stairs. Sammuel had been gone for hours, much longer than she had expected. Although she was disturbed by his presence, his absence brought about an angst foreign to her. She had hyperventilated, taking in too much air during the anxious panic associated with worrying about him. She had come up with some lame excuse to explain the attack to Beatrice.

Sammuel's eyes immediately found hers when he entered the room. They visibly became lighter. Perhaps he was as concerned about her as she was for him. There was a bond between them that defied logic. He was a vampire and she was human — prey and the predator. There should be nothing more between them, but something was.

She dressed in the blue gown she had worn the first day. Sammuel had barely been able to take his eyes off her. The last two days he barely glanced in her direction, but she had caught him casting furtive glances her way when he assumed she was not paying attention.

Every evening he found a means to be alone with her and take her blood. Miranda continued to grow in strength with each feeding. Physically, Sammuel did not seem altered by the exchange. She felt safe in his arms and bereft when he left, while Sammuel fought whatever was between them. Miranda could only hope he would not abandon her until he had successfully delivered her and Beatrice to Lorenz's community.

"I hope to be on our way tomorrow at sunset," Sammuel said. "With the energy that passes between us, you have the strength to help protect your sister, the babies, and the other women. Join me above and I will show you some defensive moves should we find ourselves under attack."

Miranda was excited about the opportunity to learn how to fight. She needed to be able to defend Beatrice and herself should Sammuel decide to take the others and go their separate ways. From this moment on, she would keep one of the many swords hanging from the day shelter's wall close at hand.

She grabbed the sword closest to her and followed Sammuel up the stairs and passed Tanya as she returned. The woman barely acknowledged her presence. Although there was no outright hostility, like with Patrice, Miranda felt uncomfortable around Tanya.

Miranda was relieved when she reached the surface. It had been three days since she enjoyed the night air. Her lungs took in several large breaths of the fresh, clean air. Until that very moment, Miranda had not noticed how stale the air in the day shelter had become. It was a good thing they would be leaving tomorrow night, otherwise she would have asked for the other women and the babies to be brought to the surface in shifts.

"Let me show you the proper way to hold a sword," Sammuel said. She had been leaning on the sword, waiting for Sammuel to start the lesson. "Because of the weight and the length of the base, you should hold it with both hands. Your goal is to decapitate your opponent. As a vampire decomposes, his neck weakens. Strong strikes against the enemy's neck will prove effective. Now, try to hold it up in a ready position."

Miranda lifted the weapon. His blood gave her the strength to raise the sword. Sammuel adjusted her hold, placing her hands closer to the cross guard, rather than the pommel of the sword. She had a more balanced grip holding the sword in this manner. His close proximity made it hard to focus. Miranda had to concentrate to absorb his words.

"Most of your moves will be thrusts," Sammuel added. "Use your energy to swing when you have a good chance of bringing down the opponent. Once he is on his knees, go for the decapitation. Practice thrusting against one of the trees."

Miranda lifted her sword and whacked one of the maple trees in the grove. She barely made a dent. Sammuel came up beside her and attacked the same tree. His muscles flexed in the light of the nearly full moon. A large chunk of the tree's bark cascaded to the forest's floor.

"Imagine the vampire has his fangs at Beatrice's throat and try again," Sammuel said.

A vivid image of what Sammuel described assaulted her mind. Miranda felt a shiver run up her spine. She raised her sword, screamed, and attacked the tree. This time, power soared through her body when she swung the weapon. Her sword was now embedded halfway through the trunk.

Sammuel pulled the sword out of the mighty oak. "Very good," he said. "That strike would have decapitated your opponent. The sun will be rising soon. We should return to the shelter."

"Vampires will be seeking refuge from the sun," Miranda said. "I would like to stay here and practice a while longer."

"These woods have other dangers besides vampires," Sammuel said. "Desperate humans and wild animals prowl these forests. It will take five days to reach Lorenz's settlement. We will continue your lessons along the way."

As if responding to Sammuel's words, a rattlesnake slithered into the small meadow. Miranda had heard of such creatures, but had never seen one. She looked between the snake and Sammuel and ran for the shelter's stairwell. A laughing Sammuel followed in her wake.

Her body responded to his laughter and heat rose from her core. She did not fear his strength, but the uncontrollable way her body reacted to his. Would she be able to concentrate on the enemy when he fought beside her?

Miranda did not doubt, for a moment, that the most dangerous creature in the woods followed her down the stairs. Sammuel was a lethal being. She had yet to see him kill, but she imagined no one was his equal.

"You should sleep and we will restore each other's energy before we head out," Sammuel advised. "You are still human and require rest. I cannot explain the power you draw from my feeding on you, but I doubt it will sustain you without the regeneration sleep offers."

She walked across the common space to the bedroom she shared with Beatrice. There were plenty of cots in the outer area to accommodate everyone else. The babies remained in the cribs fashioned the first night. Sammuel had seemed relieved and Patrice overjoyed when Miranda accepted the room.

Tomorrow they would leave the safety of the shelter. There was no telling the dangers they would encounter on the journey. Miranda was uncertain what disturbed her more…the risk they accepted continuing their trek, or her growing feelings for Sammuel. She lay awake staring at the ceiling in the dark, imagining Sammuel's hands running over her body. It was not a daydream, but something she knew would occur again. How was she going to deal with what her body craved and her mind fought?

CHAPTER 5

Miranda felt the hairs on the back of her neck standup. Something was tracking them and it was no animal. They had traveled four full days without coming across another living being, vampire or human. It appeared their luck had run out. Only a large force would attempt to stalk three vampires. She was stronger than the average human, but Miranda would not kid herself into believing she could take on a vampire.

She glanced at Sammuel who had stopped to listen carefully to the forest's whispers. There were no sounds except the rustling of leaves in the wind. It was too quiet. Her heart pounded in her chest, beating faster than it had several minutes ago. This time her body was not reacting to his proximity, but the danger they faced.

The scrape of Patrice's sword leaving its sheath broke the near silence. Miranda swallowed hard. It was as if her throat were blocked with some kind of obstruction. The metallic taste of adrenaline filled her mouth. Her hands were sweaty on the sword and she took care to maintain the stance they had practiced.

"Surround the women holding the babies," Sammuel ordered. "Beatrice, get behind me; Miranda, stand to my left."

The babies limited their options, but Sammuel decided to face the enemy rather than run. They had all been walking, resting the three horses.

The women moved into formation quickly and Miranda made a slight adjustment to where she stood. Patrice and Tanya closed ranks. By this point, the four had drawn their swords, ready to defend their valuable cargo. Miranda saw movement everywhere and knew it was her nerves, not the enemy. Her imagination was running rampant, seeing things that did not exist.

Rather than wearing a dress, today she wore a light-weight tunic and leggings. Her attire made it easier to move. Miranda balanced her weight, ready for the upcoming attack. She focused on slowing her breathing and heart rate.

One of the babies started to cry, waking the remaining three. They cried often throughout their journey, but Miranda needed to concentrate. She could not allow herself to be distracted. If the infants were hungry or needed to be changed, it would have to wait.

Movement to Miranda's right grabbed her attention. Three vampires came from behind a particularly dense copse of trees. Her set of brief sword fighting lessons came charging into her mind. She would stand her ground. Running would only excite the vampires and result in her death. Being the weakest of the defenders, Miranda was their most likely target. She had to concentrate, her life depended on it, and she could not afford the luxury of turning to see how many other vampires engaged in this assault.

"Strike the tree," Miranda said aloud, remembering her training.

The vampire directly in front of her stopped at her unexpected words and her sword made contact with his shoulder. Rather than striking with the blade of her sword, she had hit him with the flat part of the weapon, an unfortunate mistake. However, her lessons included not only taking the shot, but also quickly recovering after the strike. Miranda pulled her sword back into the ready position and was prepared to strike again when Sammuel beheaded the vampire.

Her first opponent dead, Miranda prepared to strike against the second vampire. She stared into the red glowing eyes of her enemy. These creatures did not deserve her compassion. Other than Beatrice, the vampires in the lab had been the closest thing she had to family. These rabid beasts only wanted to kill and destroy. Miranda needed to strike without mercy in her heart.

Her arm pulsed with the strength provided by Sammuel's blood. Miranda raised her weapon and swung with all her might. Her sword made contact with the vampire's neck. The momentum of the blade sliced through the fragile bones that attached the vampire's head.

Centuries' long of deterioration of the creature's body made it possible for her to decapitate him in one swing.

She momentarily froze, absorbing her body's reaction to the kill. Blood rushed to her head, making her lightheaded. Now was not the time to reflect on what she had done. The training Sammuel provided was back in the forefront of her mind.

Miranda prepared for her next target when Beatrice cried out. She turned to see what had caused her sister's cry of alarm. Patrice and Tanya were engaging their opponents, but one of the human women had been cut down. No babies lay at the fallen woman's feet.

"One of the vampires grabbed two babies," Beatrice whimpered.

Without thought, Miranda ran after the vampire who had taken the little ones. She assumed he had taken the path to her right, as it was the only entry into the forest. Her newly powerful legs chased after the infants. Miranda hoped holding the valuable cargo in his arms would slow the vampire and allow her to catch up.

She entered another small clearing and the vampire stood before her. He had placed the babies on the grass, allowing him free use of both his arms. The vampire held a dagger in his right hand.

"I could smell you coming, abomination," the vampire sneered. "You are no longer protected by the scientists who naively believe you could ever hold the answer to vampires walking in the light of day again. It is said half-ling blood is the sweetest ambrosia a vampire can feast on. I believe I will enjoy drinking from a woman who can produce such an act against nature."

Miranda studied her surroundings. The babies were in no immediate danger. She could hear the sound of metal against metal as Sammuel, Patrice and Tanya, continued to fight their opponents. The vampire would have to cross the clearing and get close enough to her to use the blade or attack her neck. Her sword gave her the advantage, assuming he did not throw the dagger and make contact.

With incredible speed, the vampire cleared the distance between them and bit into her neck before she could defend herself. Almost as quickly as the vampire attacked her throat, he backed away, coughing up the blood he had consumed.

"What are you?" the vampire managed to say between gagging and spitting out her blood. She could see the revulsion in his rotting face.

Miranda stood mute and frozen in place. She had never heard of a vampire rejecting human blood. Tomas had not adversely reacted to her blood. Rather than taking advantage of the vampire's temporary state and attacking, she remained stupefied by his reaction.

A flash of black exited the forest and took down the vampire. When her eyes refocused, a large black cat was ripping at the vampire's throat with its sharp teeth. Miranda had to reach the babies before the panther realized they were there. She held out her sword and made her way to the babies, never taking her eyes off the large cat.

Amber eyes stared at Miranda as she closed in on the innocent infants. The cat made no aggressive move. Perhaps the feline's maternal instinct held her back from attacking Miranda or the babies.

"Hold back, Miranda," Sammuel called from behind her. "Slowly, start stepping away from the cat and make no sudden movements."

Miranda continued to look into the large cat's eyes. She had never seen a large predatory cat before. The intelligence she saw reflected there surprised her. Rather than taking Sammuel's advice, Miranda held her ground, her sword at the ready in case the cat attacked.

Sammuel headed for the panther, walking past her and the sleeping children. He studied the feline as Miranda continued to do. As Sammuel got closer to the animal, Miranda said a silent prayer for him not to hurt the cat. The animal had killed the vampire and made no aggressive move toward her or the babies.

"You are not as you appear," Sammuel said. Miranda assumed he was referring to the cat, not her. It seemed an odd thing to say.

He reached down and stroked the cat's head and gently pulled on one of her ears. The panther fell onto her side, exposing her stomach for Sammuel to pet. To Miranda's astonishment, Sammuel got on his knees and playfully rubbed the huge cat.

"Now I have seen everything," a male's voice came from the woods.

A handsome teenager entered the clearing. Based on his appearance, Miranda identified him as being one of Sammuel's blood brothers. He had mentioned there were four, but provided no descriptions. The vampire who stood over Sammuel and the cat could not have been more than a boy when he was converted.

The new arrival wore a blue shirt and black leather pants. Curly brown hair framed his beautiful features. None of the boys at the farm looked like him. Women would have stood in line to reproduce with this gorgeous creature, were he human. Where Sammuel had looked dangerous when she first saw him, the boy looked like he would not harm a fly. Miranda knew enough to know that appearances could be deceptive.

"Does she belong to you?" Sammuel asked his brother. He continued to pet the large animal, although the cat did not purr.

"Portia belongs to no one," the vampire answered. "We travel together now. Originally, she and Frazour were companions. Her taste in men has certainly improved."

Sammuel produced a sound Miranda longed to hear again from him—laughter; and Miranda immediately relaxed hearing its enchanting melody and the hardness in Sammuel's face seemed to soften as he relaxed.

"Frazour answered Drake's call then," Sammuel commented. "Somehow, I thought he would be the last of us to bow to Drake's demands."

"I cannot speak for our blood brother," the youth said, "but the chance to kill Wylaine was too much of a lure."

Miranda had no idea who Wylaine was, but she assumed Frazour was one of the brothers Lorenz and Drake had sent for. She walked forward, hoping Sammuel would introduce her to the boy. They could use the additional protection until they reached the settlement.

Tanya entered the small meadow and retrieved the babies. Miranda had been so captivated by Sammuel's gentleness toward the cat and the youthful vampire's appearance, she had all but forgotten about the babies.

"This is Miranda," Sammuel said and continued to rub the panther's stomach. "She and her sister escaped from Yorik's breeding farm. They seek asylum in Lorenz's settlement."

"She carries the gene," the young vampire said. "Lorenz and Afton will welcome her and her sister with open arms. I am Jace."

The vampire extended his hand and Miranda placed her small one in his. Jace bowed his head and kissed the back of her hand. He looked up at her, his eyes full of mischief.

"Are you trying to make me jealous?" Patrice asked.

The female vampire had moved so quietly Miranda had not heard her approach. With Patrice and Tanya present, the battle they fought must be over. Patrice ran into Jace's arms and kissed him.

Portia got back on her feet and growled at Jace and Patrice in his arms. The cat had not reacted aggressively when Jace kissed her hand earlier. Sammuel soothingly stroked Portia's head, but she continued to vocalize her displeasure at the attention Jace was getting from Patrice. Miranda watched as Sammuel got on his knees and whispered into the panther's ears. In response, the cat ran back into the forest.

"Come," Jace said. "Lorenz's keep is close. I am surprised you were attacked so close to his settlement."

"This was probably their last chance to recover their goods before it was too late," Sammuel commented. "We will follow you, assuming you do not have to go after your cat."

"Portia will find her way," Jace said.

Patrice turned and addressed Miranda, "You fought well today." The female vampire returned to Jace's arms. Miranda was both shocked and honored by Patrice's compliment.

Jace retraced his steps to where he had originally entered the meadow. Patrice and Beatrice walked beside him, while Tanya and the one surviving human woman followed. Miranda held back, waiting for Sammuel to join her.

"When you said Portia was not what she appeared to be, what did you mean?" Miranda inquired.

"She is a shifter," Sammuel responded. "I am surprised Jace is unaware of that fact."

Miranda had heard stories about shifters, but never expected to come across one. She had seen something in the cat's eyes making her believe she was not in jeopardy. The shifter obviously had feelings for Jace.

"Who are Afton and Wylaine?" Miranda asked.

"Wylaine is a powerful vampire who The Creator wanted destroyed," Sammuel said. "Two thousand years ago, he first converted the creature's birth brother and then the brutal Frazour to slay Wylaine. Lorenz is still the most human among my blood brothers and could not kill the vampire who was once his human brother. I believe Wylaine gets a perverse thrill out of toying with Frazour, who has unsuccessfully battled Wylaine since his conversion."

Miranda could not fathom the passing of two thousand years and wondered how long Sammuel had existed. Vampires must measure time differently than mortal beings.

"And Afton?" Miranda asked.

"I do not know," Sammuel admitted. "Lorenz has never aligned himself with a woman for more than a few nights of sex and feeding. I had heard rumors he had entered an agreement to join with Yorik's half-ling daughter. Let me see your neck. I shall heal the damage the vampire wrought."

Sammuel swept her hair from her shoulders and she found his gentleness surprising. He treated her with the same care he had displayed with the cat. Miranda tilted her head aside, giving Sammuel full access to her ravaged neck. His tongue ran across the ripped flesh and a shiver ran down Miranda's spine. She was suddenly very warm.

"We should restore ourselves," Sammuel said, between strokes of his tongue against her wound.

Sammuel took her into his arms and his lips stole away her next question before she had a chance to ask it. Whatever Miranda was going to say was lost in the sensations rocking her body. Every kiss they shared seemed to grow in intensity. Her legs gave out, but instead of steadying her, Sammuel brought her down onto the soft grass.

While his mouth devoured hers, his hands tugged at her leggings. Sammuel's hand breached her undergarment and his fingers caressed her slick feminine folds. Her body's passion lubricated his fingers as he pleasured her. His mouth captured her cries while her body readied itself for ecstasy.

"I need to be inside you," Sammuel murmured urgently. His words were spoken in broken gasps, as if he struggled to speak. "That vampire could have taken you from me today. I have to make you mine."

The thought of a vampire taking her virginity had plagued her nightmares for years. Now, she had a chance to be with a creature she craved. Their telepathic connection and ability to generate energy from each other proved they belonged together. He might leave her as soon as they reached Lorenz's settlement but, for now, he appeared to want her as badly as she desired him. She wanted this one moment, unsure of what the future held.

"Yes" was all she was able to say before her body fractured. Her response was more of a scream than a word. She hoped Sammuel understood she wanted this, too. Miranda was not certain if she would be able to utter anything else.

Sammuel removed his fingers and released his erection from the pants that had confined it. The stiff member rubbed against her, as if introducing itself. With one of her free hands, Miranda reached for his arousal and wrapped her fingers around the engorged rod. The extremity had a life of its own.

She needed him inside her to be complete. The energy they shared craved the additional strength the joining would produce. Miranda guided his erection through her glistening folds. Her body tightened around the foreign protrusion. Sammuel groaned as he entered her inch by inch.

Miranda cried out as the small membrane representing her inno-cence was breached. The slight pain did not hinder the joy of completion she felt. Her body clenched around his, suffusing her with a pleasure she could not comprehend. With each thrust, energy hummed in her veins. Sammuel plunged into and then pulled out of her body, setting an urgent pace which Miranda matched with every lift of her yearning hips.

Sammuel shifted his weight as he drove the rhythm of their bodies' movements. Miranda wished they had undressed so she could feel his flesh against hers. She widened her spread legs, giving him greater access to her.

Sensations continued to build within her core. She was close to something wonderful, just out of reach. Miranda lifted her knees and wrapped her legs around Sammuel's waist. He covered his mouth over hers and caught her cry as they came together. Strength she had not fathomed possible escaped her body and the ground below her actually quaked, or so she thought.

Nature revolted to the broken vow to his dead wife. The ground beneath Miranda growled its displeasure. Sammuel had not only betrayed his wife, but he had taken Miranda's innocence. He could not explain his actions any more than he understood the earthquake. Such disturbances were rare in the Nightshade universe, but his former world had been plagued with such seismic activity.

Sammuel withdrew from Miranda, rose onto shaky feet, and rear-ranged his clothing, tucking his betraying member away. Energy soared through him, but the impact she had on him made him unsteady both physically and mentally. He quickly handed Miranda her leggings. She uttered an unintelligible response and turned her back to him while she dressed. He could feel the hurt and uncertainty radiating from her, but Sammuel found he was unable to speak. Any comforting words he might have uttered were stuck in his throat. Many levels of guilt consumed him.

He stared at the corpse of the vampire Portia had killed, not more than ten feet from where he had taken Miranda. What had he been thinking? Some force within caused him to lose all reason. His mind had but a single focus—Miranda.

"They must be wondering what has become of us," Miranda said. Her eyes surveyed the ground, unable to look him in the eye. He had humiliated her and made her feel unsure of herself.

She raced toward the forest, following the path the others had taken earlier. He wanted to take her into his arms and comfort her. Sammuel could not understand the feelings he had for this woman. For some reason, his blood transformed her and made her stronger. She was no longer the fragile waif he first met. Energy coursed through her because of the life force she drew from him and the intimacy they shared.

He wished he could call what they just experienced making love, but he could not. Sammuel had an uncontrollable need for this woman he could not begin to explain. Although he had not been with a woman since becoming a vampire, his blood brothers had. No woman they ever shared sex and blood with ever transformed the way Miranda had.

Sammuel entered the forest and followed at a discrete distance behind Miranda. He could sense she wanted to run away from him as she struggled to maintain a steady pace. There was no doubt in his mind that he would track her down and take her again if she ran from him, the urge to claim and reclaim this woman coursed through him.

"You will not tell Jace about me?" A voice cut through his obsessive thoughts about Miranda.

He turned and saw a naked woman half hidden in the woods. She had dark mocha colored skin, black flowing hair, and was breathtakingly beautiful. Why this vision would spend her life in the body of a panther was a mystery to him.

"Your secret is safe with me, Portia," Sammuel said.

"And the woman?" Portia asked, biting her lower lip.

"I will ask her not to say anything to Jace," Sammuel said. "He is a stranger to her, so I doubt she would mention what I told her. Does Frazour know?"

"Frazour and I had mutual needs and we traveled together for many years," Portia said. "Things have now changed, as you will see when you arrive at Lorenz's. The woman is yours to protect."

Portia turned and walked deeper into the forest. Sammuel suspected she would be in her panther form the next time he saw her. What was between Jace and the shifter was none of his business. He had enough to deal with related to his budding relationship with Miranda and how unsettled he felt.

Sammuel quickened his pace. He wanted to give Miranda some privacy, but did not want to get too far behind her in case any vampires made a last ditch assault before they arrived at Lorenz's. Once they were safe, he had a life altering decision to make regarding Miranda and how he had planned to spend his immortality.

CHAPTER 6

Miranda was shocked by what she saw upon entering Lorenz's settlement. Humans worked side by side with vampires, smiles on their faces. Miranda had never seen humans appear so carefree and well fed. Even though she'd heard the stories, she still could not believe her eyes.

The vampires were dressed in the same clothing the humans wore, instead of robes. Although their flesh was decomposing, their eyes did not glow red. Some of the vampires even had smiles on their rotting faces.

Even more amazing, no one, vampire or human, seemed concerned by the black panther prancing beside her. Portia must be a regular visitor to the keep. The cat had traveled beside her the last hour. Miranda fully enjoyed the one-way conversation she had with the female shifter and was prepared to get an earful once Portia took her human form.

Miranda had been so distracted by her surroundings, she lost sight of Jace, Patrice, and her sister. When she came to a split in the path she was following, Portia nudged her to the right. It was not long before Miranda spotted cement stairs leading to the stone structure's entrance.

A breathtakingly handsome blond male stood at the building's threshold. His golden tan brought out the deep blue of his eyes. A disagreeable sound behind broke the enchantment she experienced gazing at the beautiful creature. Sammuel came up behind her and continued forward to meet the vision.

Sammuel embraced the blond and, even in the torch lit courtyard, his darkness was a stark contrast to the man he greeted. Miranda inched forward, anxious to meet the male who captured her attention.

"How is it possible?" Sammuel asked, his hand running down the stranger's tan face. "You have much to explain, Lorenz."

Miranda stopped in her tracks. She must have misheard the name Sammuel uttered. Lorenz was a vampire. Although Sammuel and his blood brother were different from the blood sucking creatures who raised her, they were still vampires.

"Enter," Lorenz said, "I have much to tell you. Afton is making ready for the babies you transported. Portia warned us of your arrival before she returned to help guide your group to our settlement."

Sammuel extended his hand, expecting her to join him. "This is Miranda. She will stay with me."

His demand was such a shock it rendered her mute. Fully expecting that Sammuel would guide them to Lorenz's and wash his hands of her, Miranda believed she would room with her sister until their situation was finalized. The fact he wanted to share quarters surprised her.

"The women will be safer in the harem," Lorenz said. "Our settlement was just attacked by rogue vampires. There may be more on the outskirts of the keep, readying a second assault."

"Miranda stays with me," Sammuel dictated. His words were so forceful, Lorenz merely nodded his understanding and consent. "I will protect her from any threat."

Having followed orders her whole life, Miranda was conditioned to do as she was told. There was a part of her that was thrilled by Sammuel's dictate. She enjoyed the physical aspects of their relationship, although she wasn't going to admit it to him.

They entered a great hall with carpets on the stone floor and colorful furniture brightening the torch-lit room. Miranda never dreamed such a place existed. Until very recently, everything in her life was either sterile or horrifying.

"I see you have made some changes since the last time I was here," Sammuel observed.

"Everything has changed," Lorenz said. "Finally! Here comes Afton, Yorik's daughter."

Miranda turned and saw a tall woman with long, flowing black curly hair enter the hall. She was as tan as Lorenz and appeared to be the epitome of health. She had heard Afton was a half-ling. It was Miranda's understanding half-human, half-vampires were sickly beings.

"You cannot be Afton," Miranda thought. To her horror, she said the words out loud.

"And you must be Miranda," Afton responded. There was humor in Afton's delivery which surprised her. Nothing about this place or the people who lived here were what she expected. "We were advised of your arrival."

Miranda noted Jace entered the hall. Portia was in her panther form and presently lay on a rug near a blazing fire. Her large black head turned in Jace's direction. With a huff, she rose to her feet and stalked over to Jace, wedging herself between him and Patrice.

"They said you were Yorik's half-ling at the farm," Miranda addressed Afton. "I am destined to bear his next child if you do not help me."

"What?" Afton screamed, her face reddened with anger. "I knew he had one of those horrible farms, but I didn't know he was planning on victimizing another poor woman to produce another offspring. I will not allow another woman to suffer what my mother endured."

"I do not scent the gene," Lorenz commented, confusion written on his face.

"It was present until…" Sammuel started to explain and stopped abruptly.

All eyes were now focused on Sammuel. He shifted uncomfortably on his powerful legs. Miranda remembered them pinning her down as he drove in and out of her. Her own legs became weak with the memory.

Lorenz and Afton exchanged glances. A knowing look transferred between the two of them. Rather than a scowl marring her face, Afton broke into a brilliant smile.

"You feed off each other and generate energy, don't you?" Afton asked. "The same happened between me and Lorenz, and then Frazour and Emma. Welcome to our family, sister."

Miranda was momentarily stunned. How could the woman before her possibly know what passed between her and Sammuel? Yet, Afton had claimed the same thing happened between her and Lorenz.

Afton embraced Miranda. Beatrice only held her in fear. Miranda had never been hugged with honest affection. Strong emotions overwhelmed her. Tears she could not explain ran down her cheeks.

Sammuel watched in horror as Miranda started to cry. He had seen women fall apart over the centuries, but never had he been as affected as he was now. Just prior to him forcefully pulling her from Afton's embrace, Miranda smiled.

"I am so sorry," Miranda muttered, "I do not understand what is happening to me."

Afton backed away from Miranda and pushed her blond hair away from her face. Lorenz's woman seemed to have genuine affection for… he was not sure what Miranda was to him. Sammuel had not been the same since they met. Emotions he could not control or understand coursed through him.

"We are soul mates, as are you," Afton informed them. She turned to address him, "No one else will satisfy your hunger. When you are together, you will draw incredible strength from the physical act."

Sammuel had heard various legends of soul mates since The Creator disappeared with a woman through a portal two millennia ago. He had always thought the tales were nonsense. But he could find no other reasonable explanation for what was happening between him and Miranda.

"So, you have finally deemed to grace us with your presence," a booming voice from behind bellowed. Sammuel did not have to turn to know Frazour had joined them.

Whatever retort he was going to say was lost in the shock of seeing Frazour and the little blue haired woman beside him. Frazour had been the most feral among them. This particular blood brother had never been comfortable around his own kind, preferring the company of beasts to both humans and vampires. Originally, Sammuel had been concerned about Miranda and Frazour being in the same keep. But there was a new calmness, an almost serenity, about Frazour.

The female by his side was striking with her rich blue hair, highlighted with deep red streaks. Her body was covered with markings, all water signs. She was as much a mystery to him as the changes to Frazour.

"And who do we have here?" Frazour asked.

Sammuel instinctively moved closer to Miranda. He did not miss the humor reflected in Frazour's woman's eyes. Afton was less amused and came to stand beside Miranda.

"Play nice, Frazour," Afton warned. "This is Miranda. She is Sammuel's soul mate. She was also born and raised on a human farm, so she has been very sheltered. Before she met Sammuel, Miranda was destined for my father."

Frazour's eyes widened in surprise. "Your mate is safe around me. I cannot say the same once Drake joins us."

"Drake was always a gentleman around me," Afton said. "You, however, tried to compel me when we first met. Although, based on Lorenz's description of you, I was expecting to be terrorized by the sight of you. So, I guess you did me a favor with your outlandish behavior."

"It was all good fun, my sister," Frazour said, as he embraced Afton. "The blue haired beauty is my soul mate, Emma."

Sammuel watched the interplay with growing interest. He must have missed a lot and had much catching up to do. They had all been summoned to Lorenz's for a particular reason. That was a good starting point to find out what was going on.

"It is nice to meet you, Emma. What of Wylaine?" Sammuel asked. "Has he attacked? You mentioned earlier you had been attacked by rogue vampires."

Frazour and Afton exchanged glances. However, it was Lorenz who answered his question. "My brother met the sun," he replied. "We have much to share with you, but let us get you settled first."

The women in his blood brothers' lives created a new dynamic. Lorenz and Frazour seemed almost human. They appeared to feel deeply for their women. However, if their females were threatened, Sammuel believed they would become more vicious than they had been before. Miranda stood stationary, absorbing everything happening around her.

"Where do you wish to be housed?" Afton asked Miranda. "You can stay in the harem with your sister and the other women, or with Sammuel. The choice is yours, not his."

A growl came from within Sammuel, a sound he had never generated before. No one was going to separate him from his mate. He did not miss the warning look Lorenz threw in his direction.

"Don't you snarl at me," Afton scolded him. "I spent weeks in my father's hive as his prisoner. You are a pussy cat compared to that monster. Everyone who resides within these walls has free will, including Miranda."

"She stays with me," Sammuel reiterated. He put just enough edge in his voice not to excite Lorenz.

For an instant, Afton's eyes glowed red. She raised her hand and pointed toward the fireplace. The fire raged out of control, as if an accelerant had been thrown on it.

"Care to modify your answer?" Afton asked.

Sammuel presumed Afton's trick with the fire just now could be part of the answers he had been promised, but Afton was right. Miranda needed to be settled and get some rest. He could feel her anxiety flowing through their link. She was uncomfortable with his behavior toward Afton.

Miranda placed her hand on his forearm. "I would like to stay with Sammuel."

He was not sure if rooming with him was her desire or to facilitate peace between him and Afton. Sammuel had to admit he liked Afton and her emotional strength. Although he did not appreciate her trying to separate him from Miranda, he liked the fact she put Miranda first.

"Come," Afton finally said to Miranda. "I will show you where you will be staying and where you can find your sister. You are free to move around this keep as you desire. If you change your mind and wish quarters of your own, you have only to ask. We also need to get you something to wear."

Sammuel allowed Miranda to leave with Afton. She needed to be cared for and all he wanted to do was bury himself deeply inside her. His body burned for hers. Whatever guilt he possessed over betraying his long dead wife was overshadowed by his uncontrollable attraction to Miranda.

"We have an uneasy peace with Yorik," Lorenz informed him. "Should we expect him to arrive with hopes of claiming your mate? With the five of us present and Miranda no longer emitting the scent of the genetic marker, Yorik will probably back away from his claim."

The five blood brothers were vampire royalty in the eyes of most vampires. They had been the only live humans converted by The Creator. All others had been either dead and reanimated or created by a reanimated creature. Sammuel and his brothers were the only vampires who appeared human. Tanya and Patrice shared the same blood, being spared the decomposition all other vampires experienced. Since they were women and fed off vampires, they were unwelcome in most vampire hives.

"I understand the feeding synergy between us," Sammuel said, "but not the elimination of the gene from her body."

"Afton's control of fire did not give you a hint to what you are now dealing with?" Frazour asked. "We are evolving into elementals. The women are transitioning quicker than we are. Afton controls fire, while Emma gathers her strength from water. It was Afton and her elemental gift that brought Wylaine down."

Sammuel immediately recalled the ground trembling after he had sex with Miranda. He wondered if that after affect would continue. The stone structure they now lived in would become problematic when he wanted to have relations with Miranda.

"Is there a way to minimize elemental powers?" Sammuel inquired.

"Why?" Lorenz asked.

"I believe Miranda is a land elemental," Sammuel answered. "The ground quaked the first time we were together."

"Wonderful," Lorenz replied, looking at the walls and ceilings of his home. "We will have Emma visit with her. Her element is water and she had to learn to control her elemental gift from overtaking her."

Sammuel's world was spinning out of control. The woman he had mated with had the ability to destroy everything Lorenz had built. Worse, he had little self-control to prevent Miranda from destroying the stone structure when they had intercourse.

"There is more we need to share with you," Frazour said.

He imagined they were going to explain Lorenz's tan, Frazour's calmness, and Emma's hair. In the short time he had known Miranda, he witnessed how her body had changed before his eyes. What else was in store for him?

CHAPTER 7

Miranda looked around the large quarters she would be sharing with Sammuel. Her eyes kept returning to the enormous bed that dominated the room. She could almost sense Sammuel's hands exploring her needy body. Why did she feel incomplete without him beside her? None of this made any sense.

"There are modern bathrooms behind the door to your right," Afton said.

"Bathrooms in a vampire's keep?" Miranda questioned. She was used to using chamber pots when she had to relieve herself. The vampires had promised her a rudimentary bathroom because they had running water in the lab, but never followed through. She had never expected such a luxury in a settlement populated primarily by vampires.

"Vampires are not the only beings who live in this community," Afton assured her. "A human's comfort is essential in maintaining harmony in our settlement. They donate their blood and the vampires see to it they are well cared for. No one is a prisoner behind these walls."

Miranda had witnessed how healthy and happy the people who lived in this settlement appeared. The vampires at the farm were only concerned with the blood their subjects would supply, not their quality of life.

"A couple of my dresses are being shortened," Afton told her. "You look to be five or six inches shorter than me. Nothing of Emma's will fit you. In the meantime, you can wear this."

Afton was probably six feet tall and Emma was significantly shorter. Fortunately, Afton was also powerfully built. Miranda knew her body grew more muscular by the hour. The garment Afton handed her was made of the softest material she had ever felt.

Miranda quickly removed the clothing she borrowed from Tanya, not bashful to undress before the woman. Although she'd had her own quarters before, modesty was an extravagance that even Miranda did not possess. Vampires would enter her room without knocking to draw her blood, lead her to the lab, or take whatever they desired from her.

She slipped the dress on over her head and the luxurious material cascaded down her body. The silky cloth molded to and caressed her newly curvy figure. She had been a stick with no shape before she encountered Sammuel.

Afton eyed her curiously. "We need to talk. You left a sheltered life at the farm, although I can't imagine what kind of existence that was. Now you are a soul mate of a powerful being. More importantly, you are evolving into a nearly unstoppable force."

"I do not understand what you mean," Miranda responded. She possessed no powers, other than feeding Sammuel.

Afton pulled a nasty looking bejeweled dagger from within her dress's pocket. Miranda gasped in fear and took a step back. The ground trembled below Afton's feet, cracking the stone floor.

"Interesting," Afton mumbled. Her response was so disciplined, while Miranda was alarmed by what occurred. This time, she knew she was responsible for what had occurred. "You're the first land elemental among us. I mean you no harm. Do you trust me?"

Miranda's gaze shifted between the knife in Afton's hand and her eyes. There was no reflection of malicious intent reflected in her eyes. Miranda was about to respond when Afton sliced her own forearm.

Shocked, Miranda lunged forward to offer what aid she could. She watched in wonder as the cut healed before her eyes. How was such a thing possible? Miranda cautiously extended her arm, now understanding Afton's original intent.

The cold steel cut through her skin, followed by a sharp pain. Afton wiped the blood that flowed from the wound and Miranda watched it miraculously heal. Within a minute, there was no evidence she had ever been injured.

"How? Why?" Miranda uttered, unable to finish a thought. She continued to look at her forearm dumbfounded.

"He gifted you with immortality," Afton responded. "Well, at least the ability to heal remarkably fast. I wouldn't recommend getting decapitated or hemorrhaging and bleeding out. Those two things will definitely kill you. Unfortunately, you are still susceptible to pain."

Miranda considered everything Afton shared. She had always been weak and had decisions forced upon her. Since leaving the farm, decisions were now hers to make. Although she allowed Sammuel to decide what the group would do, it was still her choice to follow.

Was she now tied to Sammuel for eternity? The thought of unlimited time was overwhelming. However, the prospect was not as horrifying as she originally imagined. Spending most of the day in his arms was an alluring thought. It seemed he wanted to keep her around.

"What have I gifted Sammuel?" Miranda asked. It had to be more than fueling him with energy. Nature always had a balance, at least that was her impression in the limited experience she had.

"The sun," Afton responded.

That simple answer explained Lorenz's tan. A whole new world was now open for Sammuel to discover; his movements were no longer relegated to the night. She knew he was still emotionally tied to the vampire women he traveled with and could not imagine him leaving Patrice and Tanya behind.

A banging on the door captured Miranda's attention. The door opened and a breathtakingly beautiful woman entered the chamber. Her mocha colored skin was flawless and her curly black hair fell over her shoulders. She was tall, with muscular legs. When Miranda looked into her amber eyes, she knew Portia stood before her.

"I brought a garment you can use until yours are completed," Portia said. "It is short on me, so it will suit your height. You look very nice in Afton's gown."

Miranda was not used to the kindness of others or their compliments. She searched for a full length mirror in the enormous chamber. Finally, she spotted one on the far side of the room, partially hidden by a partition.

Afton stepped aside, understanding Miranda's destination when she finally moved. Miranda stared at her reflection in disbelief. Everything about her had changed, except for the shape and color of her eyes.

"Most of your physical transformation is complete," Afton commented. "However, your powers will continue to grow in strength." Miranda did not miss Afton glancing at the crack in the stone floor. "The initial blood exchanged started your physical change. It was the intercourse that initiated the elemental evolution. Those are the two stages of what is call the joining. As your gifts develop, you need to learn to control, as well as wield your power.

"Things are getting too serious," Portia complained. "Let us head to the harem and luxuriate in the soothing waters there."

Afton laughed, "Your vocabulary continues to improve. Maybe you should spend more time in your human form. One of these days, you have to reveal yourself to Jace."

"Not today, or any time soon," Portia said. "I want to swim and enjoy myself while we are here."

Portia grabbed Miranda's arm and led her from the room. The sound of Afton's laughter faded as they headed away from the quarters she was to share with Sammuel. She allowed Portia to drag her through endless stone hallways. It was unlikely Miranda would be able to find her way back to her chamber.

Every human they encountered appeared healthy and free of visible vampire violence on their bodies. When the vampires fed at the farm, they seldom healed their victims. Wounds often festered and became infected. Considering the value their blood held, the humans were treated despicably.

Miranda did not realize there was anything to do in water but bathe. Once a week she was allowed a bath, rather than the usual bowl and towel she was provided. Most of the humans on the farm lived in squalor, unless a vampire wished to feed on them. Miranda spent most of her time in the lab, since the stench where the rest of the humans resided was offensive. She did, however, find spots outside in the sun where other humans were not allowed. Only human guards frequented the area and they left her alone.

When they entered the harem, Miranda could not believe what she saw. Women lay in various stages of undress, lounging on couches or relaxing in multiple pools. There were two waterfalls that fed the largest pool. The water cascading down the stone structure produced a relaxing sound. The vast room had curtained alcoves bordering it and doors leading to private chambers Miranda surmised.

"There are articles of swimwear you can wear if you do not wish to undress completely," Portia told her. The shifter pointed to the area where she indicated Miranda could change.

Portia removed her dress, revealing her naked body, and entered one of the pools. The woman was absolutely stunning, it was hard to take her eyes off her. Her physical activity when she was in her cat form was evident. Miranda needed to get more exercise in order to tone her own body.

Not being familiar with the rules of the harem, Miranda chose to partially cover her body. She did not know if vampires entered this sanctuary in order to feed off the women or relieve their other needs on any given schedule. Having Portia present relieved some of her anxiety over Sammuel's absence. She had seen the shifter destroy a vampire with her powerful jaws. Although she did not understand the mechanics behind Portia's ability to change forms, she felt safer in her presence.

Miranda tried on several tops before she found one large enough to sufficiently cup her now large breasts. As it was, her breasts still spilled out of the top she wore. She slipped on a bottom that came to her hips, providing adequate coverage.

She headed for the pool Portia entered and stopped dead in her tracks. A devastatingly handsome male prowled toward her. His dark eyes drank in her appearance. Miranda knew without an introduction, Sammuel's last blood brother, Drake, approached.

"What have we here?" Drake's voice was smooth and seductive. "Another beauty to taste and savor."

Good God, it was as if his words stroked her. Miranda's knees grew weak and she involuntarily moved forward. She had a sudden overwhelming desire to kiss his lips and run her hands through his midnight black hair. Her nipples hardened in anticipation of his touch.

In a flash, Drake was no longer in front of her. A black blur of two figures struggling for dominance crossed her field of vision. Inhuman sounds came from the mayhem before her.

Finally, the skirmish was over and Sammuel was plastered against the wall, Drake's hands around his neck. Miranda stepped forward wanting to aid her mate. Sammuel's glare warned her not to interfere. A power was building within her, demanding to be released. Sammuel was in danger and she was not impotent in her ability to protect him.

"Hello, brother," Drake drawled.

Drake looked behind him and smiled at her. The man had a lethal charm, but a different kind of lethal was reflected in Sammuel's eyes. Her anxiety lessened, as did the fire from within.

"I assume the beauty is yours," Drake continued, his delivery as smooth as it was earlier. "Brothers share, you know."

"Never," Sammuel answered through gritted teeth. His jaw was so tight, she half expected his teeth to shatter.

Miranda could see the playfulness coming from Drake, but she sensed a very different emotion emitting from Sammuel. He would kill Drake if he had the chance.

Hate raged through him, unlike anything he experienced before. His blood brother had tried to compel Miranda. Even after his family had been slaughtered, he had not felt the uncontrollable need to kill. Sammuel knew he was going to erupt, the power overwhelming.

Miranda came to stand next to Drake and placed her hand on Sammuel's cheek. Power channeled from him into his mate. She screamed as the dark elemental fuel escaped him and overwhelmed her. It was not a sexual release that caused her to yell, but the strain of unbridled energy.

Drake grabbed her wrist and severed the contact between them. Sammuel shuddered to think what would have occurred had Drake not broken the flow of power. His blood brother caught her in his arms before she collapsed. Sammuel did not view it as an aggressive act and continued to get his rage under control. Miranda had absorbed most of his dark power.

Drake placed Miranda on a nearby lounge and draped a blanket over her. From where Sammuel stooped, he could see her wan face devoid of all color. He did not understand what was occurring between him and Miranda, but he did not like it. They normally generated power with one another, not drain it.

"You need to feed her your life force," Drake said. "Whatever she pulled from you nearly drained the life from her. Each soul mate pairing appears to have stark differences. This type of negative power transfer has not occurred between Lorenz and Afton, nor Frazour and Emma."

Sammuel rose to his feet and staggered to where Miranda lay. She was so spent, even her lips were gray. He instinctively knew physical contact would be insufficient. Drake was right, she needed his blood.

He accepted the knife Drake offered and cut deeply into his lower forearm. The bone-exposing gash would provide her ample blood before it healed. Sammuel brought his arm to her lips and urged her to drink. The light suction of her lips against his skin brought an indescribable pleasure coursing through his body.

It was a different energy produced by feeding his mate than when he feared she was in danger. He had unlimited capacity to absorb the magic they produced when they were together. The energy was positive, life affirming.

He watched in awe as color returned to her cheeks. Sammuel could feel her growing energy mirroring his own. Miranda regained consciousness and was alert. His urgency to carry her to one of the adjacent rooms and thrust into her was almost palpable.

Sammuel removed his arm from her grasp and gathered her into his arms. There were various chambers they could use to slake his growing hunger for her. As he walked away from the lounge, his need only grew more intense. Sammuel could sense the same urgency emanating from Miranda. He was quickly losing control. Even a room was too distant for his lust to be satisfied.

He entered one of the curtained areas. It provided a minuscule amount of privacy, but he could no longer reason or consider such an incidental factor when his body cried out to connect with his soul mate. Sammuel placed Miranda on the elaborate bed that populated the area.

Miranda had the presence of mind to start removing the tight material restraining her plump breasts. He grabbed the cloth and ripped it down the middle, freeing her from its constraints. Sammuel lifted her hips and removed what covered his reward. He tried to be as gentle as possible but was barely in control of his desire.

He plunged into her with a single thrust, pushing her ruthlessly into the mattress. Miranda wrapped her legs around his hips, taking him deeper into her core. She pounded her fisted hands against his back, demanding more of him.

Her urgency fueled his rhythm as he drove in and out of her. His body slid sensuously against hers as passion-produced sweat saturated their skin. When her breathing became labored Sammuel slowed his pace.

Miranda frowned her disapproval. "I want to be on top," she boldly pronounced.

Sammuel immediately responded to her demand. In a matter of seconds, Miranda straddled him, Sammuel still buried deeply inside her. A troubled look crossed her face. He knew she was not quite sure how to ride him. He grabbed her hips and aided her in finding her own tempo.

Her breasts shook as she rode him. He was not sure what was more satisfying, watching her breasts or her face, glorious in its obvious pleasure. Miranda set an urgent pace gasping for air. He not only felt her orgasm build, but also the rise of a different, more destructive, release.

Their pace was so excessive, Sammuel was not sure he would be able to communicate his concerns to Miranda before she reduced the keep to a pile of rubble. Lorenz had mentioned he had the ability to telepathically communicate with his soul mate, similar to the ability shared between the five blood brothers. He knew such a link existed between him and Miranda from her earlier ability to read his mind.

Sammuel focused on her and pushed his thoughts toward Miranda, as he did when he communicated telepathically with his brothers. He could already feel her emotions washing over him. Her urgency had been as great as his, driven by the blood he had fed her.

"There are two forces rising within you, Miranda," Sammuel communicated telepathically. *"That sexual climax you feel is going to shatter you in a million pieces and can be pushed out as you fracture. Something else has been building inside you. You need to release it into me, like you took my energy earlier."*

He was not certain she was capable of understanding him. She was in some type of primal state, her body's elemental nature erasing all ability to reason. Miranda continued to ride him with a manic fervor. It was doubtful she understood what he communicated, assuming he had been able to link into their special channel.

Miranda threw her head back and screamed her release. Her hands came down against his chest as the orgasm rocked her body. Power shot through her palms into his torso. The energy soared through him, causing his own climax to amplify. His shouts echoed through the harem accompanying those of his soul mate's.

She collapsed on top of him, totally spent from the cataclysmic release. Her elemental power still swirled within her, but the excess had been absorbed within him, intermingling with his growing ability to gather energy. This time the ground did not quake in reaction to Miranda's saturation of elemental power. He had absorbed her power, as he had hoped.

Sammuel brought his lips to hers and fed energy to his mate, restoring her strength. He no longer craved blood, all he desired was her. After three centuries of feeding off vampires to exist, a new world presented itself to him. He actually looked forward to whatever tomorrow would bring, with Miranda by his side.

"Afton said you are now a day walker." His mate had used the terminology vampires called a being who existed on blood, but was able to withstand the rays of the sun.

Sammuel had always loved the night. Even as a boy, he would gaze at the sky, seeing shapes forming in the stars. His father often told him stories associated with the figures in the night's sky. When he had children of his own, he shared those same tales.

The light of day had always presented the risk of the village being attacked. It was on just such a day that his family had been slaughtered and his surviving daughter was abducted. Night brought his salvation and the means to seek his revenge.

He rarely left a shelter during the day. Nightshade settlements had purple canopies protecting the vampires from the sun's harmful rays. Sammuel had never been drawn to the filtered warmth of the sun. Daylight weakened a vampire and the fabric that protected them painted the sky a light shade of purple.

Now, theoretically, he could venture out without feeling the orb weaken him or fear a blue sky might be the last thing he saw before being turned to dust. Over the years, he had considered meeting such an end, but could not leave Patrice and Tanya behind.

His fingers caressed the small of Miranda's back and then slowly drifted up her spine. Small mewls escaped from the woman who sheltered his body with her own. They could live here for eternity, feeding off each other when either weakened. They needed nothing and no one else.

Patrice and Tanya did not need him and had not for a long time. If he had been honest with himself, he would have realized, it was the other way around. The women had a purpose for their immortal life, while he had not. Everything changed when Miranda entered his life.

"What do you want?" Sammuel asked curiously.

She stared at him, bewildered by his question. He should not be surprised, considering she grew up on a human farm. Miranda had not made a single decision in her entire life, until she decided to run.

"Beatrice's safety," Miranda finally answered.

Miranda's mission in life now became his own. They had one obstacle to overcome before they could truly start their life together. Yorik must be destroyed.

CHAPTER 8

A fton stood a top Lorenz's battlements. Her father's men surrounded the keep, his force enormous and comprised of vampires from the newly united Venture-Bertram hive. She fought alongside her father to rescue Emma. Yorik became more powerful by aiding her.

She loathed Yorik for what he had done, continuously raping her mother until she conceived a child — a half-ling. Lorenz and a crystal telepath rescued her mother first from The League's clutches and then from Yorik.

Crystal telepaths were beings able to navigate inter-dimensional portals. One took her mother and an infant Afton to Earth, Gingko Terra. That parallel dimension was vampire-free, but her mother was broken beyond repair and took her own life when Afton was but three years old.

Another crystal telepath and a mind control telepath had tricked Afton into returning to the Nightshade universe. She was slowly dying on Earth, blood barely sustaining her. When Afton joined with Lorenz, her life had changed. She was no longer a weak half-ling. Now, she was a powerful fire elemental.

Once again, Yorik wished to mate with a human capable of bearing him an offspring. Afton was not going to allow another woman to suffer her mother's fate. Yorik was prepared to attack their settlement to retrieve what he viewed as his property. It was highly unlikely Miranda would be able to bear Yorik's child since her conversion, but

Afton doubted her father cared. What belonged to him was his until he released it. Afton had belonged to him until he gave her to Lorenz.

"Your father is approaching the gate and has requested an audience," her soul mate said. "If we explain what has occurred, perhaps he will back down."

Afton turned to address her mate. His beauty still caused her to pause. She had often dreamed of a perfect lover and he stood before her. Their joining had saved her life and she had dedicated her immortality to changing the quality of life for humans residing in the Nightshade universe. Lorenz's settlement proved vampires and humans could coexist in harmony.

"You have more faith in my father than I do," Afton replied. "Yorik is not going to leave without Miranda and I will not give her up. The treaty between the two of you should protect us. After all, it forced you to join with me."

"Yes, and it has been such a hardship," Lorenz said, as he took her in his arms. Every now and then her soul mate would say things in a playful manner. It happened on rare occasions, and she cherished those instances. "The treaty has always been to Yorik's advantage. Even though he has left my settlement alone as agreed, I paid the yearly tribute until I finally fulfilled my obligation concerning you. When it is no longer convenient for him, the parchment and blood that represents the treaty will be worthless."

Her father would not wait long to speak to them. For a short time, she would enjoy what Lorenz's lips were doing to the nape of her neck. Whatever he did to her physically, always transported her mind to a glorious world, escaping from the horrors of the Nightshade universe. Time was a luxury she currently did not have.

"Let's get this over with," Afton said. "Make sure Drake is present."

Several times Afton had been close to letting Drake destroy her father, but in weak moments she stayed Drake's arm of vengeance. The charming vampire had forged an alliance with a human from another dimensional realm, pledging to kill Yorik. Today would be the day she released Drake of his promise and finally end her father's miserable existence.

Drake stood alongside his four blood brothers, watching Yorik enter Lorenz's great hall. The master vampire was flanked by a small army.

A greater force surrounded the keep. Yorik was displaying his strength. Whether he would attack was another question, entirely.

The three female soul mates stood behind them, each capable of causing major destruction. Yorik already knew of the fire and water elemental women who were present. Boiling caldrons were scattered throughout the room, ready for Emma's use if push came to shove.

Yorik was unaware a third elemental was among them. Even Drake was unsure of Miranda's power. He had been present when she absorbed the tremendous energy Sammuel generated in his rage. Not for the first time, Drake wondered what his own soul mate would evolve into once he completed their joining.

His mate still resided in her mother's womb in a parallel realm. Every time he came near Alexandra, he could feel the unborn child reach out to him. His soul mate, Star, could somehow feel his need across dimensional boundaries. Star was going to be a force to be reckoned with when she reached maturity.

"I have come for my property," Yorik demanded.

"I am not your property, Daddy Dear," Afton's voice dripping with sarcasm.

"Best you not mind my business, little girl," Yorik growled. "Miranda was taken from me and I have come to retrieve my property."

Drake could feel the rage rise within Sammuel and knew he was about to speak. He grabbed his blood brother's shoulder. *"Leave this to me, brother. Nothing gives me greater pleasure than annoying this creature. I will not have many more opportunities to enjoy myself at his expense."*

"You are too late, Yorik," Drake said. "My brother has joined with his soul mate. Miranda is no longer human and will only be able to bear offspring with her mate."

Drake was not all together sure what he claimed was true. Up until a short while ago, soul mates were stories of legends. The tales were fueled by The Creator's joining with a human woman bearing the genetic marker and the two subsequently left the Nightshade universe through a portal two thousand years ago.

"She stands behind me," Sammuel said "Can you smell her fertility? You are too late. Miranda can no longer provide you with what you desire."

Drake could see Yorik's contemplating his next move, a frown present on his already decomposing forehead. The master vampire did not like to be denied. In Yorik's eyes, it diminished his perceived power.

"Nonetheless," Yorik said, "I will take her and the four babies stolen from me. Their life blood belongs to me. You may keep the two human breeders as a token of my generosity."

"You will leave with nothing," Afton informed her father.

In the next instant, the vampire who stood beside Yorik burst into flames. Before Yorik could react, another of his minions erupted.

Yorik seemed unfazed by what Afton had done. "How long can you keep that up, daughter?" Yorik asked. "Is your strength already diminishing? I have hundreds outside these walls, thousands if necessary."

What stopped Afton from destroying her father was anyone's guess. It had been a tug of war between father and daughter since Afton returned to the Nightshade universe. One minute the monster was threatening his daughter and the next he did something to safeguard or aid her.

"The treaty you signed in blood states you will protect this keep and all the humans in it," Lorenz stated. "I have held up to my end of the bargain and you were able to double the size of your force through our association. What is the loss of one woman and a few children? You can no longer breed with Miranda, and four human babies are nothing compared to what you have gained."

"And what have you got to lose, Lorenz?" Yorik asked. "I have not forgotten you are responsible for the loss of my previous breeder and her offspring."

Drake did not miss Afton's gasp and two more vampires burst into flames, while scalding water showered over four others. However, it was the earth trembling beneath his feet that alarmed their adversary.

"I will return in two days' time," Yorik said, preparing for a hasty retreat. "Consider how much you have to lose while I am gone."

No one moved as Yorik exited the hall. There would be no question of surrender. The blood brothers would rally around Sammuel's mate. They had two days to come up with a plan to defeat Yorik.

Afton came to stand in front of Drake. "I release you from your pledge," she said.

Drake did not have to ask which one of the many promises he had made to Afton. She had finally given him permission to destroy her father.

"My beautiful crystal telepath, Shirl, should be returning to our dimension," Drake said. "I must honor another pledge when I destroy your father. Benko Jarlyn must witness his demise."

Drake had forged an alliance with the future ruler of the Troyk universe, another parallel dimension. Yorik had brutalized Benko's mate, Chartail, in the short period of time she was in the Nightshade universe. Shirl was also the best friend of his soul mate's mother, and was also close to Afton.

They had a battle to plan. Yorik was a formidable enemy. If he said he would return in two days, Yorik would do exactly that.

CHAPTER 9

THE TROYK PENAL COLONY

Miranda could not believe she was in a parallel dimension where vampires were nonexistent. She had never realized how much stress she felt while living in the Nightshade universe, until she spent time in this little village. Afton and Drake were meeting with Benko Jarlyn to discuss strategies to defeat Yorik. This dimension had once been a penal colony populated by the undesirables from the world Benko hoped to rule one day.

They had transported the babies through the portal and they would stay behind when the rest of them returned to the Nightshade universe. She could not understand why they could not all stay. These people lived a simple life, free from the threat of vampires.

Afton and Emma had both sworn to change the universe ruled over by vampires and would not abandon the humans trapped there. Miranda could not help but think about other teenage girls, like Beatrice, who were used as breeding stock. She had witnessed, firsthand, the result of what they had to endure.

She was mesmerized by this safe haven. It was a world Lorenz and Drake had helped to free of the dangerous criminals who had been sentenced to live out their lives here after committing crimes in the Troyk universe. All who remained were the freedom fighters dedicated to overthrowing the mind control telepathic government of their home world. Miranda had no idea what a mind control telepath was, but it did not sound good.

"Would you like more to drink?" a girl around her age asked. "I'm Cassie Jarlyn, by the way."

Miranda looked up to see a lovely girl with mahogany brown hair and bright blue eyes. She had a welcoming smile, something Miranda was not used to. It was hard not to immediately like the girl.

Cassie talked like Afton and Emma, combining and abbreviating words together. All three women had been born or raised on Ginkgo Terra, Earth. After spending time with Afton, Miranda had begun mimicking her speech patterns.

"Thank you," Miranda replied, "I'd like that. I'm Miranda."

The girl looked like she wanted to say something more, but was unsure how to start. Miranda had spent a lifetime holding back questions and comments. She imagined Cassie would speak her mind when she was ready.

Miranda had never had a friend. Humans and vampires alike avoided her. She was different, courtesy of the genetic marker. Until she saw Afton and Emma interact with each other, Miranda had not realized what she was missing and how lonely she truly was.

"Would you like to walk to the lake?" Cassie asked. "The moon is bright and there are torches to guide our way."

She rose to her feet, a silent acceptance of her desire to join Cassie. It would provide them the opportunity to spend time together. Besides, Miranda was happy to get away from the discussion to kill Yorik. She had nothing to add to the discussion and felt out of place.

Miranda reached through their channel to communicate her plans to Sammuel. He was absorbed in debates related to Yorik's fate. Rather than responding telepathically with words, he pushed emotions toward her. She felt contentment radiating from Sammuel indicating his pleasure in her desire to become friends with Cassie.

After living almost her whole existence on the farm, Miranda could not wait to see a large body of water. She just wished it were light out so she could really enjoy it, but there were still members of their party who could only travel at night.

"We are very much alike," Cassie said, breaking the silence that had fallen between them. "Both of us have unimaginable power and people shy away from us because of it. At least your soul mate touches you. Darden will do little more than kiss me. He's afraid of what he will unleash once we are together. When telepathic soul mates make love for the first time, our brains excrete a hormone that unleashes additional telepathic abilities. I'm already a powerful mind control telepath."

The girl spoke so rapidly, Miranda had to concentrate to catch everything she said. Miranda had never met telepathic people before, although she did share a telepathic connection with Sammuel. She understood what a crystal telepath was, but had no clue what Cassie's ability was.

"What exactly is a mind control telepath?" Miranda asked.

Cassie stared at her for a moment. "You just decided to return to the Nightshade universe when the rest return there with my father to witness Yorik's death."

Miranda was shocked. She had been debating what she wanted to do and had finally made a decision. Sammuel told her he would support whatever she decided. The girls who were victimized on the farm finally swayed her decision.

"How did you know that? Can you read minds?" Miranda asked.

Rather than feeling violated, Miranda was intrigued. Cassie shook her head. She was having trouble looking directly at Miranda. Her eyes wandered everywhere but at Miranda's face. It was obvious her new friend felt awkward about what she had just done.

"I was able to sense you were struggling with making a decision and I made it for you. Those girls need your strength, support, and power," Cassie said. "It feels like you made your own decision, but I made it for you."

Miranda continued to stare at Cassie Jarlyn. She was uncertain what to say or how to react. At no point had she sensed the other girl in her mind. As far as she was concerned, returning to the Nightshade universe was her idea.

"Generally, I shy away from groups. I can make decisions for a collective without even being aware I'm doing it," Cassie admitted. "I've seen people do some stupid things over the years because of me. I watch their faces as they wonder what had possessed them. The answer is easy, it was me."

"Wow! I'm just struggling with not bringing down buildings when I cause the ground to shake," Miranda laughed.

It felt good telling someone else her fears, even in a joking manner. She had never felt so comfortable and relaxed with anyone before she met Cassie. They were kindred spirits.

"You are not messing with my emotions, are you?" Miranda asked.

Cassie smiled. "No. I can only make decisions. I guess that can help sway someone's mood, but it's indirectly."

"What else can you do?" Miranda asked.

"I try not to do anything," Cassie admitted. "People look at me in fear, so I intentionally try not to use any of my powers. I don't want to harm anyone. Controlling my powers requires practice and I can't do that. What can you do?"

"This is all new to me," Miranda admitted. "I am evolving into a land elemental. So far the ground shakes when I am overly excited or angry. Recently, I have learned to funnel excess power into Sammuel, so I do not damage the buildings I am in. Afton said I will gain more powers in time, which frightens me. Emma struggles with her burgeoning powers as well."

Talking to Cassie was freeing. Miranda felt the pressure in her neck and shoulders continue to ease. Shirl traveled between dimensions on a regular basis. Maybe Miranda could see more of Cassie. They both needed a friend to confide in.

"Will you be joining your father when he enters the Nightshade universe with us?" Miranda asked.

"No, not this time," Cassie said. "It may get violent and my dad said I was to remain here, where it's safe. He loves Chartail and wants revenge. But when Shirl and Alexandra go to see Afton, I'll try to catch a ride through the portal. When they travel from the Troyk universe, they can make a detour here before they open a gateway to the Nightshade realm."

They decided to head back before one of their men came after them. Even though they lived in different dimensions, Miranda knew she had a friend in Cassie. If ever her friend needed her, Miranda would be there for her.

Sammuel released a sigh of relief when Miranda and the other girl returned to the village. His soul mate appeared to be more relaxed, even happy. She needed more than he could singlehandedly provide. Miranda needed female companionship. He figured the female elementals, along with the women from this and the Troyk universes were a good beginning.

He wanted her to have a rich life. She was no longer the isolated girl from the human farm he originally met. Miranda was beginning to see what the broader universes had to offer and she desired more. Sammuel looked forward to introducing her to new experiences, both in and outside of their bedroom.

They had been debating strategies for over two hours about how to eliminate Yorik. Shirl, the female crystal telepath, wanted to be involved. She had spent time in the Nightshade universe and witnessed the treatment Chartail had been subjected to. Had it not been for Drake claiming her, Shirl could have easily fallen prey to Yorik's horrific handling. The crystal telepath assured the men she could wield incomprehensible power if it became absolutely necessary. Her soul mate, Starc, confirmed her unparalleled abilities, but would not provide details. Starc's only demand was that all would obey without hesitation should he shout for everyone to hit the ground.

Based upon everything he had witnessed since joining with Miranda, Sammuel was not going to discount what Shirl was capable of. Soul mates were able to generate power stronger than he ever dreamed possible.

As much as Sammuel would have preferred to leave Miranda safe in this universe, she had the right to fight for her own safety and freedom. Although, he would have liked more time to hone her powers. Regardless, he had given her the option and he had to abide by her answer.

Miranda came to sit beside him. He placed his hand over hers. Sammuel needed to touch her. Shards of power trickled through the link that existed between them.

"Has anyone considered what will happen after Yorik is eliminated?" Frazour asked.

His brother rarely spoke, but when he did it was relevant and not a means to fill silence with inconsequential chatter. Frazour had been a warrior his whole existence. He saw the world differently. It was only recently, with Emma by his side, his feral brother had mellowed. However, Sammuel knew no one would be more deadly than Frazour if his Emma were threatened.

Sammuel had to correct himself—if Miranda was in danger, no creature would be more lethal. He could feel his rage building at the mere thought.

Miranda squeezed his hand, sensing his disquiet. Sammuel doubted he would be able to breathe without feeling her next to him. His life was now tied to hers…a thought that should terrorize him, instead it gave him a sense of peace.

"Chaos," Lorenz finally responded to Frazour's question. "No one is powerful enough to step in and take over Yorik's holdings. Wars will breakout between factions for control of the two hives and the human farm. The alliances he cultivated will fall apart. Smaller keeps, like my settlement, will be under constant attack as vampires rally to build small armies. It will all take a tremendous amount of blood."

"We are strong enough," Afton said.

"You cannot be serious," Lorenz responded to his soul mate's comment.

"Not all at once," Afton replied. "We liberate the human farm and develop relationships with any of Yorik's lieutenants who attempt to take over the Venture Hive. We can show them how the residents in Lorenz's settlement, vampire and human, can live together in harmony. No vampires are starving in our keep, unlike the condition of the vampires in other hives. Humans from the farm can experience how pleasurable giving blood can be. We'll lose the Bertram Hive for now, but that can't be helped."

Silence followed Afton's suggestion. Each of them digesting her vision. It would not be easy, but nothing worthwhile seldom was. When Sammuel was alone with Miranda, they would discuss the idea without others influencing her.

"Afton is right," Miranda whispered. Sammuel doubted anyone but him heard her barely audible words. It was his turn to squeeze her hand in encouragement. "Unless Shirl can open a portal and transfer all the farm occupants to this world, their best hope is living as the humans do in Lorenz's settlement. I grew up on the farm. What you have to offer is paradise compared to their pathetic existence."

Afton smiled at Miranda. Sammuel could feel the warmth radiating from her at Afton's simple action. Some of that contentment soaked through their bond into him. She continued to gift him with emotions and sensations he had not felt since he was human.

"I sat at my father's side for two interminable weeks," Afton shared. "Yorik is hated. No one will seek to revenge his death, but many will try to grab their own piece of the pie."

It was an odd term to use, but Sammuel understood her meaning. Where the people before him would unite, the hive vampires would scatter until a number of dominant future masters emerged. Other than them, there were no conspiracies brewing to overthrow Yorik, who had an uncanny ability to identify and neutralize any threats to his empire.

"Taking into consideration only the Venture Hive," Emma said, "there are not enough humans to properly feed their numbers."

"Vampires tend to gorge, taking more than they need," Afton said. "Ironically, all that excess blood does little to stay their thirst. In the beginning, we will limit the amount of blood each vampire can consume. If we have to, we'll use the serum that causes humans to replace their blood at ten times the usual rate. If we enforce the humane treatment of the farm occupants, ensure a pleasurable experience giving blood, and strictly adhere to the rules Lorenz instituted in the settlement, we should be fine."

"This is nothing but a pleasant dream if we are not successful in killing Yorik," Emma said. "Never again will I stand aside and watch humans be slaughtered by vampires to repopulate a hive after a battle."

In his delay answering his blood brother's summons, Sammuel had missed the battle to rescue Emma from the Bertram Hive and the installation of Yorik as the new master. He knew the toll a vampire war took and the human blood required to replenish the forces.

"We will channel our power through our soul mates and Benko will finish him off," Afton said. "Jace, Drake, and the rest of the settlement vampires will hold back any of Yorik's force stupid enough to try and stop us."

Sammuel was not sure what Benko Jarlyn was capable of doing. Whatever it was, he would not be using a sword, but his telepathic mind control powers. Everything was dependent on their being able to incapacitate Yorik.

There was no structure in this settlement that could withstand the sun's rays. While, theoretically, he was now immune to its destructive power. Sammuel was not willing to test that theory and Drake was still at risk, not having a mate. Therefore, they would begin their return to the Nightshade universe just prior to sunrise.

Until they were ready to leave, there was plenty of work that needed to be done. The four blood brothers would be able to accomplish in hours what it would take humans weeks of manual effort to achieve.

The hard work reminded Sammuel of when he was human. Those were brutal, difficult times. How the human race survived in his birth dimension amazed him. Whole villages were slaughtered to gain property that would later fall to a more powerful clan. Those who did not die in battle were ravaged by disease.

In Benko's former world, it was not a body's destruction, but the corruption of the mind the freedom fighters fought. He was supposedly a powerful mind control telepath who chose not to use his gifts for political gain, but a promise for a better tomorrow. It was a noble cause to be part of.

But Benko's next battle would be strictly one of vengeance. It was a feeling Sammuel understood all too well. He had given up his mortality to seek his own. The problem was, it had not brought back his wife and children, nor had becoming a vampire healed the terrible void in his life. Only time eased the emptiness he felt. And Miranda completed him.

She seemed relaxed with Benko's daughter. Every once in a while Miranda laughed. His heart warmed at the merry sound. There had been too little laughter in her life up until this point. From here forward, Sammuel's sole purpose was to guarantee she lived a joyous life where laughter was a regular occurrence.

Cassie was showing Miranda how to bake bread. The women prepared the morning meal while the men constructed the additional huts they needed. They would be returning to the Nightshade universe before the humans sat to feast.

Miranda was safe in this world. He wished he could leave her here while they dealt with Yorik and the aftermath of their actions. Whether he liked it or not—win or lose, it was going to be bloody. Drake's hand had been stayed by Afton for too long. His blood brother had made a promise to Benko Jarlyn and Drake did not like the pledge hanging over his head.

It was time to return to the Nightshade universe. Now that the work aiding the Troyk freedom fighters was behind them, Sammuel could see the stark fear in their women's eyes. Shirl opened the portal and they returned to meet their destinies.

CHAPTER 10

THE NIGHTSHADE UNIVERSE

Yorik was true to his word. The master vampire stood before Lorenz and Afton two days to the minute after his promise to return. Sammuel and Miranda stood directly behind their host, flanked by Frazour and Emma. His soul mate's fear leaked through their connection.

Drake and Jace stood further behind them, with their Troyk guests close by. Benko Jarlyn, the crystal telepath, and Shirl's mate were also guarded by Portia. The cat was almost as effective killing vampires as he and his brothers. Portia's preternatural speed and powerful jaws made her a voracious hunter.

Everyone was in their position and awaiting Afton's signal. Patrice and Tanya were in the harem protecting the women in case it was attacked. There was no telling what the ramifications might be if they failed to destroy Yorik.

Regardless of Yorik's crimes, he was still Afton's father. Yorik had abided by the treaty with Lorenz for eighteen years, even though it was doubtful his half-ling daughter had survived. Sammuel had also been told Yorik came to the rescue when Lorenz's troops were about to lose a battle against Wylaine's minions and Afton's life had been in peril. Yorik had not returned to the Venture Hive until his daughter was back on her feet.

More recently, the vampire had aided in Emma's rescue. His blood brothers had willingly turned over the Bertram Hive to him when he named it as the price for his assistance. That battle was what caused Yorik to begin an unscheduled harvest at his human farm in order to feed his starving soldiers. Had that not occurred, he never would have met Miranda...a fortunate twist of fate.

Yorik's crimes were too numerous to list. One did not become the master of a hive without incurring a high human death toll. He had terrorized his daughter and victimized Benko's soul mate.

"I have come for my property, little girl," Yorik said. He enjoyed belittling the powerful fire elemental. "Relinquish what is mine and no one needs to die today. Bring me my bride and I will leave in peace."

"Your 'bride' seeks sanctuary within these walls," Afton sneered. "Leave now, before I avenge my mother in the manner she so rightly deserves. I would never turn Miranda over to you, so you could do to her what you did to my mother. No matter the consequence, that will never happen again."

Afton's voice grew louder with each word she uttered. By the time she was done speaking, Afton was on her feet, her hands were raised, and fire surrounded Yorik. All the vampires who had stood in the ring's circumference were now ash. For some reason, the containment ring was able to destroy more vampires than when she singled out individual creatures.

"Release me or you will all be destroyed!" Yorik shouted.

Yorik's threat was met with scalding water raining down over his entire army. The verbena-laced water weakened all the vampires drenched in the mixture. Frazour and Drake, backed by a contingent of Lorenz's resident vampires, systematically eliminated any vampires attempting to release Yorik. The only thing feeding the fire was Afton's strength, and her contact with her soul mate. Jace stayed behind to safeguard Shirl, her soul mate, and Benko Jarlyn. Sammuel guarded the three female elementals.

The great hall's air was already beginning to become thick with smoke from the inferno, making it more difficult to see in the already dark chamber. Sammuel searched along their telepathic connection to ensure Miranda's health. Fortunately, Miranda no longer had human lungs and tolerated breathing the polluted air with relative ease. Even her eyes were not watering.

Miranda had her hand on Sammuel's shoulder transferring her excess energy to him. They had yet to discover a way for her to use her element indoors. Sammuel's sword sliced through the unfortunate vampires who attempted to attack what they perceived to be the easiest target—the women.

Emma placed her hands on one vampire who got past him. Her mere touch caused what little liquid was contained in the vampire's body to evaporate, leaving a dehydrated husk. This distracted the vampires battling Sammuel temporarily and he took advantage of their ill-timed lapse and decapitated three vampires with a single stroke.

Vampires started to back out of the hall, abandoning their master. The troops outside would see their retreat as a sign Yorik was dead or no longer master of the Venture Hive. His troops would scatter across the local area, unless Yorik's lieutenants could salvage what remained.

Jace came forward, accompanied by Benko Jarlyn. The crystal telepath opened a portal behind the future leader of the Troyk universe; for what reason, Sammuel was not sure. Drake came to stand beside Benko, offering him additional protection.

Benko stood before his greatest nemesis. He merely stared at Afton's father. At first, it appeared nothing was happening. Perhaps the telepathic power Benko possessed only worked on humans. Sammuel lifted his sword, ready to jump through the flames and eliminate the threat to his mate. Before he could move, Yorik cried out in pain. Yorik shoved back his robe's hood, his hands cradling his head. Before Sammuel's eyes, the master vampire's skull began to crack, his brain matter escaping as the organ deteriorated.

It was a slow and agonizing process, which Benko purposely prolonged, making Yorik suffer as Chartail had suffered. Lorenz carried Afton from the room against her will, fully understanding she would later regret seeing her father die while doing nothing to stop it. He rightfully took her choice away. In his mind, Lorenz had made the right decision.

Where his soul mate was concerned, Sammuel knew that Miranda needed to witness Yorik's destruction, so she could be certain the threat to her future was no more. Sammuel took her hand, not to siphon energy, but to offer support. She leaned her body against his. He released her hand and wrapped both his arms around her waist, resting his chin on the crown of her head.

Sammuel could feel every cell in her being, and as usual, she was thinking of her sister. The creature who owned them was dying. Their future, however, was only as strong as Lorenz's settlement's walls.

The flames that had surrounded Yorik died as soon as Afton was taken from the room. Benko's hold on the vampire no longer needed fire to contain him. His victim's brain had been destroyed.

When Yorik's heart stopped and he breathed his last breath, Benko turned to Drake. "You have fulfilled your promise to me. I will continue to honor your right to see Alexandra and be near her child even, after she is born."

Sammuel did not miss the look of disgust on the crystal telepath's face, but did not understand the dynamics at play. It was clear Shirl did not like Drake having access to her friend and Drake's unborn soul mate. The agreement was now one sided. Benko could change his mind any time and Drake would be helpless, no longer having the latitude to travel between dimensions to be with his soul mate. Sammuel could not imagine being separated from Miranda for any length of time.

Miranda stood over Yorik's corpse. At one point she stood right before him and he did not realize who she was. Not once had he traveled to the farm to develop any type of relationship with her. She would have been merely a vessel to bear him a child. A shiver ran through her upon the realization that, had Sammuel had not come along, her future would be very different.

It was Afton's fury that led to her father's downfall. Had Miranda not escaped when she did, Yorik would still be alive. The master vampire might have called for Miranda several days after the harvest to impregnate her and an ignorant Afton would have been powerless to stop him.

Miranda never voiced her fears about being forced to be with Yorik or giving birth to a half-ling. There was no one with whom she could talk. Beatrice always came to her to be comforted, but it never dawned on Beatrice that Miranda was in need of support or comfort.

Sensing her vulnerability, Sammuel tightened his hold on her. He comforted her without uttering a word. What could he say? The immediate danger was over, but they still lived in a world ruled by vampires.

"I can take you with me," Shirl said.

Miranda could feel Sammuel's grip on her tighten, his hold on her so constricting it made it difficult for her to breathe. It was an involuntary reaction to the crystal telepath's words. He immediately released her when he sensed her discomfort.

She turned and placed a gentle kiss on his lips. Miranda knew she could not leave this man. However, it would be a relief knowing Beatrice was safe. The girl factored into every decision and thought she had.

"My place is here," Miranda admitted, "but I would be eternally grateful if you took my sister with you."

"I will take her back to the penal colony dimension," Shirl said. "They rarely use their telepathic gifts as often as those in the Troyk universe. And, in case your sister becomes uncomfortable not having the power, there is a community not far from where you were where using telepathy is outlawed."

Tears welled up in Miranda's eyes. She was not used to the kindness visited upon her by Sammuel's brothers' soul mates or the Troyk women. Miranda could not help drawing comparisons between the women she recently met and the desperate females who merely existed at the Ventura Hive Farm.

Anger rose in her, similar to the build-up of her elemental strength. Miranda needed to control her emotions before she accidently brought down Lorenz's keep.

"Let us send for your sister," Sammuel offered. He had an uncanny ability to redirect her thoughts., although he usually employed physical distractions.

A thousand thoughts flooded her mind while they waited for her sister. Miranda knew she was doing the right thing for Beatrice. Self-doubt about her own path was what plagued her. The changes that were occurring to her body and her growing powers confirmed she needed to stay with Sammuel. It was which world they should reside in that she continued to question. Would a sane, rational person purposely live in the Nightshade universe?

Cassie had told her a mind control telepath's influence was negated when new data or a stimulus caused the person to reconsider their decision. It had been peaceful not being plagued by having to make a decision.

It was not long before Beatrice was before her. Although Patrice and Tanya protected all within the harem during the battle, her sister looked pale as death. Beatrice swooned when she saw what remained of Yorik's body. Miranda should have had his remains covered before Beatrice entered the hall.

"Yorik is dead and the Nightshade universe will become even more dangerous for humans while vampires fight for control of his holdings," Miranda said. "I am sending you to a parallel dimension where vampires do not exist. This is Shirl. She can travel between worlds and will take you somewhere safe. Beatrice, I will visit you as often as I can."

"No!" her sister cried. "You need to come with me. It is not safe for you in this world either. We are family, we need to be together."

Miranda embraced her sister. "Something is happening to me I cannot explain," she said. "I need to be with Sammuel and his brothers. The change has made me powerful and I cannot turn my back on all the humans who suffer in this dimension. When you enter the new world, ask for Cassie. She is very nice and she desperately needs a friend. Will you do that for me?"

Giving Beatrice a mission would hopefully make the separation more palatable for her sister. Now was not the time to tell her sister she had become immortal thanks to the bond with Sammuel. As always, she needed to focus on Beatrice.

"I will, if that is what you really want," the young girl responded. "It will be nice to have a friend. You have to promise me you will visit as often as you can."

"Promise," Miranda replied.

Miranda nodded to Shirl and the crystal telepath opened a portal. She watched her sister's eyes opened wide in amazement. For the first time in her young life, Beatrice had hope. It was difficult knowing she would not be by her side when she experienced positive, wonderful things. Miranda somehow knew Cassie would welcome Beatrice with open arms. Miranda felt a stab of jealousy when her younger sister walked through the gateway.

"Are you all right?" Sammuel asked.

"I have to be," Miranda responded. "There is not a doubt in my mind I did right by my sister. Her safety has always been what kept me going. It stopped me from dwelling on my own horrific fate. I am on a different path now, and she cannot travel alongside me any longer."

Sammuel's eyes surveyed her face. He did not look at her with lust, but with understanding. Miranda knew that few would understand what she just sacrificed, but Sammuel did. Ultimately, she knew he also faced leaving his daughter and sister-in-law behind one day.

"As soon as Afton has processed her own loss, we need to head for the human farm," Sammuel said. "It is too big a target to delay its liberation."

Afton stared at the blazing fire, her own emotions feeding the raging flames. Their mission was successful, so why did she feel horrible? The only violence she had been subjected to in Yorik's keep was by his own hand. Yet, he contracted Lorenz to join with her, knowing he had been the one who rescued her mother. There were so many contradictions where her father was concerned.

"You have nothing to feel guilty about," Lorenz said. "Yorik used you as a pawn. Afton, you represented the continuation of his line and that was it. He was a monster who held a woman hostage forcing the Troyk men into tricking you into returning to the Nightshade universe. For all he knew, you could have been happy and healthy."

She knew everything Lorenz said was true, but her mind kept focusing on everything he did to safeguard her. They fought side by side. First against the crazed Wylaine and then rescuing Emma.

"What will they do with his body?" Afton asked.

"The same thing we do with all the fallen. We will burn what is left until only ash remains. If you still question what you orchestrated, look long and hard at Miranda."

Her grandmother had told Afton she had her mother's eyes. Every time she looked in a mirror, she saw her mother. She knew a certain peace would now come to her, knowing her mother had been avenged.

"We should join the others and start planning a strategy to liberate the human farm," Afton said. "They should have completed removing all the bodies by now."

Lorenz placed his lips on hers. Between the passion and the power that was exchanged, Afton was momentarily stunned. She grabbed ahold of his arms in order to keep her balance.

"Maybe we should restore our energy first," Lorenz suggested.

He said it in such a sexy voice, her knees grew weak. How she wished they had time to fool around. The kiss had restored what little energy she lost restraining Yorik's movement. Every day she grew more powerful. The containment ring had been a new tool in her ever growing elemental arsenal.

"News of Yorik's demise will travel quickly," Afton said. "The human farm will be one of the earliest targets of a power hungry vampire. Unfortunately, we do not have time to enjoy ourselves. After we've liberated the farm, I will make it up to you."

Afton gave Lorenz a kiss on the cheek and exited their chamber. She had little self-control where her mate was concerned and did not want to risk falling for his ample charms. They could not afford any delays. Hundreds of human lives were at risk.

The loss of her sister was written all over Miranda's face. She had done the most unselfish act of love he had ever witnessed. Sammuel had not had the strength to let Patrice or Tanya go all those years ago. Patrice had only been sixteen when he transformed her into a monster. His daughter would never age, never have children, or enjoy a real relationship with a man. Sammuel had stripped her of the chance when he converted her, a selfish and uncaring act.

Miranda placed her hand on his cheek. Their bond must have made her aware of his thoughts. Compassion for his suffering swam in her eyes.

"You should not dwell on the past," Miranda said. "We need to safeguard the humans at Yorik's farm and find a place where they will be safe for the time being. Afton has such ambitious plans for this world and there is not a minute to waste."

Lorenz and Afton entered and the small group began planning their next moves. The soot in the air discolored all their faces. Other than that, no one was harmed during the short battle. This was only the beginning of what was to come as Yorik's holdings were claimed.

"We need to reach the farm before vampires start creating alliances," Lorenz said. "Their nature will cause them to fight individually now that their master is dead. It will not take long before they start banding together and factions develop. It is unlikely the smaller groups will wait until there is a new master before they try to acquire the humans at the farm."

"Should we all go with you or will some of us need to stay behind to protect the humans here?" Sammuel asked. He knew Patrice and Tanya would want to fight to liberate the souls on the farm.

"The sheer number of resident vampires here should be a large enough force to protect the keep," Lorenz answered. "My concern is where to take the humans after they are liberated. Yorik's stronghold lies between us and the farm."

"Sammuel, Tanya, and I have a community in the mountains by the East Sea," Patrice suggested. "There are a few small vampire hives we will have to pass, but our home is well fortified and defensible."

"How long will it take to get there?" Frazour asked.

"Two weeks on foot," Tanya answered. "There are too many humans to provide horses, and that is assuming they even know how to ride."

"We should travel by day," Emma said. "Jace, Drake, Patrice, and Tanya can follow at night, rounding up any stragglers or vampires who try to follow us. Once we free the humans, most of the pursuers will assume we will head back here, putting those left behind in greater peril."

Once they liberated the farm, Sammuel would test out his ability to withstand the sun's rays for the first time. It made sense for those who could travel during the day to put as many miles behind them as they could. This time of year, the Nightshade universe had longer daylight hours, making nighttime travel more difficult for the slower humans.

"Our opponents may be many," Afton said, "but they will not be united. Any attacks upon the settlement, as well as any who dare accost us along the way, will be small in number and poorly planned. The vampires who live here will be sufficiently armed to withstand any attack a disintegrated hive will throw at them."

"And newly formed vampire clusters will not fight with the precision of a hive," Frazour added.

"We leave now," Drake said. "We can continue devising our strategy to liberate the farm and the resulting exodus along the way. I am sure there are any number of beautiful humans who will need comforting."

In all the centuries Sammuel had known Drake, he had changed little. He was truly a wolf in sheep's clothing. Anyone listening to Drake would have no clue what he was capable of. His charm disarmed his victims and then Drake would attack.

"No seducing the women, with or without compelling them," Afton warned Drake. "They have been victimized enough. Besides, it's high time you start being faithful to your mate. I will have many exploits to share with her in a number of years when she comes of age."

A playful smile crossed Drake's face. Sammuel did not know if he was thinking of his unborn mate or enjoying the verbal fencing with

Afton. He noted a similar expression on Drake's face when Shirl had lit into him. His blood brother enjoyed the women scolding him.

"Let us start our journey," Lorenz said, getting the group back on track. "Arm yourselves and be prepared to leave within the hour. Miranda, I need you to draw a diagram of the farm. The buildings, where the guards are posted, and anything you feel will help in the assault. Work with Emma on a drawing. Frazour and Sammuel will pack for the women and make sure they are properly equipped."

Sammuel did not like Lorenz giving orders to Miranda. For the time being, Lorenz was in charge and he had to respect this authority. However, when they were preparing for battle, no one would be making decisions for Miranda except him.

CHAPTER 11

They traveled as a group for five nights. Miranda now had her own mount, which Sammuel cared for before they went to ground. As they made their way to the farm, they picked off any vampires that crossed their path. Tanya and Patrice needed them for nourishment. Besides, there would be less of them to deal with once the humans were free.

Miranda took a handful of soil and rolled it in her palm. She did not generate power from her element the way Emma was able to become stronger with direct contact with water. So far, she could only make the ground quake. She was not altogether sure how ground tremors could be used as a weapon when liberating the farm.

Portia approached and rubbed against her leg. Miranda reached down and petted the panther's head. Portia usually ran beside Miranda and her horse while they traveled. The cat viewed her to be the weakest member of the group and acted as her protection. While in human form, the shifter had befriended Miranda and as a feline she deepened their relationship.

Miranda got down on her knees and massaged the cat's shoulders. Portia was a beautiful animal and administering to the panther relaxed her. When the cat began to growl, Miranda did not have to turn to know it was Patrice who approached.

"Why does she not like me?" Patrice asked.

"Oh, I suppose she is jealous of your relationship with Jace," Miranda responded.

When Miranda got back on her feet, Portia took off into the forest. It was not Miranda's place to tell Patrice what Portia truly was. The shifter would reveal herself to Jace in her own time, and then finally to Patrice.

"She is a cat," Patrice said, stating the obvious.

"A very protective one," Miranda said. "Who knows what she can sense? We all react differently to our surroundings. I have not been exposed to many animals in my life, just vampires and humans. I get different impressions from each person I come in contact with, their reactions to me and how in turn I behave toward them."

"What do you get from me?" Patrice said.

"It's funny, but I feel you are protective of me," Miranda answered. "Beatrice told me you did not want your father to turn me. I was a perfect stranger and you did not want me to suffer as you have."

If vampires could blush, it sure looked like Patrice was. "I have to apologize for how I initially reacted to you," Patrice said. "You were the first woman my father showed any interest in since my mother's death. Although it was so long ago, it was still a shock and I overreacted."

It must have been difficult for Patrice to admit her feelings. Patrice could have moved forward in their relationship without ever apologizing and simply changed her behavior. She could not help liking Patrice a little bit more for that declaration.

"Thank you for that," Miranda said. "Your father loves you and I really want to be your friend. I never want to be the reason for any friction between the two of you."

Patrice gave her a critical look. "What about Tanya. What do you sense from her?" Patrice asked.

Miranda hesitated. Sharing feelings with another being was new to her. It had become easy with Sammuel because he could sense what she was feeling through their link. Talking about the negative vibes she picked off Tanya made her uncomfortable.

"Tanya was your mother's sister and I am afraid, in her eyes, she thinks I have replaced your mother," Miranda admitted. "Maybe not at first, but now…" She had felt uncomfortable around Tanya from the start. Patrice's earlier obvious dislike of her changed over time, but Tanya's attitude was more subtly masked with civility.

Patrice did not answer, she merely nodded. She had seen the same thing. It was nice to know it was not just her imagination.

"All those years ago," Patrice said, "my father originally showed interest in Tanya, but ultimately chose my mother. Maybe she thought my father would begin a relationship with her after a reasonable amount of time. Until you came along, he was dedicated to my mother's memory."

"And you don't resent me?" Miranda asked. She needed to be sure Patrice was comfortable with her relationship with Sammuel. The earlier apology went a long way to heal the division between them, but Miranda wanted to reinforce Patrice's comfort in what was occurring.

"It has been three thousand years!" Patrice answered. "I think that is an adequate mourning time. When I met Jace, we spent time together. He has become like a brother to me since I lost my own. We are not creatures that should love. My father is no longer a vampire, so he can."

Miranda could not help but feel sorry for Patrice, although she knew the other woman would not want that. Three of the blood brothers had found their soul mates and Drake was certain the Troyk woman carried his in her womb. Maybe there were equivalent mates for Patrice and Tanya out there.

Sammuel approached them and hugged his daughter. Since Miranda had entered his life, Sammuel was conscientious about showing Patrice the affection he had for her. Miranda loved that aspect of the man before her. She had never known the love of a mother or father.

The same was not true regarding Tanya. Miranda could see the female vampire pulling away from Sammuel. There was nothing in her behavior that caused Miranda any concern; she simply became unsettled around Tanya.

"The sun will be rising soon," Sammuel said to his daughter. "You need to go into the day shelter. Miranda and I will join you and the others shortly. It is time I finally see if I can, once again, walk in the light of day."

Patrice left them and headed for the shelter. She seemed unconcerned about her father testing his ability to withstand daylight. Miranda, on the other hand, was having a very different reaction.

Panic started to rise in Miranda. She had been told both Lorenz and Frazour had tested the sun's effect on their bodies while they were still within Lorenz's keep. They both validated the sun did not drain their strength before heading to the purple tarp protected courtyard. Only after those two stages did they venture into full sunlight. Sammuel was going forward with no failsafe.

"You should first feel the impact of the sun from the protected stairs of the day shelter," Miranda pleaded. "I have seen vampires burst into flames or turn to ash as soon as the sun had contact with their bodies. The farm was also used as a makeshift prison and I saw vampires forced into the sun."

The thought of losing Sammuel was overwhelming. She began to have problems breathing and began to hyperventilate. Miranda could sense the rising of the sun. The dirt around them started to move, as if blown by the wind. Slowly, a shelter of soil began to form around Sammuel. He understood what she was subconsciously doing and made no attempt to move.

Although there was nothing supporting the dirt shelter, it stood firm and would protect Sammuel against the harmful rays of the sun were Afton wrong about Miranda gifting him daylight. Miranda turned and watched the eastern sky slowly brighten. She had never seen the sun rise before and was awestruck by its beauty. The vampires had often locked Miranda in her room during daylight hours, ensuring she would not try to escape while they were in their weakened state. Occasionally, she would see its rays cascade over the east wall.

Vicious dogs patrolled most vampire farms during the day. The poor animals were horribly mistreated as puppies and then set free while the sun shone to stop humans from trying to escape the farm's walls. The dogs would not leave since they were well fed each evening.

The dogs worked in concert with human guards. Vampires did not totally trust humans guarding humans, so the dogs had been introduced. The farm's residents hated the men who betrayed them for a better quality of life.

"How do you feel?" Miranda inquired telepathically. She was not confident Sammuel would have heard her otherwise.

"I do not feel weakened in any way," Sammuel responded. *"Release some of the dirt surrounding me and we will see if I feel any different."*

Miranda concentrated on the mound before her and slowly soil started to fall from the fortress of earth she had constructed. She continued the process until only a thin layer of dirt stood between Sammuel and the elements.

"Keep going, Miranda. I can feel the sun's warmth, but am not weakened by it."

Miranda held her breath and let the remaining dirt fall to the ground. Sammuel stood and faced the rising sun. Her heart raced as his profile became visible out of the shadows and into the light of day as the sun continued its journey into the sky.

Sammuel was consumed by warmth, so distant in his memory, he had forgotten how much he enjoyed it. He had not realized what giving up the sun truly meant until this moment. Emotions welled up inside him, bringing him to his knees.

Miranda stood beside him and he could feel her confusion over his momentary weakness. Recovering quickly, Sammuel stood and took his soul mate into his arms.

"Thank you for this precious gift," he said. "Let us watch the sun for a couple of minutes more and then we should return to finalize plans to attack the farm tomorrow."

"The sun just rose," Miranda said. "We should review the plans closer to sunset and enjoy the day. It is your first sunrise in three thousand years. Take this time before we are all consumed by the coming battle and enjoy what most in other worlds take for granted."

"I forgot the multitude of colors. The pinks and the oranges playing off the bright yellow," Sammuel mused. "It is almost magical."

He took Miranda into his arms and kissed the crown of her head. Together they would enjoy what he had missed since becoming a vampire. Although Lorenz and Frazour were no longer adversely affected by the sun, they stayed in the day shelter so he could enjoy this moment alone with Miranda.

In his joy, he thought of his daughter and Tanya. They were still imprisoned by the vampire curse. How could he enjoy this, when they could not?

"Do not go there, Sammuel," Miranda said. "We will find a way for Patrice and Tanya to join us, and one day they too will witness this miracle. This is my gift to you and I want you to enjoy it, not feel guilty about decisions you made in haste after your family's horrific death."

It was clear he could hide nothing from Miranda. She felt his moods, just as he did hers. There was something freeing about the ability to be that close to another being, especially one as beautiful as his Miranda.

"Afton has asked Lorenz to build a pool outside his settlement," Miranda commented. "Can you imagine swimming under the sun's warmth? The pools in the harem are nice, but it would be wonderful to float on one's back and look into the beautiful blue sky and the intense sun. In the world where Afton grew up, such pools were common. Can you believe that?"

"Tomorrow we attack the farm," Sammuel said. "We need to have a sharp focus and not daydream about such things. When this is over and we can let down our guard, I promise we will watch another sunrise, swim in pools, and everything else you want to experience together."

Sammuel saw her acceptance of his words in her simple nod. He could not let his overwhelming emotions impact how he fought. There would always be another sunrise they could witness together. They had eternity. Today, they needed to focus solely on the upcoming battle. It was the only way he would be able to concentrate on what needed to be done.

He placed his arm around Miranda's waist and together they approached the entrance to the day shelter. They descended the stairs holding hands. Halfway down, Sammuel closed the iron gate that filtered out sunlight. Torches were lit to guide them the rest of the way down the corridor.

When they entered the large single room, everyone stood huddled around the table holding the map of the farm that Emma drew based on Miranda's input. There was a tall stone wall around the facility and a single entrance to the fortress. The structure was created to keep out non-hive vampires and to eliminate any chance of humans escaping.

The entry had a large carved stone that required several vampires to pull three ropes to lift the massive barrier. Dogs entered and exited the farm from the facility through the gate just prior to dawn and dusk. The only other time the gate was opened more often was during the quarterly harvest.

"Oh good, you are here," Frazour said. "There are more questions we need to ask. You mentioned the laboratory was underground and it was also where you were kept. Can you explain the layout of the subterranean shelter where the vampires will be congregating during our attack?"

"I only have knowledge of the area between the lab and my quarters. My room was near the entry to the underground section of the farm." Miranda wished she could provide more information. In the last several years, she opted to spend as little time underground with the vampires as possible. Even though she was not welcome by the other humans, Miranda enjoyed being in the sun when she was released from her room.

"What humans are kept underground during the day?" Afton asked. "There is nothing in the lab we want and the babies were rescued already. The farm was not designed for an attack by humans and I am not certain the vampires are aware we have day walkers among us. If we anger Miranda, she can destroy the underground bunker with an earthquake."

His soul mate was certainly capable of wielding such power. She was such a kind, gentle woman, yet she possessed enough energy to destroy the monsters who had held her and other human captives their whole lives. To his surprise, she was neither disturbed by the question nor by what Afton asked her to do.

"Vampires have a strong sense of smell," Miranda answered. "They try to stay away from the farm occupants because they are not given the means to bathe regularly. Other than Beatrice, and women giving birth, humans do not venture into the subterranean areas. It should be another month or more before any of the others have their babies. However, that doesn't mean a woman has not gone into premature labor and is underground in the birthing room."

Afton's gaze scanned the room and the faces of her co-conspirators. "We are just going to have to risk that no human is below. Miranda, do you have any idea how far the farm's underground chambers go? Collapsing its entry will buy us time. If we bring down the whole subterranean areas, we will significantly reduce the number of vampires that might follow us if they are rescued."

"They will not be rescued," Drake said. "Without hive affiliation, those vampires are expendable. Trapped, they will turn on each other and the strongest among them will feed off the weak. No vampire will set free whatever remains."

Drake spoke the truth. In a world overcrowded with vampires and not enough humans to sustain them, the vampires trapped were not worth saving. Unless the vampire was a master or lieutenant, it was forbidden for vampires to feed off each other. An infraction of the feeding rights resulted in an immediate death sentence. Naturally, the blood brothers were exempt from all vampire laws and only had to follow The Creator's dictates.

"I don't know," Miranda finally answered. "There is no telling. I might bring down other structures and accidentally create exit routes for the vampires trapped below. The point is moot until the dogs and guards are in our control."

"I will handle the dogs before the sun rises," Jace said. "The rest of you take care of the human guards."

His brother, Jace, had an uncanny ability to calm animals. They hoped he would be able to contain the dogs and ultimately use them to protect the humans during the daylight hours when the four vampires among them had to seek shelter. It was not unlike the shifters who protected the mountains surrounding his home. Sammuel did not like the idea of killing the dogs unless there was no other way.

"No one has said this, so I will," Emma said. "Why would the humans we rescue follow us, rather than scattering and pray they'd be safe on their own. I saw the humans they dragged into the Bertram Hive after we won the battle and Yorik had to restock the blood. They were petrified. It is still a vision that haunts me."

"We will save the ones that wish to come with us," Sammuel said. "In the past, we have liberated smaller farms and it is true, many humans blindingly ran. It is instinctual."

"Lorenz's settlement is known among the humans in this farm," Miranda advised them. "If we assure them who he is and what we plan to do, they may follow. They may also be aware of the babies that were rescued. Beatrice told me stories they shared about hope and a special vampire named Lorenz. He is a folk hero to these people."

"One problem," Sammuel said, "Lorenz does not look like a vampire with that tan face. We should have Drake or Jace pose as Lorenz. I am fairly certain they would never expect a blond vampire, regardless."

"Jace will have his hands full with the dogs," Drake said. "I will be happy to pretend to be Lorenz. It will be my opportunity to spend more quality time with Afton."

"Dream on, Romeo," Afton said under her breath. "I have to admit, Sammuel and Drake are both right. Besides, with me beside you, it is less likely you will manipulate any of the poor women."

"I am wounded, my love," Drake said, laughter in his voice. "If I behave, will you convince Shirl to bring Alexandra back to the Nightshade universe, so I can be near my soul mate?"

Afton shot Drake one of the dirtiest looks Sammuel had seen in the three thousand years he had lived. Women usually swooned over Drake, so it was nice seeing one stand up to him.

"No deal. You will do this and then I will consider your request. Not before," Afton said.

"We should all get some rest and restore our energy," Lorenz said. "Next sunrise we will get things underway."

The small shelter offered him and Miranda no privacy. All the furniture had been claimed while he and Miranda were watching the sunrise. He grabbed several blankets and created a cozy spot in one of the corners. Sammuel situated himself and then raised his hand to Miranda, who took it and joined him on the floor. He took her into his arms and held her tightly.

Later today, they would rescue people who had shunned Miranda because she carried the genetic marker. If it were up to him, the humans would be left behind and they would head home without them; but this was what Miranda wanted. He only hoped she did not regret her decision.

CHAPTER 12

The farm's stone wall was high and seemed impenetrable. Miranda could not imagine she had enough built up power inside her to bring down its walls. They did have a contingency plan — Frazour would scale the wall and pull up the entry stone were she to fail.

To her amazement, Jace had corralled the six massive dogs and charmed them. The beasts jumped around Jace like puppies. He had collected the dogs as they were released and immediately took them to a nearby day shelter. The animal-loving vampire and the dogs would spend the daylight hours safely inside the bunker. They were fortunate the dogs had been released early, so Jace made it to safety long before the sun rose. Drake, Tanya, and Patrice would follow him at sunrise, ensuring any stray vampires were quickly dispatched.

Miranda stood before the stone entry and concentrated. Although she focused, nothing happened. She could not generate enough powerful emotions on her own.

"What would those guards have done to Beatrice had you not escaped?" Afton asked. "One of those men would have claimed Beatrice and taken her against her will. He would have held her down and violated her, regardless of her pleas. Is that happening right now on the other side of that gate to another young girl?"

She knew what Afton was trying to do and the fire elemental was successful. Miranda could feel the anger grow inside her. It was as if she could hear Beatrice's screams and energy built until the maelstrom within her threatened to overpower her.

The ground beneath her began to quake. She walked to the stone entry, placed her hands against the cold marble, and then screamed out her anguish. Power flowed through her, penetrating deep into the rock. The large slab began to crack and Miranda substituted her sister's cries with her mother's. Her imagination continued to fuel her elemental strength.

Crushed stone started to fall at her feet as the entryway disintegrated. Frazour, Lorenz, and Sammuel all ran past her with their swords drawn. They would make quick work of the two dozen human guards. Afton and Emma would only use their elemental powers if necessary. At this point, their role was to guard a depleted Miranda. The three women stood at the farm's threshold.

Miranda needed to restore her energy. She knelt down and picked up a handful of dirt, hoping to finally be able to draw energy directly from her element, but she was, once again, unsuccessful. Before she could bring down the underground lab, she would have to pull power from Sammuel, who was presently battling the human sentinels.

All the guards had to be executed had they had any hope the other humans would follow. That had been the biggest bone of contention and they had argued for hours. The idea of killing the men left a bad taste in Miranda's mouth. She would have preferred if they were left to run free and try to survive on their own against any vampires they were sure to come across. It seemed a more fitting death than the swift ending the elemental males would dole out.

Several of the farm's occupants came running in their direction, stopping in their tracks when they saw Miranda. Clearly they knew who she was and were confused by her presence.

"I have come from Lorenz's settlement," Miranda shouted. "Yorik is dead and we are freeing you. We will protect you and escort you to a place you will be safe from vampire violence. Please, trust us. There are other vampires out there who will kill or capture you for your blood."

Two of the men took off running, but the others remained. Miranda could not force anyone to come with them, she could only offer them an option. The rest of the group turned and watched the men cutting down the guards everyone feared and loathed, a better argument for them to remain than anything Miranda could add.

Other humans ran from the farm and the original group of humans urged them to stay. Like before, there were a handful of them that took off running for the forest and a short-lived freedom.

Sounds from inside the farm quieted, as more of the prisoners left the stone confines. The group stood around talking about the men who liberated them and Lorenz, their savior. Although she had only known Drake for a short period of time, Miranda knew he was going to enjoy the adoration that would soon come his way—particularly, the idolization that would come from any number of the females.

The group of humans parted as Sammuel made his way toward her. His sword was stained red with the guard's blood and she could not take her eyes off the gore-covered blade. The reality of what they were attempting hit her hard. Miranda was weighed down with the responsibility for so many human lives.

"There are three guards who refused to fight and fell to their knees begging for mercy," Sammuel said. "We have some decisions to make. Before we deal with them, you need to bring down the entry to the subterranean lab and quarters."

Miranda followed him into the farm. The fallen guards were easy to find, since they wore black uniforms. A number of other humans were also dead. They were collateral damage, held hostage and killed by the guards in an unsuccessful attempt to save themselves.

In the middle of the large yard, three men were on their knees. Each man had their hands behind their heads, continuing to beg for mercy. They had never given mercy; why should they be given a pardon for their crimes? Miranda did not want to make the decision. She walked past them, in the direction of her former quarters, not bothering to look at the guards who still lived.

Sammuel came to stand beside her and took her hand. Energy flowed between them, but not enough for what she needed to accomplish. Miranda brought her lips to his and drew in power their intimacy generated. It did not take long to restore her strength.

Miranda stood before the stairs she had taken so many times over the years. A million emotions flooded her brain as memories of her life here came raging back. So many years without hope, simply existing. The one bright light in her life up until her escape had been finding and helping to raise Beatrice. Although only two years separated them, Miranda had been the parental figure from the start.

"Do I need to make you angry again?" Afton inquired. Rather than asking the question in a serious tone, Afton's delivery was playful.

"No," Miranda answered. "I just need to bring down the stairwell."

"Can you pulverize the stone into sand?" Afton inquired. "When I was a little girl, my grandmother took me to see an artist blow glass. We can finish the cave-in with a sheet of glass. It's the only thing I can think of that allows me to participate. I don't know if it's the right combination of materials, but I can give it a try."

Miranda had no idea how Afton was going to make glass from sand, but she could not deny her new friend. She took Afton's hand and concentrated on the walls supporting the stairwell.

"How do you call your element without emotion?" Miranda asked. She needed to be able to control her ability over land without always getting angry or being enraptured.

"Let me answer that," Emma said. "Your element is part of you. That portion that you release into Sammuel when you feel overloaded is what you need to connect with. Right now, it's probably only a small flame. You need to find that little spark and let your mind imagine it growing bigger and bigger. Then direct that power, like you send telepathic communication to your soul mate."

It seemed too simple. Could it really be that easy to control her power? Emma was right, it was part of her. Miranda searched for the energy that continually grew inside her. She imagined it growing larger, but contained. Controlling her breathing, she worked to manage her elemental gift.

The sides of the stairwell began to crumble, but the earth did not shake. Areas adjacent to the entry began to cave in as well. As Afton requested, the stone broke down into sand. More and more of the area began to collapse.

Fire sprang from Afton's hands and heated the sand Miranda had created. The silt started to glow red from the flames attacking it. Miranda halted the generation of more sand until Afton's work was done. A tremendous amount of heat was coming from the pit.

"Go ahead and cover it," Afton said. "The layer of glass should be a nice obstacle if the vampires from below try to escape."

Miranda once again concentrated on the power within her and brought down more of the rock the vampires used to construct the underground sections of the farm. She had reached the point where her energy was no longer required and it seemed the earthen tomb imploded on its own.

Sammuel came to stand beside her. "Nicely done," he commented. "They will not be able to come up from that unless they have help.

Lucky for us, it is doubtful any such assistance will arrive. We just need to determine the fate of the three guards that surrendered, and then we start the journey to my fortress with whatever humans who wish to come with us."

Together they walked to the center of the yard. A large number of the farm's inhabitants stayed to witness the fate of the guards who surrendered. For the first time in her life, they looked at her with respect, rather than revulsion.

Miranda stood before the three prisoners, recognizing the one in the middle. The guard had light brown hair, dark eyes, and a sneer on his face as soon as he saw her. He had been one of the guards who had his eye on Beatrice. The fiend even went so far as to say lewd things to her little sister. When she thought about Beatrice being violated earlier, it was his visage she saw in her mind. Miranda wondered if Beatrice's nightmares bore the same face.

Miranda pointed to Beatrice's tormenter and said, "He dies. Ask the crowd what should happen to the other two and tell them their options. I have to get out of here."

As Miranda left the farm, she heard many voices screaming out for justice. Afton and Emma walked along side her, offering her what support they could. Just having them near was a comfort. They both were dressed for battle and looked fierce. The elemental women wore leather tops, leggings, and chainmail for protection. Each one had a metal collar protecting their necks from vampire bites. The outfits had various places weapons were stored. She would have to ask Sammuel to get her a similar outfit for future use. This was just the first of many battles to come to change the face of the Nightshade universe.

Sammuel watched as several of the armed humans finished the three remaining guards. It was poetic justice that the poor souls they had helped victimize were the ones that ended their lives. The one Miranda had sentenced to death met the same fate the rest of the community had demanded. If she felt guilty later over her decision, Sammuel would let her know he would have died regardless.

Lorenz spoke eloquently to the crowd. Telling of the community he had started decades before and how humans and vampires were able to live together in harmony. Although Drake would later pose as Lorenz, his brother was proud of what he had accomplished. The majority of the humans decided to go with them.

Since no one knew the location of Lorenz's settlement, they would be unaware they were not heading in the correct direction. Sammuel's fortress was a greater distance, but was a less dangerous journey to make with a large group of humans. Afton hoped for more settlements like Lorenz's and his home would eventually adopt the winning philosophy. Currently, no vampires lived within the mountain oasis he created, other than his daughter and former sister-in-law. Sammuel was open to allowing peace-loving vampires to enter one day, but their first priority was resettling the humans.

Sammuel and Miranda had already committed to the next phase of Afton's plan— taking over the Venture Hive. However, it was a long walk to their new home and a lot more planning was necessary before they attempted such a large undertaking. For now, Afton would have to be content with the liberation of her father's human farm.

The bodies of the twenty-four guards and ten other humans were collected and burned. They wanted to leave nothing behind for any starving vampires to salvage. Dead blood did not feed the cells the way fresh blood did, but would provide partial nourishment for a desperate vampire.

Their elemental mates waited outside the walls, ready to leave. They had a number of horses with them that would be used for weaker humans unable to walk any real distance. A number of the children ran to Afton and wanted to see her produce fire from her hands. There was a lot of explaining to be done, but for now they needed to be on their way.

A small group of humans approached Miranda and asked for her forgiveness for the way she was treated. They thanked her for coming back and liberating them from their prison. Miranda graciously accepted their apology with tears in her eyes.

"Come," Sammuel said, addressing the humans before him, "we have a long walk ahead of us. It will take at least two weeks of walking every day to reach Lorenz's settlement. A number of friendly vampires will protect us at night, so you have little to fear. We are also re-training the dogs, who will also protect you."

Fortunately, no one questioned the number of days it would take to get to his fortress or the number of days Miranda had been gone from the farm. These humans were uneducated and would not grasp the discrepancy. They took him at his word and followed blindly.

"I am going to take four of the healthier men and teach them to hunt," Frazour said. "We have a large number of humans to feed, so it would be prudent to collect fruit as we make our way. We will need to make frequent stops and limit their food intake until their systems become accustomed to their new diet. These people are barely surviving."

No one knew better how to survive in the wilderness than Frazour and Portia, whose shared experiences would shape their decisions going forward. Portia brought up the rear, keeping out of sight. Sammuel doubted she would take her human form, even with Jace not around during daylight hours.

"It's funny," Miranda commented, "we spent so much time planning their liberation, I don't believe we discussed what it would take to get everyone to your fortress."

"There were discussions," Sammuel said. "I did not want you burdened with this part of the plan. We needed you to concentrate on your portion of the rescue. You were amazing today and I am very proud of you."

Sammuel always enjoyed watching Miranda blush. Her ivory complexion was suffused with color and her blue eyes more vibrant. The next two weeks were going to be horrendous because he would not be able to be intimate with her.

The former residents of the farm became anxious and agitated when the sun began to set. Miranda could hardly blame them; in their shoes, she would be wary as well. Although the group was reassured they were protected from vampires, the humans associated the setting of the sun with danger. It was ingrained in their psyches.

While orchestrating the rescue, Sammuel and his brothers planned for the introduction of the friendly vampires into their midst. The blood brothers, Tanya, and Patrice, did not resemble the decomposing creatures the humans were accustomed to.

A birdcall cried out, a signal that Jace and the others were approaching. It was Lorenz's responsibility to inform the humans of the approaching vampires. The dogs would be spread out around the perimeter and remain hidden for the time being. The humans needed to get comfortable with the vampires before the newly trained dogs were reintroduced to them. Although it was unlikely any shifters would be visible once they reached the mountains, the humans must be informed about these special beings as well.

"My friends," Lorenz called out, "I'd like to introduce you to your future host. The sun has set and he has been able to leave the confines of the day shelter. The vampires you are about to meet are different than the ones who victimized you in the past. They were converted by The Creator himself and appear human."

Drake, Jace, Patrice, and Tanya walked into the make-shift camp they set up for the evening. The group fell quiet as the four vampires entered the clearing. Miranda looked around at the stunned faces around her. These beings were as beautiful, as they were powerful and deadly. The fact that two of them had been converted as teenagers also made them appear less threatening.

"I am pleased you have all agreed to join me in my settlement," a smooth talking Drake said. "We have found harmony between a vampire's need for blood and a human's desire for a good quality of life. In my community, a vampire who takes blood must make it an enjoyable experience and heal the donor after he feeds. Any vampire who fails these two simple duties is thrown out of the keep and is allowed to starve with the rest of the vampires in this dimension. If a human is accidently killed, the vampire is executed. Are there any questions?"

The freedom to ask questions was foreign to the humans raised on the farm. They were given orders and failure to comply meant death at the next harvest. Miranda wanted to make the former occupants comfortable by asking the first question.

"What rights does a woman have in your community?" Miranda asked. She knew the victimized women needed to understand they could say no and it would have to be respected.

"No woman will be taken against her will, by either a vampire or a human male," Drake answered. "There is a zero tolerance threshold where this is concerned. I love and respect women and will not tolerate physical assaults against them. Any being found guilty of such a crime will be punished severely. There are various options available to women as to where and how they want to live within my community."

"It is time you meet the rest of us," Lorenz said. "This is Lorenz's mate, Afton. She was a half-ling. When she mated, the element Fire chose her to wield its power. Many of you witnessed her generating fire from her hands."

Lorenz's voice got a bit of an edge to it when Drake took Afton into his arms. She smiled gracefully when Drake kissed her on the cheek. He realized the role he had to play and did not want to agitate Lorenz or Afton with anything more than a simple peck on the cheek.

"This is Lorenz's blood brother, Jace," Lorenz continued. It was agreed only Jace would be introduced as a blood brother. Emma, Frazour, and Sammuel would be introduced as humans from the settlement who were here to support them. "Lastly, we have two female vampires who will help protect you. Patrice and Tanya were the ones who rescued several babies during the last harvest. They travel across the Nightshade universe saving our precious young."

Slowly, a handful of the farm humans came forward to meet the vampires. As the first few touched the vampires and suffered no injury, more gathered to meet them. Relief and joy were on their faces as they walked away from their new protectors.

The group became more comfortable and talkative as the evening progressed. The children had stood and watched as Afton started a fire with flames darting from her fingers. Fresh game had been caught and cooked over the raging fire and small portions were doled out, so their stomachs could tolerate the meat.

Dogs barking and an angry feline cry in the distance warned of danger approaching. The five blood brothers grabbed their weapons and ventured out to meet the enemy. The powerful elemental women and the two female vampires stayed behind to protect the humans. They pleaded for everyone to stay in place, but a few ran in the opposite direction the warriors went. Miranda would make sure that those who trusted her and remained in the camp would be safe, even if the cost was her life.

CHAPTER 13

Sammuel's feet traversed the rugged terrain with ease. Fallen trees and thick underbrush did not hinder his progress toward the barking dogs. His blood brothers were around him and also had no difficulty navigating the woods. When he entered a clearing a single vampire lay dead on the ground, Portia's teeth still embedded in his throat. Several of the dogs surrounded the cat and her prey, barking with excitement.

"Where are the rest of them?" Frazour yelled.

Portia released the vampire and took off into the woods with Frazour fast on her heels. It appeared the synergy between the two former traveling companions had not been lost. Sammuel did not see the need for them all to follow the panther. If they were dealing with a small group of vampires, the creatures would have separated at this point.

"Spread out and see if you can find more," Sammuel ordered. "Start heading back in the direction of the camp, as you make your way through the woods. Destroy every vampire you come across."

Sammuel knew Portia would not have left the clearing if she had taken down a vampire traveling alone. Lorenz and Jace raced after Frazour and the cat, while Sammuel and Drake headed in the opposite direction.

"You like to play with fire, Drake," Sammuel commented as the two looked for signs of the other vampires. "Be careful not to push Lorenz or Afton too far, particularly Afton."

"I like to play, period," Drake replied. "How else am I going to entertain myself until Star comes of age?"

"Star?"

"My soul mate," Drake answered. "Starla was Alexandra's mother's name. She named her daughter after the woman, but calls her Star for short. Where are the other dogs? It appears Portia did all the work and they were merely observers."

"I do not see any signs anyone or anything has been this way," Sammuel said. "Go several hundred yards east and I will continue going this way. We can meet back at camp if we come up empty handed."

Drake nodded and they both took off looking for any signs of other vampires. Sammuel turned once he reached five hundred yards and headed back to the clearing where they established camp for the evening. He was on what appeared to be a well-traveled path, but there did not appear to be any recent signs of use.

A birdcall some distance away alerted him that Drake had discovered something. He headed off the path and went in the direction of Drake's summons. Sammuel picked up the pace when he heard metal meeting metal.

When he came across Drake, his brother was battling two vampires. With a swing of his sword, Sammuel decapitated the one closest to him. Before the vampire's corpse hit the ground, Drake had dispatched the other.

Screams were heard from a distance and both men started running in the direction of the camp. Sammuel's mind was crazed with worry about Miranda. He should have continued her weapon training, and not relied so heavily on her elemental gift.

When they entered the camp, he nearly fell over a dilapidated corpse that Emma must have wrung dry. Several vampires were on fire and the ground shook, swallowing two more. Sammuel jumped into the makeshift grave and made quick work of decapitating the two creatures.

He watched as Miranda swung her sword and it made contact with a vampire's shoulder. She recovered and finished off her opponent as Sammuel leapt out of the hole she had created. It was obvious Miranda's physical strength had increased by the way she handled the sword.

Tanya and Patrice were protecting the humans who remained untouched. The men who Frazour had taught to hunt had weapons drawn and stood next to the two female vampires. It was clear they needed to train additional humans.

All the vampires who attacked the camp were dead. Sammuel started carrying their bodies to the hole in the ground Miranda had opened. Drake used his charm to calm the women, while the men assisted Sammuel. Afton incinerated the remains of the vampires and they waited for the others to return.

Jace entered the camp with four of the dogs playing at his side. The humans immediately became alarmed by the appearance of the animals. They quickly calmed as they watched Jace play with the mutts. A fearless boy came forward and started to pet one of the hounds. When the dog licked his face, more children came forward.

Frazour returned to the camp from the opposite direction, having circumnavigated the camp to assess the damage. There was a glum look on his face, making it clear there had been casualties.

"I figure there were a total of twenty vampires that circled the encampment before the dogs and Portia became aware of them," Frazour reported. "To the west of camp, seven humans who ran off were drained dry by the vampires. We also lost two of the dogs."

A human male who had been listening came forward. The former farm resident was dreadfully thin. He was one of the men Frazour had taught to hunt and helped to protect the camp. "I will talk to my people and tell them running off during a vampire attack means certain death. Those that stayed lived."

"What is your name, friend?" Sammuel asked.

"Benja," the man answered. "All we were taught by the vampires at the farm was how to plant vegetables so we could eat. There is much we need to learn. Frazour, I thank you for what you taught me today. For the first time in my life, I feel worthy of living. We were all forced to do terrible things, and I want to help safeguard my people."

The human looked in the direction the women congregated. There was much for the men to atone for. They did what they had to in order to survive, but they had difficult times ahead. It would take a lot of effort for the women to trust the men who would ultimately protect and care for them in the future.

"We must travel during the day," Frazour said, "but we can train at night before you all rest. Have your friends pick up the weapons the vampires used. I doubt we will be attacked every night, but there will be other assaults."

"We should retire for the night," Miranda said. "Men and women should be separated to reduce as much anxiety as possible. We will scatter ourselves around the camp to offer protection."

Sammuel could see the stress and fatigue written on Miranda's face. *Do you need to restore energy?*

Miranda subtly nodded and headed toward the outskirts of the camp. Sammuel followed his mate, and as soon as they were clear of the encampment, he took her into his arms. He brought his lips down to hers and kissed her with pent up passion. Energy soared between them, but he also felt greatly relieved holding her. She had done an admirable job protecting herself and the humans this evening.

"I don't know if I can handle two weeks of attacks and safeguarding these people," Miranda admitted to him. "There are so many lives I am responsible for."

"No, Miranda, my blood brothers and I hold the responsibility," Sammuel admitted. "The creatures that crave human blood come from the same entity that created us. We should have continued destroying them as Drake and The Creator originally started. Nature never intended such beings to exist. Maybe humans and vampires living in harmony should not be the answer, but the total annihilation of the species."

Miranda held on to her soul mate and absorbed the power he provided. She had been terrified this evening when the vampires attacked. There were not many, but so many souls depended on her…it was overwhelming.

She was not sure how to respond to what Sammuel said about destroying all vampires. Even with their heightened powers, it was a daunting task he suggested. Miranda had met several vampires who lived in Lorenz's settlement and did not fear them, and vampires had raised her.

"Afton's plan, although ambitious, seems more realistic," Miranda said. "I don't want to declare war on the whole vampire species. Lorenz proved coexistence between humans and vampires can be achieved. I don't want to talk about vampires and wars, right now. Please, just hold me."

Sammuel tightened his grip on her. When she was with Sammuel like this, she felt safe and cherished. Her mind could rest for however long they could steal away. The power they shared revived her physically, but she also needed time to recover emotionally.

Sounds of laughter came from the camp. After the attack, it was reassuring to know some were still capable of experiencing joy. Several more people joined in the cheerful sound and her curiosity was peaked.

"Let's go see what is happening," Miranda said.

Hand in hand, they headed back to camp. Energy still passed between them, restoring her physically. It was too bad her beleaguered mind was not as easily relieved. When they entered the camp, Emma was throwing three large rocks into the air and catching them.

"What is she doing?" Miranda asked.

"She is juggling," Sammuel answered. "But more importantly, she is taking their minds off the attack."

The people gathered around the fire were mesmerized by Emma's skill and concentration. Miranda joined the group watching the water elemental. Emma was not using her gift, but an ability honed long before her transformation. A number of children scurried around the camp looking for rocks to try their hand at the skill.

"Go to sleep now and I will teach some of you how to juggle tomorrow night after the evening meal, while others learn to fight," Emma said. "Everyone will have something to learn. Some of the things taught will be helpful in your survival, while other pursuits are just for fun."

Having fun would be a new concept for many humans. There was a time when they were young, before the reality of their situation sank in, that these humans enjoyed themselves. The quarterly harvests were constant reminders of the fate each person had in store. It was a new beginning for everyone.

Afton stole away with Lorenz. The closeness to her mate restored her. She had accomplished the first thing she had set her mind on after her father died. This was the first time she fought without the hope of Yorik coming to her rescue. Her father's death was her fault.

"Your thoughts are leaking through, Afton," Lorenz communicated telepathically, not wanting anyone in the camp to overhear him. He held her a little tighter.

She had not mourned for her father, a creature who raped her mother and manipulated her return to the Nightshade universe. He had been a vicious and cruel master vampire. When Shirl had told her what Yorik had done to Chartail, she supported Benko's desire for vengeance. However, no one would lay a hand on her father without her approval. What he had planned for Miranda had been the tipping point. She knew she made the right decision, but it was something she had yet to come to terms with.

"You can't stop me from feeling guilty about what I set in motion," Afton responded, *"any more than I can stop my conscience from continually questioning my decision. It is something I will have to live with. And trust me, I can."*

"Return to the others," Lorenz said as he kissed her lips. *"I have warned Drake he better not take advantage of this situation."*

She was no longer one of them. Although, in reality, she never was. Miranda sat alone on the outskirts of the encampment where they spent the seventh night of their journey. Except for the four men helping to guard the camp, most humans slumbered peacefully. Those four were not necessary to safeguard those asleep, but the humans wanted to be part of everything that was done to protect and provide for them while they were on the road, as well as when they reached their final destination.

Miranda rarely slept. The energy she shared with Sammuel seemed to provide everything she needed, including whatever she derived from the healing, restful sleep humans required. Then again, she was no longer human. It was evident that the former farm residents saw that as well. Rather than looking at her in disgust, they looked at her in awe. All she ever wanted was to be one of them, but she never was and never would be.

Afton, Emma, and the blood brothers accepted her into the family because of the link that existed between her and Sammuel. Even Portia seemed to take a liking to her. So, why was she disheartened the humans still would not accept her?

"You need to give your mind some rest," Sammuel told her telepathically. In consideration of the sleeping humans, he did not utter the words out loud. He joined her on the ground and placed his arm around her shoulders.

"My brain will not turn off long enough for me to fall asleep," Miranda admitted. *"Besides, I have too much energy churning within to even attempt to get any rest."*

Sammuel grabbed her hand and removed the soil she had been unconsciously playing with. *"You are pulling additional strength from your element."*

Originally, she had been unable to gather power from the ground. Over the last few days, she noticed that was no longer the case. Her powers were evolving, just as Afton said they would.

"How am I not to have contact with the ground we walk, sleep, and live on? Have you noticed the forest is denser after we travel through it?"

Miranda originally thought what she saw when she looked behind her had been her imagination. More undergrowth was evident, the plants were greener, and the area lusher. It appeared she did not just take energy from the land, but gave it back as well. Physically, she felt no different. Whatever she was doing unconsciously was not draining energy from her.

"Afton said your powers will grow," Sammuel admitted. *"She can feed fire as you seem to help plants grow at a faster rate. Perhaps you need to spend part of tomorrow walking with Emma and discuss managing your element as she does with water. You both have regular physical contact with your element, unlike Afton."*

What he said made sense. Over the last week, she had spent hours with Emma trying to learn from her experiences. She felt comfortable asking Emma questions about her relationship with water, but had not confided in the other woman what she was feeling and experiencing.

It was easy, natural, to confide in Sammuel. What she did not tell him, he generally was able to pull from the link between them. Keeping a secret from her mate was next to impossible.

"There will be more mouths to feed once we reach your fortress. Maybe my ability to make things grow faster is a good thing," Miranda said. *"I'm just concerned I will not be able to control the power I am ultimately given."*

"Nature is about balance," Sammuel said. *"There are two of us. I am already able to absorb your excess power, as you are able to take mine. Maybe as you become more powerful, so will my ability to soak in the excess energy. Lorenz, Frazour, and I are no longer vampires. Clearly we are also transforming. Who knows what we will ultimately become, but I know there will be synergy between us. I need to make my rounds, try and get some rest."*

Sammuel kissed her and rather than sharing energy, he pulled power from her. She was suddenly weary and ready to sleep. Miranda gave Sammuel a questioning look, but he simply smiled and walked off. Her mate knew what she needed and provided it without comment.

They had another week of traveling before they reached their destination. Although they had come across several small bands of vampires, there was no attack like the first night. Sammuel had been right. The number of vampires diminished as they neared his fortress. Miranda wondered what became of the vampires trapped in the underground lab and if an army of vampires were close by to reclaim what they believed belonged to them.

CHAPTER 14

The attack Miranda dreaded never came to pass. They now stood before the foothills of the mountain range where Sammuel's fortress was located. She had never seen a more awe-inspiring sight than these majestic mountains. For the first time in her life, Miranda saw snow covered peaks at the higher elevations.

"I have never led such a large group through the pass," Sammuel said. "There are parts of the trail where we must travel single file, so we should spread our protection throughout the group, with more at the rear. I think we should wait until morning before we venture any further as the sun will set in a couple hours."

"It is not advantageous to have the mountains at our back, closing off an escape route in case we are attacked," Frazour said. "We should divide the group into thirds and spread out tonight. Tomorrow we will take one group at a time up the trail. Sammuel and Miranda should head out tonight and gather more support from within the fortress. This is not over yet."

She did not like the thought of leaving the humans behind, but what Frazour suggested made sense. However, if the group was attacked this evening, Miranda was not sure if she could live with herself if any humans were killed in the raid.

"Perhaps I should stay behind," Miranda said. "You need all the assistance you can get in case they attack tonight."

"Miranda," Frazour said, "there are portions of the mountain pass you may be able to widen with your elemental powers. The longer it takes to get everyone through the mountain trail, the more dangerous it is for the ones in the rear of the group. I want to get everyone through the pass while the sun is up tomorrow. You can make that happen by leaving now."

Miranda had not thought past the threat a single evening presented. Frazour was correct in his analysis. If she could use her powers to widen the narrowest portions of the trail before the humans started making their way through the pass, then it was wisest she left now. The sooner they got everyone to his fortress, the better.

The skills and abilities of the blood brothers and their mates continued to amaze her. She needed to stop thinking about the here and now, and start looking at the bigger picture—what was best in the long run. In her former world, it was never good to look beyond where you were at that moment. Miranda needed to change her perspective and began planning for the future.

"We will take two of the horses and will return with more," Sammuel said. "Be safe tonight, we should return before daybreak tomorrow to start moving the humans through the pass."

Sammuel gave Miranda a leg up onto one of the horses and then mounted his own steed. They entered a trail hidden by thick vegetation. The sheer number of people stomping through the pass may destroy the shrouded entrance. She looked on the other side of the trees to see if she could widen the path through the rocks. Miranda was ill-equipped to know what to do.

Her thoughts of self-doubt were temporarily halted by Portia running past her horse and coming alongside Sammuel and his stallion. Rocks fell from the side of the trail as Portia continued to disturb her environment. This initial section could create injuries if any of the humans were caught in a rock slide.

"Should I broaden the path here?" Miranda shouted. In the short time she spent examining her surroundings, Sammuel had increased the distance between them.

"The shale is precarious here," Sammuel replied. "We would be more likely to cause an avalanche and close the pass."

"I'm just concerned someone could get hurt. Besides, the natural barrier will be destroyed with all the people traipsing through," Miranda said.

"Sweetheart, with your touch, a jungle can replace the small growth that shelters the opening," Sammuel said. "We will advise everyone to watch their footing and keep their distance from the mountain face."

Once again, Miranda had not thought things through. She needed to consider all her growing powers when she looked at the situation before her.

"You need to stop beating yourself up for not having all the right answers at your fingertips," Sammuel communicated. *"This is all new to you. My brothers and I have had thousands of years to learn from our mistakes. Even I have forgotten my ability to move around during daylight hours. I continually strategize what I can do during the night. Just keep looking around for opportunities and we will discuss them as we go."*

Sammuel had the ability to build up her confidence with his words. He was a remarkable man. It was not the soul mate link, but the man himself, who she was growing to respect and have feelings for.

He had just called her "sweetheart" and she was experiencing feelings of joy to an extent she never realized possible. Miranda became warm inside and she sat up a little straighter on her mount. After all the fear and anxiety she had felt over the last two weeks, this new feeling was overwhelming, but a wide smile blossomed on her face.

Fortunately, her horse was well trained and the trail easy to follow, because Miranda was too distracted by her emotions to navigate their route. She daydreamed about the intimate times she had with Sammuel and the many future encounters she hoped to enjoy. Time flew as they moved up the trail to higher elevations.

"How about here?" Sammuel asked. His words pulled her out of one very erotic reverie. It took a moment for her to reestablish her bearings.

Miranda looked in Sammuel's direction and was surprised to see they were on a narrow pass with a very sharp drop off. She had been so lost in her thoughts, she had not recognized how dangerous the path had become.

Sammuel came up beside her and helped her dismount. He whistled and slapped the hindquarters of the horse to move it forward. The animal ran up the path far enough for Miranda to get the lay of the land.

Portia was a good distance ahead of Sammuel. The cat had a keen sense of survival. She paced, anxious to continue their journey.

Miranda placed her hand against the mountain and closed her eyes. The stone was cold and rough. She could visualize trimming part of the stone face, but the trick was not to get caught in the shower of rocks and dirt that would be produced.

Miranda headed back to where the trail narrowed. "Stay well ahead of me," she advised her mate. Somehow she knew her element would safeguard her, but she was not sure if Sammuel would be as well. Miranda was not willing to chance endangering his life.

She moved forward, trailing her fingers along the mountain's face. Vibrations began deep within the mountain while Miranda moved forward, still caressing its mass. It felt strange, she became one with her element. Rocks fell behind her, but a good enough distance away that she was not in danger of being struck by the falling debris.

When Miranda reached a part of the trail that was already relatively wide, she turned around to examine the pristine and much safer mountain ledge she had created. There were not even little pebbles along the trail. All the stone had fallen into the cavern below.

"Impressive," Sammuel commented. "Let us stretch our legs and walk this next stretch. The tree sheltered path we are about to enter is wide enough for our purposes."

"I feel invincible," Miranda said. "It is a miracle what just happened."

"We live in a dangerous world," Sammuel commented. "Enjoy this success, but always be aware that peril waits around every corner. I do not want to downplay what you just accomplished, but what you feel now could get you hurt…or worse."

Sammuel felt terrible about destroying Miranda's wonderful mood. He should have let her bask in her success a little longer, but he needed to stress the perils of letting down her guard. There was no better motivator than fear.

He could feel her inside him, reaching out to gauge how he felt. It was a strange sensation having her accessing his emotions. She could hide nothing from him, so it only seemed fair Miranda was able to do the same.

She came up beside him and wrapped an arm around his waist. Sammuel brought her closer against his body, placing his arm around her shoulders. He kissed the crown of her head. They needed to push forward to make the timeline he created in his head to support Frazour's plan. If he were not pressed for time, he would have properly kissed the woman in his arms.

"How much farther until we reach your fortress?" Miranda asked.

"We have another hour in our ascent, it will level off for a while, and then we will descend into the valley where the fortress is located.

There is only one pathway into the valley. The mountain cliffs that surround it are too steep to traverse. We should be entering the territory of—"

His words were cut off by the sound of animalistic growls and howls ahead of them. Sammuel took off running, with Miranda at his heels. He was about to tell her they were entering the territory of the wolf shifters. In hindsight, he should have warned Portia about what she would encounter in these mountains. The cat shifters' territory was closer to his fortress.

Sammuel stopped running when he spotted Portia twenty feet in front of him, confronting two wolf shifters. From the sound of howls in the background, more were on their way.

"Portia, settle down," Sammuel said. "These are friends of mine. They help guard the entry to my stronghold against rogue vampires. Good evening, Basil and Ivan. Please shift, so Portia can see who she is dealing with."

At Sammuel's request, both wolf shifters immediately changed into their human form. If anything, Portia's agitation increased at the sight of the two naked men standing before her. Sammuel turned to Miranda and saw how surprise she was. He was not pleased she was looking at two unclothed men with unabashed appreciation.

"This is our territory," Basil complained. "What is *she* doing here?"

It was clear his friend recognized Portia as another shifter. She did not cease growling after the two took their human forms. The conversation they participated in did not lessen the cat's reaction to her surroundings either.

"Portia," Miranda said, "come here and help to protect me. That's why you are here."

The panther turned in Miranda's direction, still internally debating what she was going to do next. If Portia chose to attack, he had exposed his neighbors to a deadly predator—they would be no match in their human form. The panther held her ground, considering Miranda's words.

Years ago, Ivan had explained that shifters used the magic of their ancestors to change forms. The transformation was usually instantaneous, unless something interrupted the conversion. There were all kinds of shifters, but Sammuel had only met wolf and feline shifters who had been caught in the portal's grasp.

Portia shifted to her human form and stood behind Miranda, sheltering herself from Basil and Ivan. "What are these dogs doing here?" Portia asked with such contempt in her voice it surprised him.

"Like you, they were brought here by one of the three active portals in this world," Sammuel replied. "They make their home here and protect the human children we bring to my home to raise. We also have panther, jaguar, and tiger shifters. Their settlement is closer to my home."

Miranda seemed taken aback by the knowledge cat shifters existed in this dimension. She must have felt she was alone in the Nightshade universe, which could have been the reason she had traveled so long with Frazour.

"At least they have the good sense to stay away from the stench these dogs give off," Portia spit out.

"This needless arguing is wasting too much time. Your dislike of the other shifters does not help the humans from the farm make it to safety," Miranda said. "Sammuel, we need to continue our trek to your fortress and prepare to escort the rest of our party to your home. Portia, we will have to deal with your…issues later."

Miranda started walking toward the two wolf shifters. She kept her back straight, head high, and regally continued up the path. Ivan stepped aside to let her pass. Portia turned back into her panther form and followed closely behind. The wolf shifters had the good sense not to confront the cat as she ran past.

"I have close to two hundred and fifty humans we rescued from a farm coming through here tomorrow morning. Any assistance you can provide will be appreciated. Stay alert and out of sight. I do not know if we are going to have unwelcome company as we make our way."

"Gareth will be alerted to the humans coming, as well as the existence of the female shifter," Ivan said. "We have very few females among our numbers. He will not be pleased the cats will be adding one."

"It is doubtful she will join Callum's community," Sammuel advised. "She travels with one of my blood brothers."

"Has she mated?" Basil asked. "Having an unmated female within range may create problems."

The last thing Sammuel needed was a war brewing between the cats and the wolves over an unclaimed female. Gareth was difficult enough to manage when there was peace between the two shifter communities. He needed to get Portia behind the fortress walls before things spun out of control. Their focus must be on any vampires that may be trailing the large group of humans.

"I need the area between the entry and the far reaches of your territory searched for hostile vampires. Feel free to kill any that you come across. The reward for each vampire body will triple over the next two days. We will renegotiate the bounties after all the humans make it safely to the fortress," Sammuel advised.

By the time he caught up with Miranda, she had her hands around both sets of reins and was cooing to the horses. He helped her remount and they continued on their way. Portia ran beside them, still agitated. Sammuel set a faster pace to make up for the time they lost speaking with the wolf shifters.

At least, now he understood the difficulties having Portia with them might bring. The only things that might have made the timing worse were if the confrontation took place with either Jace or the humans nearby. Sammuel was not sure of Jace's feelings toward Portia or the chaos that was sure to ensue regarding Portia's future. He knew Jace's reaction to Portia's secret would not be a minor incident.

"What was all of that about?" Miranda asked. She used the telepathic channel in order not to have Portia hear their conversation.

"Female shifters of mating age are essentially property of their father or the alpha of the pack or pride," Sammuel explained. *"In essence, the parental authority sells the female to anyone willing to pay the dowry for the right to reproduce with her. Generally, the cats and the wolves avoid each other whenever possible. However, Portia is a prize over which either side will go to war."*

He could feel Miranda's turmoil over what he had explained. It was not too dissimilar to what happened at the vampire human farms. Sammuel would protect Portia's right to choose the life she wished to have and would do his utmost to protect her secret from Jace. He was just not sure how he was going to do all of that.

CHAPTER 15

Miranda looked down in wonderment at the large green valley below and the stone fortress nestled against the far mountain cliff. There were areas of the valley that were cultivated to grow the food necessary to feed the human population. Various barns held animals that provided milk, sustenance, and other products for the community.

Lorenz's settlement was a safe haven; this place was somewhere out of her dreams. They started their descent into the valley. Portia still pranced alongside her horse, keeping perfect pace. Along their journey, Miranda had assured the shifter that they would protect her with the same zeal as the humans. Miranda hoped they would not encounter any of the feline shifters she had been warned about, preferring to fight one battle at a time.

The horses expertly navigated the path with steady legs. They had been down this trail hundreds of times. Although the descent made Miranda nervous, her mount seemed confident in what he was doing. At times, she closed her eyes and let the horse traverse the tricky trail.

It was not long before they were off the mountain and entered the flat surface of the valley. The horses moved at a faster clip, releasing the caution they had earlier exhibited. Miranda loved the speed and the wind blowing through her hair.

When they got closer to the fortress, she could see people working the farm and children playing outside the walls. As they entered, more youngsters were visible playing a variety of games. They were well fed, clothed, clean, and happy. Many of them had been born on vampire farms and rescued by Sammuel and his women, unaware of the horror that took place outside this secluded valley.

Miranda followed Sammuel to the fortress's stable and turned over her horse to one of the stable boys. Sammuel walked toward the entrance of his home with Miranda and Portia at his side. Various people stopped and gaped at them. They were used to Sammuel being accompanied by two vampires, not a woman who appeared human and a black panther. She imagined shifters only entered the fortress in their human form.

The main hall of Sammuel's keep was illuminated by large metal structures containing lit candles, rather than the torches she witnessed everywhere else. Like Lorenz's, the floor was covered with various rugs and comfortable furniture was scattered around the massive room. Was this to be her new home? Miranda was speechless.

"This is Hellen, my housekeeper," Sammuel said. "May I introduce my two special guests. Miranda will be sharing my quarters and the female shifter should be given a room in the East Tower. Her identity is to be kept quiet. I will show Miranda to my rooms and, if you would, please show Portia to her chambers."

The housekeeper was a middle-aged woman with graying hair. Humans rarely reached her age on the farm before they were led away during a harvest. She smiled warmly in Miranda's direction.

"It will be my pleasure," Hellen said. "Welcome to Stone Meadow."

"You named your fortress?" Miranda asked.

"Several centuries ago," Sammuel said. "Patrice wanted to call our home something other than Sammuel's Fortress, so she came up with Stone Meadow. It stuck."

Miranda could not help but smile. It brought a homey feeling to the stone fortress. Most properties in the Nightshade universe were named after the hive or the vampire that currently resided in the property.

She followed Sammuel to the second floor and down a long hallway. He entered the last door on the left and Miranda followed, looking forward to a room similar to the one with the charm of the main hall. His room had a single enormous bed and a large chest, nothing more. Obviously, someone other than Sammuel decorated the large common room.

Before she had a chance to ask him why his room was so bare, Sammuel picked her up and carried her to the bed. Prepared for battle, she had once again worn a simple shirt and leggings. Sammuel quickly removed his clothing while she watched, fascinated, lying on the bed. He had always taken her partially clothed when they had sex, so she never had the opportunity to see him naked. After seeing the shifters, Miranda wondered how Sammuel would compare.

There was no comparison! Sammuel was breathtaking. His chest was wide with several old healed scars he must have received when he was human. The vampire he later became allowed new injuries to heal with amazing speed, but the former scars upon his body were there for eternity.

Her eyes fell to his massive erection. Miranda could not believe she had been able to accommodate his size. She was grateful he had not fully revealed himself until after they had intercourse several times. If she had been a virgin and saw his swollen member in all its glory, she would have run off.

"Would you care to remove your clothing, or should I?" Sammuel asked. "If I do, there may not be anything left for you to put back on. We should head back to the others within the hour."

Miranda swiftly removed her leggings when presented the threat he might destroy the one outfit she had with her. She was wriggling out of her top when he pulled her legs toward him, placed his knees on the bed, and draped her legs over his shoulders. With so little time available to them, he entered her with a single thrust.

She cried out his name as he filled her. Barely having time to take in another breath, Sammuel pulled from her warm recesses and re-entered her, pushing her body further into the mattress. The friction that built in her body multiplied with each thrust. She tightened her grip as her legs fell down to his hips. He had set a frantic pace and she was barely keeping up.

They had not been together like this for two long weeks and his urgency to be with her again was obvious. He was a man possessed, allowing his animalistic side to have full rein over their joining. During the fortnight they traveled, Miranda's strength continued to grow and she was able to meet his frenzied tempo.

In record time, they both fractured, filled with a rapture they had never experienced before. They had not fueled each other; this was raw need. With no strength to maintain her legs around his hips, they fell onto the bed next to Sammuel. She was totally spent.

"I am sorry," Sammuel said, kissing her to restore her depleted power.

She treasured the last instant when their love making had exhausted her. In that cherished period, Miranda felt like she was floating. Her body was weightless and her mind was devoid of all thought. It was almost as if she was free of her earthly confines and worries.

As he kissed her, restoring her, Sammuel continued to touch her body. Taking all he could before he had to take on the burden of the humans they rescued. Miranda wondered if he achieved the same nirvana she had.

"We better dress and head back to join the others," Sammuel said. "It was a selfish thing to do, but I had to have you before we left. I may have cost our friends precious moments if they are under attack by the time we reach them."

That thought caused her to sit up quickly and grab her leggings. They needed to get back to Afton and the rest of the group and lead them to safety. How could she lie in Sammuel's bed celebrating what they had together when her friends were in danger?

Sammuel had given instructions for all the horses to be saddled and ready to go upon his return to the stable. The time spent making love with Miranda allowed the stable hands to accomplish the task. They mounted and started on their journey back to the entry of the mountain pass.

The trip back should be faster since they were not looking for opportunities for Miranda to broaden the path or contend with the wolf shifters. Gareth's men would already be in place to support them in case they needed assistance. The shifters would not leave the confines of the mountains. If the humans were under attack, they would have to bring them onto the mountain trail in the dark.

His horses were well trained and able to make the trip during the light of day or on a moonless night. Fortunately, there was nearly a full moon in the sky illuminating the trail. They made better time than he expected. He and Miranda should be back with their friends an hour before the sun began to rise.

He could hear the cries before they reached the bottom of the trail. Miranda wailed out in alarm, as she heard the same screams. The horses, feeling their urgency, quickened their pace down the mountain.

They had another thousand feet to go when they encountered Lorenz leading a group of humans up the pass. "Emma and I started bringing the children up as soon as Jace signaled we had hostile company. They started attacking us not long ago. I am not sure how many of the enemy they are up against. Afton stayed behind to flame the creatures. Continue leading the children up the trail and I will return to assist the others."

"Lorenz," Sammuel said, "Afton knew what she was doing when she asked you to lead the children to safety. I am better with a sword and Miranda can close the pass if we are desperate. Continue on your way with no delay. We are losing valuable time."

Even with the little light available, Sammuel could see the anguish in Lorenz's eyes. He knew what Sammuel said was true and he nodded in defeat. Lorenz would continue leading the children to safety and all he could do was hope his soul mate would soon join him.

"I thought your name was Drake," one of the children said.

"Does everyone want to hear a story about an arrogant vampire and a half-ling falling in love?" Sammuel heard Lorenz answer the boy just before he was out of earshot.

The blood brothers had the telepathic gift to communicate, similar to what existed between him and Miranda. Sammuel would let Lorenz know when Afton was safe. In the meantime, he needed to reach the others and help defend the humans against the vampire attack.

When he reached the trailhead, Sammuel pulled Miranda's horse's reins toward him. "I need you to stay here. If I give the signal, bring down the shale and close the mountain pass. Our first priority is the children Lorenz guards. We will try to send as many humans up the trail as possible."

"But I can help," Miranda cried.

"I know you can," Sammuel answered, "but only you can bring down the face of this mountain and safeguard the humans we were able to free. We will win this battle, but I need to know my contingency plan is in place."

Miranda leaned over and kissed him. He saw everything she wanted to say reflected in her expression. Sammuel grabbed her head and deepened the kiss, drawing as much energy as he could to confront the enemy.

Sammuel left her without further adieu, needing to destroy as many vampires necessary to end this battle. For the first time in three thousand years, he had something to fight for.

Afton flamed another two vampires. Although she had a tremendous amount of power, she could not bring down more than two vampires at a time. Drake and Frazour had her back, cutting down vampires each time they came for her. Being Yorik's daughter, made her their prime target. Somehow word got out that she was responsible for her father's death. Any vampire that captured her was that much closer to being able to take over the Venture Hive. Ironically, she was going to use that same argument when it came time to claim her birthright.

She had sent Lorenz and Emma ahead with the children. The little ones needed an escort, they were the two weakest fighters and able to walk in daylight. The sun would be rising in less than an hour. Unfortunately, this meant she and Frazour were unable to recoup energy from their soul mates.

Once the sun rose, she could generate additional power. There was also a pond nearby and, like Emma, Frazour had learned to draw strength from the element-albeit to a lesser degree.

The humans were back against the mountain pass. When they divided into groups earlier, they positioned the children closest to the trailhead and were able to move the kids out of harm's way as soon as they heard Jace's warning. The two other groups were moved to provide them protection and try to evacuate as many as possible up the trail.

Afton was relieved when Sammuel joined the fight. She knew Miranda remained behind to guard the pass, ready to block the entrance if Afton signaled all was lost.

Another two vampires were now toast. But more kept coming. She had underestimated one of Yorik's lieutenant's ability to band together part of the hive and come after her. This contingent must have been following them for the past two weeks, just waiting for the best opportunity to attack. Not only were they vulnerable where they stood, but she had also exposed Sammuel's fortress to the Venture Hive.

Howls came from behind her and before she could determine what animal made the sound, a pack of wolves attacked the vampires. They were as efficient as Portia at killing. The wolves leapt for the vampires' necks and brought the creatures down, ripping out their throats before its body hit the ground.

Patrice and Tanya both moved with lethal grace, taking down vampire after vampire. Afton torched one that came up behind Patrice, ready to strike a deadly blow. They were as efficient as Frazour with their swords.

The earth quaked, opening a crevasse between them and the vampire reinforcements. Miranda must have left her post, but the gulf she created slowed the remaining vampires. Afton had to know that Miranda was back in place, ready to bring down the mountain if necessary.

"Is Miranda back where she is supposed to be?" Afton shouted at Sammuel to be heard over all the noise of the swordplay.

"Yes," Sammuel responded.

"Great!" Afton said. "Thank her and then tell her not to leave her post again until I give her the all clear."

The wolves gathered before them, waiting for the next wave to mount an assault. Afton could feel the weak effects of the sun ready to rise. It would still be some time, but a shelter had to be constructed so the vampires in their party would be safe from the sun's rays. Miranda could construct an earth shelter for the women, Drake, and Jace at the last minute to protect them from the sun. Yorik's lieutenant probably had time for one more assault before they had to retire for the day.

A force of one hundred or more vampires stormed out of the woods, headed in their direction. As the first group jumped the gap, hot lava and molten rock came spewing from the fissure. Afton was thrilled that Miranda had difficulty following orders.

"Back up against the mountain," Afton commanded. She could feel the heat of Miranda's handiwork. Although the air around them started to cool soon after, Afton wanted to be as far away from the rift in the ground as possible.

Plumes of smoke hovered over the chasm, which the wind pushed away from the mountain. Afton heard shouts, but she could not make out any specific words. The sun would be rising soon.

"Ask Miranda if she can build a day shelter for the women, Drake, and Jace somewhere along the mountain trail," Afton commanded.

"Yes, I can," Miranda responded, as she came up beside Afton.

"I don't know whether to hug you or smack you for not following my orders," Afton smiled. "That was some display you just pulled off. You should have mentioned you could create volcanic activity."

"Hopefully, you are leaning toward a hug," Miranda responded. "I do not know what a volcano is, and I certainly did not know I could do that. I knew those vampires needed to be stopped, so I opened myself to my element."

"If you were to bring down the entry to the pass, how difficult would it be to clear the trail again?" Afton inquired.

"I'm not sure what will fall from the mountain. I imagine with the strength of our men, we should be able to clear the path," Miranda answered.

"When the last of us is through, close the pass," Afton ordered. "We can use a little down time to recover."

A group of naked men stood before her and Afton knew she was looking at the wolf shifters who aided in the fight against what was left of the Venture Hive.

"Thank you seems an insignificant response for what you did," Afton said. "If there is anything I can ever do for you, just ask."

A powerfully built male stood before her. He had black hair, sun kissed bronze skin, and glistening pale yellow-brown eyes. He was a magnificent specimen, but he paled in comparison to her blond, blue-eyed soul mate.

"My name is Gareth," the shifter said. "I have but one request for the service my pack provided today. There is an unmated shifter among your party and you will give her to me."

Afton knew Gareth referred to Portia and there was no way in hell she intended to turn *anyone* over to this man — and never Portia. She glanced at Jace who looked like he was going to explode. Drake held him back before he did something they would all regret. She had finished one battle and it appeared she was about to begin another.

CHAPTER 16

H is great hall was in chaos. Gareth and his people were verbally sparing with the cat shifters. Callum, the leader of the cat pride, had not yet arrived. Sammuel knew Callum had been at the far reaches of his territory and better soon appear; or he would shortly have a war on his hands.

Fortunately, Jace was still within the day shelter that Miranda had constructed from dirt and rocks to protect the vampires among them. Sammuel had seen the expressions chase themselves over Jace's face when he realized whom Gareth was talking about. What should have been a moment of wonderment was, in reality, first a look of betrayal and then anger.

Sammuel could not turn Portia over to Gareth or Callum, and he hoped she would not be subjected to Jace's wrath. He had never seen his blood brother look so angry. Above all else, Jace was still a vampire and could easily destroy everything Sammuel had built.

There was a special bond between Drake and Jace. Sammuel hoped that both Drake and Patrice were requesting that Jace see reason. Sammuel had always hoped Patrice and Jace would end up together as they had so much in common.

Miranda entered the hall and sat beside him. She looked wiped out. Between using her elemental powers and trying to protect Portia, his soul mate was spent.

"Have you talked to Portia?" Sammuel asked.

"She refuses to talk to anyone," Miranda answered. "Portia has locked the door to her chamber and I do not want to force it open. What little she has communicated, she wants Shirl to send her to another world where she can run free."

Running away never solved anything. He had discovered little about Portia, but knew she had been running since she left her home world in the Delani universe — the same world the shifters protecting his home were from. Maybe it was time she lived among her own people. He would not, however, allow a forced mating.

Callum entered the hall, determination on his face. The jaguar shifter was once his friend. He had been no more than a boy when he was dragged from his world into the Nightshade universe. When they found more of his kind, Sammuel brought them here to live in a safe environment. Overtime, he and Callum had drifted apart; and when Callum became leader of his pride, Sammuel had been pleased for his old friend. The shifter's new role just seemed to create a wider division between them.

The jaguar shifter was powerfully built, a requisite an alpha needed to control his pride. But more importantly, Callum was intelligent. He knew his friend was attractive to women with his jet black hair and emerald green eyes. His skin was a little darker than Portia's.

"I understand you have a feline shifter from the Delani universe under your protection," Callum said. "Under no circumstances do you turn her over to the dogs. She belongs with her own kind. We have many single males in need of a mate. The woman will not be forced to mate with any of them. It will be her choice."

"Do not presume to make demands of my brother within his own fortress," Frazour demanded. "Portia has been in this universe for five years. She is my friend and was my travel companion until I found my mate." Composing himself, Frazour continued, "I will support anything my friend wishes, including not being with her own kind."

"We accomplish nothing. I will not discuss Portia's future until I understand what she wants," Sammuel stated. "Leave my hall for the time being. As soon as I know Portia's desires, I will call you all back and give you my decision."

Sammuel could only hope Miranda would be able to get through to Portia and get the young woman to talk. They seemed to have developed a bond over the short time they had known each other. He needed to pacify his mate, come up with a solution that would make Portia happy, and not have everything he had worked so hard to build fall apart over a single female shifter.

Miranda stood outside Portia's quarters, begging the shifter to allow her into her room in order to talk. Concentrating on Portia allowed her to delay facing her own problems. She had called up elements below the ground's surface. Her growing strength was beginning to terrify her and erode whatever confidence she possessed that her powers were controllable.

"Portia," Miranda pleaded, "I need to make sure you are all right. You have to have faith that we will not turn you over to the cats or the wolf shifters."

"Is Jace with you?" Portia asked.

"No," Miranda replied, "it is only me. No one else is going to bother you, I promise."

Several moments passed and Miranda heard the lock release. Portia opened the door and motioned for her to enter. Her new friend's eyes were red from crying.

"Does he hate me?" Portia asked.

It was clear she was referring to Jace. Jace had arrived an hour ago with Drake and Patrice, soon after sunset. He demanded to see Portia, but Sammuel honored her wish to to make her decision alone. Jace stormed out of the fortress and was somewhere in the mountains. The youthful appearing vampire would go to ground outside the keep. Sammuel had numerous day shelters scattered around his territory.

"He feels betrayed," Miranda told her. "It would not have been so bad had Frazour not been aware of what you were. Sammuel's property is surrounded by shifters, so he was able to recognize what you were immediately. Why haven't you run off? I know you are more comfortable in your panther form in this world."

Miranda looked around the large chamber. It was evident Portia had spent part of the time in this room as a feline. There were areas where the furniture was clawed and a number of pillows had been shredded.

"They will hunt me down if I run," Portia replied. "Whoever catches me will have parental rights to me, including forcing me to mate. For the time being, I am safer here."

"These are Sammuel's lands and his fortress," Miranda said. "If he adopts you, or whatever the correct terminology is, the cats and the wolves will have no power over you. In fact, if you wanted to live with your own kind, only Sammuel would be able to approve a mating. Correct me if I am wrong."

Portia looked at Miranda with a critical eye. The shifter was considering what she had said. Slowly, Miranda could see Portia's face light up.

"I would not mind living within the pride," Portia said, "assuming I would not be forced to mate. I already know who I wish to mate with, but I am not ready to make such a commitment."

Miranda believed she meant Jace, but she did not want to redirect the conversation. They had a temporary resolution, assuming Callum agreed to the terms. All she had to do was run it past Sammuel. Miranda could not imagine why he would disagree with what she proposed.

"Thank you for interfering," Portia said. "I am not always the easiest person to live with. Can I be here for you as well? You have been so generous to your half-sister, but who is there for you? How did it feel to create a volcanic eruption?"

"How did you know about that?" Miranda asked. Portia had stayed in the fortress during the last battle because of the wolf shifters.

"I am a panther shifter," Portia said. "My hearing is outstanding and little else was discussed when the humans entered the fortress. Volcanic eruptions are not uncommon in my world, so I know how disruptive they can be. My people had to migrate several times over the years because of lava flows. I have never experienced one myself, but our folklore is full of such stories."

It would be so nice to talk to another person about her feelings. Cassie was in another dimension and she needed Shirl's assistance to see her. Afton had a world to change. She still did not feel close enough to Emma to approach her. Fortunately, Patrice had warmed to her, but that did not mean she felt comfortable confiding in Sammuel's daughter. Lastly, she always felt Tanya did not care for her...at all.

Perhaps sharing her fears would help relieve some of the stress Portia was under. It had certainly helped Miranda take her mind off her own problems listening to Cassie. Maybe voicing her own worries to another person would help Miranda manage her own feelings of uncertainty and inadequacy.

"Everything has happened so fast," Miranda admitted. "Only weeks ago I was living on the Venture farm waiting to be claimed by Yorik. Now he is dead and Sammuel has entered my life. The power we draw from each other is frightening. I did not know what I was doing when I started the eruption. All I did was solicit help from my element."

"Yes, I see the changes that you and Emma have gone through," Portia said. "That is why I am not ready to reveal myself to Jace. Somehow, I know that when we are together I will go through the same change. I do not know that I would survive if I were unable to transform into my panther. She is part of me."

The tables had turned. Her problems now seemed minor compared to what Portia faced. Until this point, the female soul mates had been human. Two carried the genetic marker and Afton had been a half-ling. There was no telling what would happen to a shifter once she became an elemental.

"Why don't we just face one problem at a time," Miranda suggested. "I will talk to Sammuel about claiming guardianship rights over you. You can choose to remain here or live with the pride. No choice you make between the two has to be permanent. If you choose to live with the cats, you are welcome to return here if things do not turn out as you hope. We have not made a decision when we will open the mountain path and claim the Venture Hive for Afton."

"Thank you for everything," Portia said. "Remember I am here for you, regardless of where I decide to live."

"You are welcome," Miranda said. "I will go and discuss this with Sammuel and then return. Feel free to lock the door behind me if it will make you feel safer."

Representatives from both pride and pack entered the great hall. Sammuel had sent for the cats and the wolves as soon as Miranda explained what she and Portia discussed. He knew Miranda was keeping part of their conversation confidential, particularly the part related to Jace. His blood brother had yet to return to the fortress.

It was hard to treat Callum as the pride leader instead of his friend, but knew he had to remain fair and impartial when dealing with both communities. This time around, his main concern was Portia's well-being. The panther had saved Miranda's life and he owed her more than he could ever repay.

"Thank you for responding to my summons so quickly," Sammuel said to both parties. "Portia comes from a world where the cats separate themselves from the wolf packs. She will not consider mating with any wolf."

"The Delani universe has sections that keep to age old prejudices," Gareth explained. "Those of us who fell through the portal have moved on."

"Yet you still live in separate villages and have staked out territory for yourselves, rather than sharing hunting grounds." Sammuel was not going to fall for the nonsense Gareth spewed. "These are my lands and this is my home. Portia requested asylum and I have taken guardianship over her."

"Then you are in the position to reward me with the opportunity to mate with her in payment for the assistance we provided you against the vampires," Gareth said.

"Had we come to some kind of arrangement prior to the battle and it was clear Portia was the prize, we would not be having this conversation," Sammuel assured him. "However, no such bargain was struck. Although, I certainly appreciate the assistance you provided, I will not be handing the panther shifter over to you."

Sammuel could tell Gareth was about to open his mouth and challenge his dictate. Before the wolf was able to utter a single word, Sammuel stood and drew his sword. "Mind the next words that come out of your mouth, friend. I owe you a debt for your assistance, but my memory will be short lived should you continue to disrespect me. Get out of here before you regret coming before me today."

The animal within Gareth must have sensed the dark power within Sammuel, who needed to calm down before he released the energy. Both Lorenz and Frazour had started to draw power from their soul mate's elements. Although he had not called upon the land's power, he knew he was dangerously close to doing just that.

Gareth left the great hall and his pack members followed. Callum had remained quiet during the entire exchange. Sammuel did not miss the snickering grin his former friend had on his face. Had Gareth seen the same expression, a fight may have broken out between the two. An uneasy peace existed between the two shifter communities. If not handled correctly, the Portia situation may very well bring war to his tranquil valley.

"Do you recognize the guardianship I hold over Portia?" Sammuel asked Callum.

"The girl came under your protection," Callum said, "so yes, I do."

Sammuel knew Callum well enough to know his old friend was sizing him up and his commitment to Portia. Very few female shifters had been caught in the portal's grasp over the years. The panther was quite a prize.

"Portia has been traveling with my blood brother for years and has accepted my authority," Sammuel continued. "My new mate and the shifter have become quite close. Miranda has drawn out certain demands from her friend."

"Continue," Callum said. He could tell his friend was becoming impatient, but did not want to appear so.

"The woman is considering living within your pride's community as an unmated female," Sammuel informed him. "It will give her the freedom and time to get to know the feline males. If one captures her heart, she will let me know and I will agree to a mating. Until that time, she is to remain untouched and provided a hut for her sole use."

At first, Callum said nothing. Sammuel knew different scenarios were playing in his mind. His former friend was a tactical master. Callum was trying to ascertain how he could get the upper hand in the negotiation.

"Portia will be welcomed into my pride as an unmated female," Callum said. "She has been in this universe for many years and has managed to stay alive. That is quite an accomplishment. She will be considered a fellow warrior and afforded her own living quarters. You have my word no one will touch her in an inappropriate manner. I only request to meet her now and personally welcome her."

Rather than making the decision alone, Sammuel turned to Miranda who had observed both shifter groups since they entered. No one would know Portia's state of mind better than his own mate. Portia trusted Miranda.

"We discussed the remote possibility that such a request would be made," Miranda advised them. "Portia is willing to meet the pride leader. Be advised, you have one chance to get this right. If you fail, she will not join your pride. You were right, she has lived in this dimension for five years and was brilliant enough to survive."

Miranda led the way, while Sammuel and Callum followed close behind. Sammuel felt her anxiety through their connection. His mate was concerned about Portia and what she may do. He was not all together sure whether Portia would be in panther or human form when they entered her quarters. The cat could easily attack the man walking beside him. He would have to make sure he protected his friend against Portia if that came to pass.

They entered the east tower and started to ascend the stairs to the third floor where Portia's quarters were located. Miranda knocked on the door and Portia bid them enter. Sammuel was relieved to see Portia was in her human form and able to communicate.

Portia was dressed in a beautiful flowing white gown. She was not the half wild shifter he was used to seeing. The woman was stunning. Sammuel could tell Callum was shocked by the sight of her. Whoever had the idea to present her in such a fashion had made a terrible miscalculation.

"This is Portia," Miranda said. "Portia, I would like to introduce you to Callum, the pride leader I told you about. As you can see, she is more than a survivor, but a gem worth earning. Callum, only you will have the privilege of seeing Portia like this."

"May I approach?" Callum asked. He was playing this to perfection.

Portia nodded. Sammuel knew her well enough to know she was not comfortable in the dress or the situation. Shifters were not embarrassed by their naked bodies. The woman would probably have been more at ease in her natural state.

Callum went down on one knee before Portia. "I welcome you to my pride. You will be safe and respected among us. It is understood that a mating will only be arranged with your consent and Sammuel's approval. A hut will be constructed over the next several days for your comfort. You may use my home until yours is completed. I will stay with one of our single men. Join us when you are ready."

The pride leader rose and left the chamber. His hasty departure surprised Sammuel and the two women. When Portia started laughing, Sammuel released a breath of relief. He imagined Callum was close enough to hear her reaction.

"This may turn out better than I hoped," Portia commented.

Sammuel was relieved Portia seemed satisfied with her current situation. He still had a war brewing between the cat and wolf shifters. Not to mention Jace's reaction when he returned and found Portia missing.

CHAPTER 17

Sammuel gazed over his lands with satisfaction. The humans were settling in well. Although Drake walked among them, they considered him different from the creatures that had corralled and fed off them. There were no complaints about continuing to separate the men from the females. They were slowly beginning to interact with each other in order to get tasks completed.

New housing was constructed outside the fortress with the help of Callum's pride. Portia had moved into his settlement in the mountains to the east. He figured the assistance was a means to thank Sammuel for having faith in Callum's ability to protect Portia.

Rather than joining the other cat shifters helping to settle the humans, Portia stayed in the mountains. Sammuel wondered if Jace had approached her, as his brother had yet to return to the settlement.

The wolf shifters did not join the effort. It was not surprising, since the wolves and the cats rarely did anything together. Sammuel believed there would still be some kind of fall out over Portia choosing to join the pride.

Miranda took daily walks through the fields. Due to her presence, the growth of the crops was miraculous. They had many more mouths to feed and it appeared there would be ample amounts of grain, corn, and other crops to aid their burgeoning population. This aspect of her power thrilled Miranda. Sammuel could still feel her struggles with the more destructive sides of her elemental gift.

Afton did not push the next phase of her plan—taking control of the Venture Hive. She understood they needed to get the humans settled before they could leave. Her father had victimized these people and it was another crusade of hers to make restitution. The humans knew who she was and welcomed her into their community.

Unfortunately, for some reason, the same was not true of Miranda. It was clear both the men and the women were discomfited by her presence. Perhaps it was the physical change to Miranda they did not understand and feared, as they had not witnessed Afton's metamorphosis.

When Miranda was not with him or walking through the fields, she spent time with Patrice. Jace had all but disappeared into the mountains with the dogs. Patrice had reached out to Miranda, not understanding why Jace was suffering. Sammuel found it odd that his daughter had not gone to Tanya for comfort, but was glad Patrice and Miranda were becoming closer.

Sammuel caught very few glimpses of Tanya since their return. His sister-in-law had cloistered herself in the nursery. It was hard not to notice the growing coldness Tanya directed toward Miranda. He assumed it was the budding friendship that arose between his mate and Patrice.

There was so much work to be done, even the humans had little rest. Huts had to be built, crops planted, clothing to be sewn, weapons made, and a myriad of other tasks to be completed. However, it was crucial the humans learned to fight.

For the time being, Sammuel and his blood brothers focused on training the men. They did not yet possess the muscle mass it took to wield a sword, so they concentrated on archery. Learning to use a bow would allow them to not only protect themselves, but hunt for game to feed their people. They set up targets and demonstrated how the bow and arrow were used. Because of the number of males to be trained, they started at daybreak and continued until several hours past sunset.

This evening he was concentrating on observing a group practicing what they had learned. There were a number among them that had the promise of becoming excellent archers. Each round of arrows produced a better result than the previous. They were making progress.

"They are getting better," Patrice commented.

Sammuel wrapped his arm around his daughter and kissed her cheek. Since there were no vampires to feed off of, Patrice had been taking small sips of blood from Drake. The powerful blood gave his daughter more color in her cheeks. Now she closer resembled the girl she once was before he took her mortality.

"I am pleased with their progress," Sammuel answered. "Has Tanya left the nursery? She isolates herself and I do not like it."

"Tanya is dedicated to the babies," Patrice responded. "You know that."

"True," Sammuel said, "but she never locked herself in with them before. She used to play with all the children and help with their lessons. She is not herself."

Although they rescued babies, those children grew and lived full lives before they died within the confines of his valley. The people of Stone Meadow welcomed the new arrivals with open arms. His people understood what happened outside the valley and did everything they could to make their transition a smooth one.

"You worry for nothing," Patrice said. "She is just overwhelmed by everything that has happened. We never accomplished a rescue of this magnitude before. I am going to see if Miranda needs anything." His daughter walked a few steps and then turned, "Have you heard from Jace?"

"No," Sammuel answered.

He did not want to dwell on the hurt and anger Jace felt where Portia was concerned. Sammuel was not sure what his daughter's true feelings for his blood brother were. He did not want to see her suffer over a relationship that may not be possible. They had known each other for two thousand years, but never seemed to be more than friends.

"He will return after he handles whatever is bothering him," Patrice said. "I should join Miranda."

It had been a week since they returned to his home and he made love to Miranda that first day. Every evening they entered his chamber and exchanged energy. They transitioned to resting at night in order to be fully available to the humans during the day. Although they made love, neither had declared their feelings to one another.

Sammuel had hoped that, once things got back to normal, Miranda would be comfortable enough to admit her feelings. He was too much of a coward to say he loved her first. She struggled with so much, and he did not want to burden her with guilt if she did not return the sentiment.

Sammuel heard the swoosh of an arrow coming from a direction other than where the humans were practicing. He turned to investigate and felt a sharp pain in his neck. Warm liquid ran down from his neck. When he reached up to see what caused his pain, his hand came in contact with an arrow.

Miranda knew something was wrong, she just could not figure out what. She mentally checked off all the tasks she had to perform today. For once, she was ahead of schedule. It nagged at her that she could not determine what was bothering her.

A commotion was taking place where the men were practicing their archery skills. Frantic calls for help rang out. Patrice had just joined her and they both ran in the direction of the disturbance.

Dread ran through her when she saw Sammuel on the ground with an arrow embedded in his neck. Miranda fell on her knees beside him, helpless, not knowing what to do. She was afraid she would do more damage if she tried to pull the shaft from his neck.

"I will get Drake, Lorenz, or Frazour," Patrice said.

Miranda looked up to see Patrice frantically running to find one of Sammuel's blood brothers. They would be able to help and remove the arrow. In the meantime, all she could do was sit there and watch him bleed out.

As her tears fell from her cheeks, the ground below her started to react. Her tears dampened the soil and it flowed in Sammuel's direction. Mud closed the wound the arrow produced on both sides of his neck, stopping the bleeding. The soil continued to collect around his throat.

She heard murmurs around her about the miraculous change Sammuel had gone through that allowed him to walk during the daylight hours. Now, they were witnessing another unexplainable event. The residents of Sammuel's settlement, old and new, viewed what was occurring as a blessing brought upon their savior.

Frazour knelt beside her, witnessing what was occurring. Her element was trying to heal her soul mate. Miranda went to touch the arrow and Frazour stopped her.

"Let it do its magic," he said. "Something similar happened with Emma. I somehow knew I needed to let whatever was occurring to continue without my intervention. Water had chosen and healed her. Let the ground do the same with Sammuel. You will know when you need to take over."

Termites boiled up from the ground, surrounding the wooden shaft. She knew how destructive they could be and watched in wonder as the arrow started to disintegrate before her very eyes. The termites continued to eat the wood and more of the shaft was removed from Sammuel's neck. The element had severed the arrow in half, pulling the rod from his body.

Frazour grabbed her hand and placed it over the wound closest to where they knelt. Miranda could feel the power coursing through her arm transfer to Sammuel. Miranda was not sure what she was supposed to do or visualize. Her instincts were just to keep fueling him with energy and allow his body to repair itself.

"Just have faith," Lorenz's voice came from behind. "He may not come back to consciousness once he is healed. When Afton had nearly bled out after being attacked by a vampire horde, it seemed like an eternity before she awoke."

"Your element is the land," Frazour said. "We will keep him here as long as it takes."

"Can I help?" Emma asked. "I understand that, when I was close to death, Afton also provided elemental power."

"Love," Frazour replied, "you can try. Afton wielded fire without burning you. We cannot afford any water to wash away the soil healing him."

Emma grabbed a nearby bucket of water and knelt next to Sammuel. She placed one hand in the container and the other hand on the soil next Miranda's hand. Suddenly a third hand appeared…Afton's.

Land, water, and fire. Three of the four elements worked in concert to heal her love. With the thought of possibly losing him, Miranda realized her true feelings for Sammuel. Their attraction had been immediate and now she could name the emotion which was now swirling in her stomach.

Sammuel just lay there, so very still. She kept expecting his eyes to open and everything to be all right, but his pallor remained a ghastly gray. If she had not seen his chest expand with each breath he labored to take, Miranda would have believed him dead.

"I cannot stand here and do nothing," Drake said, in frustration. "When Sammuel wakes, I will have custody of the culprit who shot the arrow."

Various suspects came to mind. Gareth wanted Portia and Sammuel had declined his request. Although Portia resided in his pride, Callum could declare her his mate if anything happened to Sammuel. A single vampire could have followed them through the pass before she closed it and was going to pick them off one at a time. She did not know any of the humans who already lived here well enough to venture a guess at any of the motives they could have.

Drake was the oldest of the blood brothers. Even Sammuel was unsure how old he truly was. Miranda hoped he would be able to fulfill his promise and find who had done this to her soul mate. Part of her already felt incomplete with Sammuel in his present state.

Alarmed, Miranda entered the link that existed between them. She could feel him. He was fighting to survive, to heal. Sammuel was drawing from her element, as she was trying to do.

"Concentrate on the light energy inside you," Sammuel managed to communicate. *"Look past your anger and hate. Draw on the energy you push when you are walking through the crops."*

Why had she not realized she needed to build, not destroy? She had been allowing her fear to focus her emotions that caused the earth to quake or erupt, not the energy to bring life and make things grow. She had lived most of her life with creatures of darkness, rather than the humans around her who thrived in the sun. It was the same power Afton harnessed, but from a different element.

Miranda had seen so little, so she concentrated on the beauty of the fields, of the mountains, and of the little stream where she and Beatrice had drunk. She felt energy once again flowing through her arm into Sammuel. However, this time it felt so light her arm almost felt weightless.

Sammuel's color was slowly returning and he was having an easier time breathing. Miranda, Emma, and Afton also continued to push energy into Sammuel. She could feel the fire warm her soul and the water refreshing her fatigue.

She watched as Sammuel's eyes began to flutter. Miranda continued to stare at his face until she was looking into his lovely amber brown eyes. Unable to hold back her emotions any longer, Miranda wept and threw herself on top of him. He wrapped an arm around her. His grasp was weak, but it felt wonderful.

"I think the two of you need to retire to your chambers to clean up and restore yourselves," Lorenz said. "In the meantime, I will check with Drake to see how he is progressing in his hunt for the one responsible for trying to kill Sammuel."

Her soul mate rose and was unsteady on his feet. For once, she would have to support him. He had been her emotional strength from the moment they met. Now, she was going to provide him the physical strength he needed.

All she wanted was to get her hands on the being who almost killed him. She would let the ground devour him, never to release the perpetrator of such a heinous crime. There would be no mercy in her heart for whoever tried to take Sammuel from her.

His legs were becoming more steady, but he realized what helping him meant to Miranda. As he healed, he could better feel her presence. Originally, the darkness within her scared him. It was too similar to the disruptive power he tried to contain within himself.

Although Sammuel did not think he was capable of communicating with her, he managed to transfer the idea she must focus on the good things in life in order to save him. The duality of nature continued to amaze him, balancing the light with the dark. They each carried aspects of both. The land had the ability to feed them energy or syphon energy away, to create or destroy.

Upon entering their chamber, Miranda requested water be brought up for a bath. He was caked in soil, particularly his neck. The ground that gave them sustenance had saved his life.

His mate stood before him and began unbuttoning his shirt. Nothing would give him greater pleasure than stripping her naked, but he knew the servants would be back shortly with the hot water. He also knew how much it meant to her to care for him.

It did not take long for the servants to enter with buckets of steaming water. Ironically, it would have taken Afton and Emma minutes to accomplish what it took the servants close to an hour to complete. While they waited, Miranda continued to touch, massage, and sprinkle kisses on his face. Energy continued to pour into him with each gentle touch.

It felt wonderful when he was finally able to submerge himself in the hot water. His tight body began to relax, recovering from the trauma it suffered. The relaxing soak was just an appetizer for what he really wanted when all the servants finally cleared out and left them in peace.

Miranda ran a wet rag over his shoulders and cleaned all the soil from his neck. She muttered something about there being no evidence of an arrow on his pristine neck. Miranda explored his body and wanted to know the origins of all the scars. He did not remember how he received half of them, so he made up amusing stories to lighten her mood. He felt the trauma she had suffered after he was shot.

When she finally put down the washcloth, Sammuel rose from the steel tub and captured her in his arms. He carried her to the bed where he methodically removed every stitch of clothing she wore. All he wanted was to be buried deeply within her.

Sammuel pushed the wisps of hair out of her face and kissed her. Although there was passion in the kiss, he held back most of his desire. He needed to tell her something before he got carried away in their lovemaking. Because that, for the first time in his usually lust saturated mind, was what he was doing. Miranda was more than his soul mate. She was his eternal love.

He never thought he would love again. He always thought Katelyn was the love of his life, but he had not experienced true love until he met Miranda. She was everything to him.

"I love you, Miranda," Sammuel said. "It is doubtful I could count the number of times in the last three thousand years I wanted to end it all. This dark, unnatural immortality. But this evening I fought with everything I had to come back to you."

Tears welled in her beautiful blue eyes. Once again, he brushed away hair that obstructed his clear view of her face. She had been breathtaking the first time he saw her and was just as beautiful after her transformation.

With precision and care, he removed the dress she wore. One of the fortress's seamstresses had dyed the material a buttercup yellow, feeling it would complement her complexion. His people had welcomed Miranda, as they had the other former farm residents.

Sammuel entered her slowly, his eyes never leaving her face. He wanted to see every nuance of each expression that crossed her face while he loved her.

"*Sammuel, we have captured the being responsible for your injury,*" Drake communicated telepathically. "*You need to join us in the main hall immediately.*"

Sammuel lowered his head on to her forehead, sighing in frustration. He did not want to deal with the guilty party now, he wanted to make love to his woman.

"What is wrong?" Miranda asked, concern evident in her voice.

"Drake has discovered who attacked me and wants us to join him downstairs," Sammuel responded.

He lifted his head in time to see her eyes widen. She nearly pushed him off the bed in her haste to rise. Miranda moved with the speed her element's power had given her. It was obvious she wanted to know who the guilty party was. She was out for blood.

CHAPTER 18

When they entered the great hall, Sammuel was surprised to see Drake holding Tanya by the wrist while she struggled to get free, but did not see the prisoner his blood brother spoke of. Whatever game Drake was playing with his sister-in-law, he wanted it to end.

"Release Tanya and present the being who attacked me," Sammuel ordered.

He expected one of the wolf shifters to be brought forward. Although his relationship with Callum was not what it once was, he could not imagine his former friend would try to kill him. If it ever came to a confrontation, Callum would come straight at him, not hide behind a crowd and an arrow.

"Even now, you do not take me seriously," Tanya cried.

"Enough of this foolishness," Sammuel complained. "I want to confront the being who tried to kill me."

Patrice came to stand beside him and grabbed his forearm. He turned to look at her shocked, concerned face. She stared at Tanya as if she were seeing her for the first time. Sammuel turned and looked at his sister-in-law. Something in the way she looked at him warped her beauty.

"Tanya?" Sammuel asked warily.

It finally sunk in that he was looking into the cold eyes of his attacker. He could not fathom a guess why she would do such a thing.

What had he ever done to warrant her acting in so dangerous a manner. It had been three thousand years since he had converted her. It could not be because of that unforgiveable moment.

"It should have been me," Tanya said. "All those years ago when you were romancing Katelyn, it should have been me. I was the strong one. Your initial attraction was to my strength, but you fell for Katelyn's helplessness. Those boys she gave you were weak. I would have given you strong sons. The hours we spent together when I taught you how to romance her, it should have been clear I was the better choice."

Patrice's grip on his hand tightened when Tanya mentioned her dead brothers. Men with swords had struck down his boys. His daughter had witnessed their deaths, as well as her mother's. In all these years, she never once talked about it.

It was true, at first he been attracted to Tanya, but there was a hardness about her that marred her beauty. When he met her sister, Katelyn, he fell immediately in love with her. Sammuel always believed Tanya had approved and encouraged their marriage. Tanya never seemed to look back at him, and then went after the village's blacksmith.

"Afterwards, I found you—not the other way around," Tanya continued. "You were a wonderful specimen when you were human, but you were incredible as a vampire. I wanted the power you possessed, almost as much as I wanted you. It was never my intent for you to find Patrice. She was supposed to have died at the enemy's hand. We were meant to be together, just the two of us."

"Miranda, please take Patrice out of here," Sammuel requested.

He did not want his daughter to hear anymore of Tanya's poisonous words. The dark power grew within him, focused on his sister-in-law. Whatever he was going to do, he did not want Patrice to witness it.

"I am not going anywhere," Patrice said in reaction to her father's order. "He turned you to keep what little was left of my mother alive. It was *always* Katelyn while he was alive, and then well into his immortality. You are pathetic."

"Why not kill me?" Miranda asked. "After all this time pining for Sammuel, why go after him?"

Sammuel was infuriated by Miranda's question. Although Drake had a firm hold on Tanya, he did not want her focus to be on his mate. He wanted Miranda and Patrice out of harm's way while he dealt with Tanya.

"You are an innocent," Tanya answered. "There you were, dying in the clearing and he would have brought you over to this miserable existence. He took away from you the grace of death. For three thousand years, he did not look at another woman, not even me. Then he takes one look at you and he is once again attracted to another woman. I thought he was finally ready to love again. You were mortal, and I believed it would finally be my turn."

Sammuel had always thought Tanya blamed him for not allowing her a natural death. He never once imagined Tanya had sought out this existence, only to regret her decision. In saving Miranda, he had indirectly re-fueled Tanya's rage. He could see the madness in her eyes. She had hidden it well for all these years. By some miracle, she had not attacked him or others earlier.

"I am tired of this existence and it is time to finally sleep," Tanya continued. "If I cannot have you in this life, then we will be together in our afterlife."

Immortality had finally driven her insane. That was the only explanation Sammuel could come up with. He was uncertain what he was going to do with the madwoman. Today she had gone after him, and there was no guarantee she would not turn around and try to kill Patrice or Miranda. His daughter was more vulnerable than his mate.

"I will grant your right for eternal sleep, Tanya," Sammuel said, "but I will not be joining you. The risk you present to my family is too great to allow you to continue living."

Although he had sentenced her to death, he did not have the stomach to execute her. He did not know if he would ever be ready to kill the woman he had spent three thousand years with. How did he miss her deep seeded feelings for him?

"Drake," Sammuel continued, "there are several chambers below us designed to hold vampire prisoners. Lock her down there until I determine what should be done with her."

Sammuel rubbed his left hand across his forehead. He was at a loss regarding what to do. The decision was ultimately his to make. There was always the option of letting her see the last sunrise of her existence.

"She not only threatened your life, she places Miranda's at risk," Afton told him. "We are connected to our soul mates. It is unclear if one can continue living without the other. Our sustenance is now solely derived from our eternal partner."

"This is all unfortunate," Frazour added, "Tanya was a fierce fighter. We could have certainly used her in the upcoming campaign to take over the Venture Hive; but she cannot be trusted, that much is clear."

"Do you wish time alone to reflect on what you want done?" Miranda asked.

She was no doubt feeling the turmoil he suffered from within. Their link made it impossible to hide what the other was feeling. That certainly had both positive and negative aspects to it. He was never truly alone. There was comfort in that.

"No," Sammuel answered. "I wish everyone's opinion. Perhaps one of you has a solution I have not yet thought of." The decision was weighing him down both physically and mentally.

"Shirl could always open a portal to an unpopulated dimension," Emma suggested. "But it is doubtful Tanya would be able to find shelter the first time the sun rose. Never mind that recommendation. I had not thought it out completely."

"There are no bad ideas at this point," Sammuel reassured Emma. "The more suggestions I get, the more likely I will come up with a solution I can live with."

Sammuel grabbed Miranda's hand and held it. How he longed to take her back to their quarters and make love to her again. For a time, he could forget the terrible decision he had to make regarding Tanya's precarious future.

"Maybe Tanya knows how she wants to die," Afton said. "From the way she talks, she hates her existence and wants it to end. She must have been thinking about how she wanted to go out."

"I will talk to her," Patrice said. "She is more likely to talk to me."

His first reaction was to keep his daughter as far away from Tanya as possible. Yet, there had always been a strong bond between the two women. When his boys came along, Patrice spent more and more time in Tanya's household, playing with her daughters. They each had the other's support after Sammuel converted them into vampires. Tanya's earlier words about Patrice had surprised him. He saw the determination in his daughter's eyes and had no choice but to honor Patrice's request.

Sammuel nodded, indicating Patrice was free to speak to her aunt. He wondered if Patrice had similar thoughts of suicide. The two women had spent so much time together. Had they discussed various ways they both could find peace?

How he wished Jace was Patrice's soul mate. He knew that was not the case. The first time he saw Miranda he was drawn to her. There did not seem to be a strong link between the youthful looking vampire and his daughter. Their bond was due to the age they had been when they were changed, not the draw of soul mates.

Sammuel stared at his blood brothers and their women who occupied the hall. The room had fallen quiet with Patrice's exit. They were hoping as he was, Tanya would choose to meet the light of day. He could not take a sword to her delicate neck.

Miranda's gaze continued to return to where Patrice had gone. Neither she nor Drake had returned. The sun would rise in three hours. She wanted to spare Sammuel the horror of watching Tanya meet the sun, if that was her choice. Tanya had isolated herself through most of the trip to the fortress. What little time she spent with anyone, it was with Patrice.

"Tanya always gravitated to the children and the women during the two weeks it took to arrive here," Miranda said. "Perhaps if Afton, Emma, and I took her to meet the sun, Tanya would be more comfortable."

"She has not communicated how she wants her life to end," Sammuel pointed out. Miranda could hear the weight of the world in his defeated voice.

"No, she hasn't," Miranda replied. "But if it were me, that is how I would want to go. Three thousand years of not feeling the sun's warmth. I could not imagine that. When I was in a dark mood, I always left the lab and sought the brightness of day if it was possible."

"Until Patrice returns," Afton said, "let's concentrate on developing a plan to take over the Venture Hive and transform it into a haven like Lorenz's settlement."

Sammuel welcomed the distraction. It was a discussion they needed to start if they wished to claim the Venture Hive. He could see the discomfort reflected on Lorenz's face.

"I do not know," Lorenz admitted. "Perhaps we should start small and eventually take on the Venture Hive. When I started the settlement, there were just a handful of desperate vampires who would do anything to feed. I threatened immediate death to anyone of them who took a human against their will or did not heal their donor when they were done."

"How many did you end up killing?" Emma asked.

"Half the vampires who originally settled in my home," Lorenz answered. "We do not have the manpower to control the sheer volume of vampires Afton is considering. I do not mean to be negative, but I just do not see a way."

"Lorenz," Afton countered, "when you started your community, nothing like it had ever existed in the Nightshade universe. The way humans and vampires interact within your settlement is well known among both species within the Venture Hive. I heard about your home, long before I ventured there. Besides, I do not plan to take the keep by force, just provide a choice to the vampires currently in residence— feed on willing humans...or starve."

"Where are you going to get the humans to participate in your experiment?" Frazour asked. "You cannot expect the people we rescued from the farm to volunteer."

"There are already humans who reside in the hive," Afton answered. "Although, I am not sure how many survived when the vampires returned after Yorik died. They could have slaughtered them all in a blood crazed massacre. We will not know until we get there."

"It's nice here, Afton," Emma said.

"Yes, but we cannot spend the rest of our lives here," Afton commented. "Besides, we need to return to Lorenz's settlement. There is no telling what has occurred in our absence. We left the vampires behind to protect the humans, but we do not know how large a force they may have come up against."

All discussion about the Venture Hive ceased when Patrice reentered the main hall, with Drake at her side. Miranda could not read Patrice's blank expression. Drake's countenance also gave nothing away.

"Tanya has chosen to meet the sun," Patrice said.

A combination of relief and sadness crossed the faces Afton watched as Tanya's wishes were communicated. The female vampire had dedicated her immortal life to saving human babies. Yorik's death was well deserved; Tanya's was a tragedy.

Love was a very volatile emotion. Her mother had committed suicide because she had fallen in love with the crystal telepath who had rescued them, but died. Afton herself would destroy any being that even looked the wrong way at Lorenz.

Now Tanya was going to die because of a three-thousand-year-old unrequited love. Since Sammuel's attacker had been identified, she wracked her brain trying to find another solution to seal Tanya's fate. Nothing came to her.

She had so few allies in this world, losing one was devastating. The mission she set in place was overwhelming. There had to be another solution. Afton needed time to think.

"Is the chamber Tanya is held in secure?" Afton asked. "Can I have another day before the sentence is executed to come up with some other punishment? She has done so much good and I am going to need all the soldiers I can raise. There has to be a way to safeguard Sammuel and Miranda, while allowing Tanya to live."

"If I give you the time you requested, will you honor Tanya's right to see her last sunrise if you do not come up with a better solution?" Sammuel asked. "I am asking you to respect her wish to die."

"Fire is my element," Afton responded. "It only seems fitting I be with her when she meets her fate, if I cannot come up with an alternative."

"You have two risings of the sun to come up with an answer, Afton," Sammuel said. "Nothing would make me happier should you discern a permanent solution to the problem."

Afton got her wish. Now she needed a brilliant idea to come out of nowhere. She could feel Lorenz trying to hold back his feelings of displeasure. He probably believed she was interfering in something that was none of her business. What he did not realize, everything that impacted the blood brothers and the elemental women was her business. It was critical they stayed in balance. The question she needed an answer to was whether or not Tanya's life or death impacted their stability.

CHAPTER 19

There was a blazing fire in the center of the main hall when Miranda entered. It was just short of the two-day deadline Afton had requested. From the inferno in front of her, it was clear Afton had not come up with a viable alternative other than Tanya's meeting the sun.

Patrice had been the only one among them to visit her aunt. Each time she entered and left Tanya's subterranean chamber, Lorenz and Frazour were there to prevent the dangerous woman from slipping away. Although his daughter pleaded for Sammuel to talk to the condemned woman, Sammuel would not agree to see her.

"I failed," Afton whispered, defeated.

Her sad utterance was loud enough for Miranda ears alone. Afton continued to look into the dancing flames for some kind of answer. If only life was that easy.

"No one expected you to come up with another solution," Miranda admitted. "How do you imprison an immortal who tried to kill… whose word is untrustworthy? We cannot subject her to another world, when there is no guarantee it is populated somewhere beyond whatever portal a crystal telepath can open."

"I need to find a way," Afton cried. "All I seem to do is destroy. It was by my orders that my father was killed."

This was not about Tanya, but Afton's guilt over her father's death. If it had not been for the woman beside her, Miranda's life would still be at risk. It had always been unlikely Yorik would have given up his claim to her, or the next woman he found who carried the genetic marker.

"Drake's patience was wearing thin," Miranda said. "Sammuel told me had you had not given him the approval, Drake would have done it anyway. The brothers had already decided your father's fate. I, for one, rest easier with Yorik gone."

Afton shifted in her chair. The fire's intensity weakened, no longer fed by her warring emotions. Miranda knew Afton was finally starting to forgive herself.

"I talked to Lorenz," Afton said, "and we will escort Tanya to meet the sun. It is my element. Afterwards I want to leave to claim the Venture Hive. I have sent Drake to find Jace. We will need him if we face resistance to claiming my birthright. He needs to get over whatever is bothering him about Portia."

"And Portia?" Miranda asked. "Will she be joining us?"

Miranda had mixed feelings about leaving the fortress. Despite the problems with Portia and Tanya, she had never had a more peaceful time in her life. She enjoyed walking through the fields and seeing the evidence of her elemental power in the tall healthy stalks of corn and the golden wheat. Knowledgeable humans would teach the new arrivals how to bring in a harvest and then they would let the land rest before planting another crop.

Each night, she and Sammuel made love. Since the attack, Sammuel had a new lease on life. He was continually telling her how much he cared for and loved her. Although she could feel the emotions welling up inside him, it was still nice to hear the words. She gladly verbalized her feelings toward him.

In the short time Miranda had known Sammuel, her feelings had changed so much. At first she felt gratitude, almost hero-worship. As her powers grew and Miranda was on an equal footing with him, she realized she utterly adored and loved him. She knew how much Tanya's betrayal and ultimate fate weighed on him.

Miranda felt a hand applying pressure on her arm. "Hello, Miranda," Afton said. "Have you heard a single word I said?"

Miranda had been lost in thoughts and daydreams of her future with Sammuel. She could not believe Afton had been talking and she had not been aware of the conversation.

"It doesn't take a rocket scientist to figure out what you were thinking about," Afton said. At Miranda's blank expression, Afton started laughing. "Never mind. How much time do we need to clear the mountain pass?"

Miranda had been practicing moving soil with her mind when she took her daily walks. She had the ability the first time she created a shelter for Sammuel, but had not realized that the volume of rock and soil did not matter.

"It will take little time," Miranda responded. "I can open a path and then close it again before we leave. The passage needs to be impenetrable while we are gone. There are too many precious lives here to risk a force of vampires entering. Although the wolves and the cats offer protection, I will feel better knowing there is no easy way to enter the valley."

"Then it's settled," Afton said. "Lorenz and I will do what must be done and we will leave shortly thereafter. Drake and Jace will follow. Patrice has asked to stay behind. Someone needs to mourn Tanya."

Miranda stared at the dying flames. She was going to be a coward and retire to her rooms when Tanya was led out. Sammuel had not told her his plans. Would he be able to watch the woman who so closely resembled his long dead wife meet her death?

Frazour and Lorenz led Tanya from her chamber to the deserted main hall. Afton had not left the spot she occupied after Miranda headed for her room. Death of a vampire was nothing new to her. She had held Wylaine in her arms and brought forth her power to weaken him close to death, then Lorenz accompanied them into the sun and said goodbye to his dying brother.

Now she was going to have a hand in killing another former loved one. A human brought over to an immortal existence whose mind could no longer reason. Tanya's jealousy had been brewing for some time. After three thousand years, Sammuel's finding Miranda had been the final straw — Tanya ultimately snapped.

The woman hated her immortality, but looked past her horrible existence and tried to do some good. Afton could not help but admire Tanya for that. Perhaps what she was about to do was not an execution, but a mercy killing. Maybe if Afton kept thinking that, she'd eventually believe it.

Tanya stood tall and proud. She wore a colorful pink and yellow gown. Although the two elemental men accompanied her, they were not dragging her forward. Neither man had a hand on their prisoner. Afton swallowed hard, trying to wish away the tears welling in her eyes.

"I am ready," Tanya said. Her voice was cheerful. It was as if she was leaving on vacation rather than walking to her death.

Afton came up beside her and took Tanya's hand. Together they exited the fortress. It would not be long before the sun would start its journey across the sky. Patrice had told Afton of a location Tanya went to stargaze and it was where she would greet the sun once again.

The first sign the sun was about to rise was evident with a slight line of orange over the mountains. She watched as Tanya's face filled with joy at the sight. Afton remembered the first sunrise she had witnessed with Lorenz. He had not seen the sight in two thousand years, and his face reflected the awe she saw in Tanya's.

Hues of yellow and red joined the orange as the sun began to rise in the east. Afton thought of the sunrises she saw when she lived in Chicago, the ones she had taken for granted. The light of day crept forward.

Due to Tanya's age, Afton was not sure how much sun she would be able to take before her body was affected. She had turned away when Wylaine met the sun, giving Lorenz precious time with the creature who had once been his birth brother.

Tanya released Afton's hand and took several steps forward. The condemned woman did not want to be near Afton in case she burst into flames. Considerate of others to the last. The female vampire lifted her head to the first ray of the sun to cross her face.

"At last," Afton heard Tanya say.

Tanya's skin began to dry and crack, similar to what happened to wet soil after it dried. She did not make a sound. Afton sensed the instant Tanya's essence left her body. What remained of her became like a statute for a short period of time. Finally, the wind began to spread what was once a living human and then a vampire across the land.

A tranquil feeling came over Afton. In the end, Tanya got what she wanted. An end to an existence that became impossible to withstand once Sammuel found his soul mate. There was little hope such a future would be available to her. Perhaps she had not planned to really kill Sammuel, but harm him in such a manner that the crime could not be overlooked. Afton was going to remember Tanya that way. It was doubtful anyone would try to prove her wrong.

"Let us head back, my love," Lorenz said. "We have a hive to claim."

Sammuel stood on the battlements of his fortress and watched Tanya meet the sun. She faced her death with an elegance that surprised him. He knew she had been unhappy and considered ending her existence long before now. It was Patrice who kept her going, as well as the hope one day he would wish to be with her.

How had he never realized how she felt about him? Sammuel kept asking himself the same question. What would he have done had he known? Although he had originally felt an attraction for Tanya, once he met Katelyn, he knew he had found his future wife.

Now he had to help find reasons for Patrice to continue living. Tanya had been the anchor in her life, certainly not him. He was the reason they were forced into the existence they both hated. For three thousand years, he had seen their contempt for him reflected in their eyes.

Lorenz looked up and silently acknowledged his presence. No one else had been aware he would witness his attacker's death, and they never would. He did not want to be plagued with questions about what happened when Tanya met the sun.

The two female vampires had never been ordinary. He had converted them, a living human transformed by The Creator. Now, only Patrice bore that lone distinction.

The Creator recently returned to the Nightshade universe for two short visits after a two-thousand-year absence. He and his mate were the first to transform into elementals. Perhaps when The Creator returned, Sammuel could ask him if there was any hope for Patrice. In the thousand years The Creator lived in the same dimension as he and his women, he never commented on what Sammuel had done.

Sammuel did not have time to dwell on his thoughts. Afton wanted to start their journey to the Venture Hive as soon as Tanya was dispatched. He had one more stop before he met Miranda and prepared the horses.

His body automatically headed down from the battlements into the fortress. Patrice had set up her quarters in the west tower almost as soon as they completed construction. She had selected a chamber as far away from his as she could get.

When he stood before Patrice's door, he hesitated. Should he enter, or knock and run the risk of not being invited in? The room contained no windows and she would spend days never leaving her quarters. In the end, Sammuel entered his daughter's chambers with no warning.

Patrice was sitting behind a large table, drawing. It was a talent she only discovered after her conversion. When she was human, there was no time or resources for such a pastime. His daughter had a talent for capturing images on paper.

Although Patrice sensed his presence, she did not raise her head to greet him. She continued to draw Tanya. His sister-in-law was holding one of the babies they had rescued. The drawing was so life like.

"It is done then?" Patrice asked. She choked on her last word, consumed with emotion.

He wanted to take his daughter into his arms, but knew such an action would not be welcomed. When she was a little girl, none of his children enjoyed his hugs more than Patrice. Sammuel missed that child.

"Yes," he answered. He could find no other words to share with her. Sammuel was walking on eggshells when it came to dealing with her after Tanya's death.

"She is at peace, then," Patrice said. "I have changed my mind about helping Afton take over the Venture Hive. The idea of staying here any longer is intolerable. I need to travel and get my mind off of what happened today. Spending time with Jace will help."

It scared Sammuel that she may hold affection for Jace that he could never return. There was something between his blood brother and the shifter. Although Portia now resided with the feline shifters, Jace could claim the woman who may be his soul mate any time. It was clear such a connection did not exist between him and his daughter.

"Jace…" Sammuel was not sure what to say to Patrice. What Tanya had done was still too raw to explore and discuss with his daughter. Any topic seemed difficult for him to breach.

"Is my friend," Patrice answered, finishing his sentence. "He has always been my friend and nothing more. Jace is like a brother to me. When Jace was converted he came to me for comfort and Drake for strength. He took the place in my heart my own long lost brothers once held. I cannot remember their faces."

Patrice threw down her quill and placed her head in her hands. Sammuel closed the distance and pulled his daughter into his arms. Patrice wept for everything she had lost. Everything they had lost.

"As soon as the sun sets, I will have Drake and Jace come get you," he promised her. "Pack your outfits and weapons. There will be a lot of action before and after we reach the hive."

"I will be ready," Patrice said. "Go and start your journey. Miranda will need you. Everything is still so new to her, although she pretends otherwise. The rest of us will catch up to you. Although, knowing Drake, it will be hard to pull him away from the women. They are standing in line to donate blood. He has already demonstrated how pleasurable it can be."

Sammuel laughed, he could not help it. Today the last thing he imagined he would do was laugh. His daughter had given him an unexpected, albeit unintended, gift. Perhaps there was still hope in salvaging what was once between them.

CHAPTER 20

Miranda stared down at the building that contained the vampires of the Venture Hive. Torches were lit outside the stone structure. She was once destined to live behind those walls as Yorik's brood mare. There was no doubt in her mind, her life with the master vampire would have been a living nightmare.

"So, we are just going to walk in and claim your inheritance?" Jace asked, disbelief evident in his tone.

The youthful vampire had barely uttered a word in the seven days it took to arrive outside the Venture Hive. Miranda noticed him checking the ground alongside where he traveled, seeing if Portia was beside him. He had not uttered her name the whole trip, but it was clear the shifter was on his mind. She had been pleased to see him the first night of their journey when he arrived with Drake and Patrice. Jace needed to focus on something other than Portia.

They had made excellent time without having to slow for the humans. What few vampires they met along the way, Patrice fed from and dispatched quickly. Frazour, a warrior most of his existence, seemed discontent with the little action they encountered.

"They are not expecting us," Afton said. "Having the five blood brothers at my side, the vampires are not likely to put up a fight initially. The real question is what will happen when I explain my plans for the hive."

"I am a little disappointed your father is not alive to see your plans realized," Drake said. "It would drive Yorik insane! He always ranted about what Lorenz had done to domesticate vampires. What fun I would have at his expense."

Miranda half expected Afton to become deflated at the mention of Yorik's name. If anything, she became more animated. She sat up a little higher and drove her mount forward. She was ready to take what was hers and destroy any creature who interfered.

"Yorik would have this dimension continue to live in darkness," Afton said. "I am going to transform this world and negate his influence upon it. People will no longer live in fear, but in hope."

They continued down the small rise to the east of the hive. The keep was built on another mountain foothill surrounded by forest. Only the main path gave them easy access to the keep's entrance.

Afton led the way, her soul mate riding beside her. The torches burned a little hotter as she approached the hive's entrance. No one was outside the hive to hinder their entrance or warn the keep's occupants of their arrival.

Stepping into the Venture Hive for the first time, Miranda felt a chill run down her spine. It was cold in the entryway, but that was not what her body was reacting to. The hall was dark and smelled of death. A battle had taken place and no one bothered to pick up the dead. Vampires were usually meticulous about burning the bodies of the fallen.

When they entered the great hall, there were perhaps twenty vampires present. No one sat in the chair at the center of the room situated on a dais where Yorik had held court. She wondered, had the master vampire claimed her, would she have joined him in this room as his mate? Afton never talked to Miranda about her mother or what she had been through. Considering how much Afton loathed her father, he must have treated her terribly.

The stench in the room was worse than the passageway. Miranda thought she was going to vomit. She concentrated on breathing through her mouth, rather than bringing in more of the tainted air through her nose.

Afton made her way to her father's throne and sat upon it. The torches that flanked the back of the chamber burned with more intensity, illuminating the rest of the room. Miranda was shocked to see piles of bodies lining the great hall. A major battle had taken place within the hive. It was obvious there was no victor.

"How dare you treat my father's keep in this fashion," Afton yelled. "It is abhorrent that the dead have not been burned. I hereby declare myself mistress of the Venture Hive as my birthright. You will bow to my authority or be prepared to be destroyed."

Afton rose from where she sat. The vampires did not react to her declaration, nor did they make any aggressive move toward her or anyone else. These creatures were lost without a master to direct them. Sammuel had explained a vampire's deterioration first affected their brains, which was how master vampires kept massive armies in line. A starving vampire was easy to manipulate. There were also hordes of the creatures to support a strong hive in the Nightshade universe.

When a vampire was properly fed, their ability to reason was restored. That was why Lorenz's settlement was so successful. The vampires within his community were able to make decisions for themselves and saw the advantages of living as Lorenz dictated. In the end, the vampires monitored their own behavior, not willing to lose what they had gained.

"You drones have until I lose my patience to make up your minds," Frazour said. "Fall before your new master or prepare to die."

"I am Afton, daughter of Yorik, soul mate to Lorenz, and a fire elemental," Afton declared. "If you pledge allegiance to me, you also agree to live as the vampires live within Lorenz's community. Failure to adhere to his rules will mean your destruction."

The vampires before her did not seem capable of deciding their own fates. They immediately fell to their knees when Frazour drew his sword from his sheath. The sound of the weapon at the ready was familiar to the creatures. Each voiced their fidelity to Afton.

"Gather the rest of the vampires still within the hive and what humans still live," Afton demanded. "Return immediately, or you will be struck down as soon as Frazour can find you."

At Afton's threat, the vampires scurried from the room. Although the feral vampire had mellowed under Emma's influence, Frazour was still a terrifying sight. This powerful man, who spent his entire existence as a warrior, certainly garnered the vampires' respect. That was what the vampires ultimately responded to.

It was not long before vampires started to enter the room and fall to their knees before Afton and her lieutenants. The five blood brothers stood beside Afton, showing their support and power. They were vampire royalty in the eyes of the creatures before them.

Miranda was concerned no humans had yet entered the great hall. Their whole plan was dependent on them still being present within the hive. If they had to transport humans here, things would become more complicated.

Miranda breathed a sigh of relief when the first human entered the hall. The women of the harem had remained untouched during the war. Vampires were programmed to safeguard and never attack the harem and that conditioning had stuck. A number of servants were among them.

Lorenz moved forward and prepared to address the crowd. "My name is Lorenz, soul mate to Afton. Many may know of my settlement not far from this hive. There, vampires and humans live in harmony. If you are to stay a member of the Venture Hive, you will live by the rules instituted within my community. A human will only be fed from with their consent, the vampire will make it an enjoyable experience, and the wound inflicted will be healed with your saliva. Failure to do so will result in the vampire's death."

"You are starving and the vampires within Lorenz's community are not," Afton continued with the hive's dictates. "There are many of you and few humans. You are used to gorging, although it does not feed your hungry cells. Now, you will take little blood and build up your body's capacity to digest the bodily fluid."

Afton signaled Drake to come closer and consult with her without the vampires hearing. "You know the keep better than any of us," Afton said. "Where is the best place to house the humans until we can get things running smoothly. We will need to monitor feedings, while still giving the humans a sense of freedom during this critical period."

"The harem and its associated rooms should work," Drake said. "There is also an exit to an external courtyard the humans can enjoy during the day. With its limited entries and the vampires conditioned to safeguard the location, it will meet our purposes."

Miranda wished there was something she could say to the humans to reassure them everything would be all right. She was a stranger to them. With her elemental powers not useful within the keep, Miranda felt worthless. It was ridiculous to feel this way when the fate of the humans was involved.

Feeling isolated, Miranda moved and positioned herself next to Patrice. She imagined Sammuel's daughter would feel out of sorts in this group. The girl had been very quiet during the journey here. Patrice spent most of her time with Jace when he was not off by himself. Neither mentioned Tanya or Portia, although Miranda doubted either woman was not continually on their minds.

"I recommend our women also stay in the harem and we will keep an eye on the vampires," Drake said. "Their feeding needs to be closely monitored and any infraction quickly dealt with. We have one chance to get this right. Any sign of weakness and these creatures will turn on us."

Sammuel did not like the idea of being separated from Miranda. Patrice and the other women would protect her, but he would feel the loss of not having her beside him at night. She not only refueled him, but he was incomplete without her.

"Soul mates are meant to be together," Sammuel stated. "We must schedule time to be with each other to maximize our power, as well as provide the comfort we all need. One day, Drake and Jace will understand what our women do for us. It goes against nature to separate us and will adversely affect what we hope to do here."

"You need not continue, brother," Drake said. "What little time I have been able to spend with my unborn soul mate are moments I treasure. I can only imagine what it will be like when we are joined. It is a request that should be honored and built into our plans."

"I need to get some fresh air," Jace said. "Come, Patrice, let us enjoy the evening. Get those creatures off their knees and have them burn the dead bodies. The humans should be taken to the harem. The vampires, not the servants, need to clean up this mess."

"Go," Afton said. "Drake, please escort the humans to the harem. Emma and Miranda kindly join them and make sure Drake behaves himself."

Once Patrice left with Jace, Miranda moved next to Sammuel. She leaned over and kissed his lips. Power surged through him during the prolonged contact. He brought her closer into his body, treasuring the feel of her.

"I need to go and make myself useful," Miranda said.

"Enjoy the amenities of the harem," Sammuel said. "A large hive should have an incredible spa for the women. The size of a hive's harem and the beauty of its women is a matter of prestige. Do not act as if you are unworthy of the human company or think they are your sole responsibility."

He had felt the various emotions Miranda experienced since entering the hive. She was still feeling different. First it was the genetic marker, now it was the elemental force she possessed. His extraordinary woman yearned to be ordinary.

Miranda joined Emma, and together they accompanied the women and the servants back to the harem. He almost hoped his blood brother's outrageous behavior would distract Miranda from her self-destructive thoughts. Perhaps he needed to encourage her to spend more time with Emma to bond as women, and not conduct constant discussions concerning controlling her power. Their relationship had become too narrow in its focus.

"When should we start introducing the vampires to their new feeding practices?" Afton asked.

"I discovered having the feeding done during daylight hours was best," Lorenz said. "The humans need to begin sleeping at night and be accessible during the day, both to work and feed vampires. They need to spend more time in daylight and perform activities outside the hive. Their health is paramount if this is going to work like it did at my settlement. Humans are not nocturnal beings."

"Anything else we need to know?" Sammuel asked.

"We just need to act quickly and harshly to those who are not following the rules…make an example out of them," Lorenz said "It is not unlike a master disciplining his troops before battle. We must be vigilant until they can truly think for themselves."

"And more so when they do start thinking," Frazour said. "Then we run the risk of them trying to band together if they are unhappy with how things are going. They need to be watched constantly. Question every unexpected movement or behavior."

Sammuel understood why Lorenz had questioned the validity of trying to convert a hive as large as this one. They had a reasonable number for now, but powerful hives attracted newly made vampires, discontent lieutenants from other hives, and rogue vampires who could not continue on their own. A steady flow of vampires would be flooding in. Plus, there was always the risk of a new master from the Bertram Hive arriving to try, once again, to unite with the Venture Hive. There were unknown alliances Yorik had that could also cause an influx of vampires entering to throw a wrench in their plans.

Afton was overwhelmed with the task before her. Everything up to this point had been abstract thoughts. She had declared herself mistress of the hive, so she could not start second guessing herself now.

"We should keep the vampires in here for the time being," Afton said. "It will be easier to control them if they are all in one place."

"Miranda should block the entry for the time being," Sammuel recommended. "We cannot afford new vampires entering the keep. It will be a challenge enough trying to control this lot."

She had watched Sammuel's face earlier. Afton knew he was battling with the logistics of what she was doing and being separated from his mate. During the time she and Lorenz had been apart while he was taking the children up the mountain pass during the vampire attack, Afton had been frantic. Even though she had been in mortal danger, but all she could think about was Lorenz.

"That sounds like a sound plan," Afton said. "Does anyone else have anything to add? There are so many moving parts, I don't want to miss anything."

"The first threat will be individual vampires entering and then perhaps a full out assault," Frazour said. "Sammuel's recommendation to close the entrance is sound."

"I will divide my time between the harem and the main hall," Afton said. "After we are sure we have discussed all relevant points, I will get Miranda and she'll close the entrance. I know of a way in and out of the keep we can use. Sammuel, I would very much appreciate it if you will come and protect us while Miranda is using her elemental gift."

"The two of you should collect Miranda now and take care of our greatest risk," Frazour said. "In the meantime, Lorenz and I will start working with the vampires to dispose of the bodies. I do not know what can be done about the stench."

"We will pick wild flowers when the sun rises and create some essential oils we can burn," Afton said. "It will be a good opportunity to start exposing the humans to some direct sunlight."

"You have done well, my love," Lorenz shared through their private channel. *"Keep asking for help and guidance. My brothers and I have lived far longer than you and know how to handle vampires. When you need to rest, let me know and I will join you. We can both use recharging."*

Lorenz gave her the little boost she needed to get off the dais and start executing her plan. There was so much work to do and she was starting to question if the small group was up for the challenge—the odds were stacked against them.

CHAPTER 21

The Venture Hive's keep seemed like one huge maze. They took hallway after hallway, still not reaching their destination. At least the halls had an occasional window, covered with a purple filter to protect the vampires from the harmful rays of the sun. Since it was still night, there was no additional light to guide or brighten their trip.

Miranda was about to ask Drake where he was taking them when he opened a door to what she assumed was the harem. It took a moment for her eyes to adjust to the well lit chamber. She had spent a little time in Lorenz's settlement's harem, but this one was triple its size.

There were more pools than at Lorenz's and the center one was enormous. The lounges were large enough to serve as beds and she could only imagine what was within the curtained off areas. There were several doors on the other side of the main entry that led to the private chambers. Miranda shuddered to think what happened in the privacy of those rooms between a vampire and his victim.

"The women can stay in here while the servants will reside in the adjacent rooms," Drake said. "We should encourage everyone to make themselves comfortable. They are under a tremendous amount of stress. The sooner we get them into some kind of routine, the better."

Miranda was half expecting Drake to make some kind of ridiculous comment about personally caring for the women, but the smooth vampire's expression was serious. It only emphasized the danger they were in.

"I will take care of the servants, while the two of you can help the women feel more at ease," Drake continued. "Have them show you around and explain the differences between the pools. Do anything and everything to get their minds off what has occurred. And answer any questions they may have about Lorenz's settlement."

Emma looked at her, eyes wide in surprise. It was obvious the little blue haired woman had been as astonished by Drake's behavior as she was. Gone was Drake's charm and before them was a powerful ancient vampire with The Creator's blood coursing through his veins. His intensity made him even more devastatingly attractive.

Miranda followed the women around the harem, learning their names and what their favorite parts of the spa were. Drake was right. The more the women talked, the more relaxed they became. She was talking to a young woman who could not be much older than Beatrice when Sammuel entered the harem.

Concerned, Miranda immediately went to her mate. Afton was with him, which meant this was not a social visit. Fortunately, neither seemed overly disturbed or anxious.

"Miranda, we want you to block the entry into the keep," Afton said. "There is a possibility other vampires will try to join the hive and we cannot afford any additional vampires entering before we have the ones already in residence under control."

The idea made sense. Miranda felt reassured they were thinking ahead and not merely reacting when issues arose. She was about to head for the exit to the harem, when Afton grabbed her forearm.

"There is an exterior exit from within the harem," Afton said. "It was constructed in case the keep was attacked and the vampires lost the battle. We will not have to go through the main hall if we exit and enter through that passage."

Miranda followed Afton while Sammuel was behind her. How she wished he could wrap her in his arms. She did not need the energy, just his touch. Her mood soared as soon as he entered the harem. Until that moment, Miranda had not realized the extent of his power over her. If anything happened to him, Miranda knew she would not survive.

The passageway to the exterior exit was narrow. Sammuel somehow managed to move through the slim corridor with ease. For a big man, he was very light on his feet and was surefooted walking sideways.

They entered a covered exterior courtyard and Afton headed for the door leading to the outside. The three of them had to maneuver through dense shrubs that hid the entrance. Miranda was glad she was dressed in a shirt and leggings, allowing her more freedom of movement.

The keep was built on higher ground, so the path they took to its entrance was at an angle. From a strategic standpoint it was advantageous, but walking on the sloped trail was difficult. Afton darted along as if she walked it every day. Miranda was relieved when they finally reach the keep's entry.

"Work your magic," Afton said. "Let me know if you need additional light."

The night sky was clear and a half-moon gave off enough light Miranda was able to see well enough to close the keep's entrance. She visualized a pile of dirt and rocks in front of the entry and when she was done, a large obstruction blocked the large iron door.

"You are very handy to have around," Afton said. "When we return inside, why don't you and Sammuel spend some time together. You probably need to re-energize after expending all that energy. There is nothing much to do until the sun rises. I am sure you will return the favor when I need some time alone with Lorenz."

The trip back was much easier, considering the reward she would get once they returned. Blocking the entry took up little, if any, of her energy. However, she was not about to confess that to Afton. She wanted Sammuel too much.

When they re-entered the harem, Afton directed them to the room closest to their escape route. Drake had left the chamber free for the soul mates' usage. Miranda continued to underestimate Sammuel's blood brother. When Star came of age, Miranda planned to be Drake's biggest advocate.

The room was a smaller version of the harem. It held a single pool, several lounges near the spa, and an enormous bed. Any additional details about the room were lost to her as soon as Sammuel removed his shirt. Her eyes drank in every aspect of his powerful chest, from his muscle definition to the hairs that disappeared into his pants.

She moved forward and released the top button of his pants. His erection was straining against its confines. He reached down and unfastened the remaining two buttons, releasing himself. Miranda reached up and brought her lips to his. She loved his taste. There was something woodsy and wild in his essence.

Sammuel ran his hands up her arms until he reached the sleeves of her tunic. He pulled the material up, brought it over her head, and then tossed it aside. Without so much as a pause, he had her in his arms and carried her to the bed. Sammuel laid her on the luxurious bedspread and removed her leggings. She reveled in the silkiness of the bedcoverings, but longed to feel his flesh against hers.

Sammuel's mouth covered her left breast, and she leaned her head back and sighed in pleasure. Her hands ran up his back and nestled in the short hair at his nape. When he had been at his fortress, he instructed his housekeeper to cut it to the length it was when she first met him. It was not long enough to grab strands, but she enjoyed running her fingers through the unexpected softness.

As his mouth went to cover her other breast, Sammuel entered her with a single thrust. This time the sound that escaped her was more of a scream. She called out his name. Miranda wrapped her legs around Sammuel, never planning to release him.

Energy flowed between them. They had learned how to share, rather than drain energy, as they made love. He was deep inside her core, where he belonged. She felt a little loss every time he withdrew, only to rejoice when he drove back in. The pace he set was frantic, but she kept up with him.

Their hearts beat in unison, as did their breathing. For several moments, they were truly one being. When they both climaxed, it took them over the top and Miranda lost the feeling of harmony between their bodies. Sammuel collapsed on top of her.

That perfect moment, followed by rapture, robbed them of the energy they generated and shared, while attaining the ones for which they both strived for. Several kisses were all it took to restore what was lost.

She needed to find that perfect moment again. The point where they were one. Somehow she knew it was the elemental side of them that would continue to grow as they evolved. Afton's plan had to work. There was too much at stake for them to lose.

Sammuel lay on top of Miranda. He felt her contentment and how much she loved his weight on her. She was able to withstand more intensity in their love making each time they were together. When they reached their euphoric moment, he knew her better than he knew himself. He could even control her erratic breathing.

He turned onto his side, taking her with him. The sun would be rising soon and there was too much to do to spend more time in bed.

For several moments he just concentrated on his body and mind's response to his soul mate.

"Although I can walk in its rays, I can still sense when the sun rises," Sammuel said. "Nothing would make me happier than to stay here for several more hours, but there is much to be done. I would not be surprised if Afton comes barging through that door and starts yelling out orders."

Miranda groaned. It was adorable, as was any sound of joy, exhaustion, frustration, or other emotion she felt warranted a response. Her little mewls said more to him than if she spoke full sentences.

"You are right," Miranda admitted, sounding disappointed. "We need to take the humans out to enjoy the sunshine. I would not mind seeing a blue sky and feeling the warmth of the sun."

It still overwhelmed Sammuel that she had given the sun back to him. He missed the clarity light gave all living things. Unfortunately, he had to oversee the vampires in the main hall and was unable to join her.

They rose and quickly dressed. He was relieved he had enough self-control last night so he did not destroy the clothes Miranda had been wearing. There would be plenty of future opportunities to tear her clothing to shreds when she had ample outfits to wear afterwards. The last thing he wanted was to embarrass her.

"I am on wildflower patrol," Miranda said. "The humans at the farm had gardens and grew flowers, but I have never seen fields of them. I caught glimpses as we made our way through the woods, but did not have time to stop and appreciate their beauty. I will finally be able to enjoy how lovely they are growing in the wild."

Through so much of her life, Miranda was not given the ability to experience joy. Sammuel would make sure she would never again miss the opportunity. While at his fortress, they had not taken the time to walk along the path down to the ocean. The vast body of water lay at the foothills to the east. He had never seen a grander sight than the sea before a storm, waves soaring to shore and lightning illuminating the sky.

He was pleased Miranda had a delightful task ahead of her. Sammuel, on the other hand, had to check the progress of the great hall's clean-up. It was doubtful the burning of the bodies eliminated the rancid odor overpowering the hall.

Before he headed off, Sammuel gave Miranda one more kiss to tide them over until they could be intimate again. He did not want to let her loose, but knew the longer he held her, the more difficult it would become to let her go. Sammuel released her and headed for the harem's exit and made his way to the great hall.

He smelled the smoke long before he entered the large chamber. The decayed vampire bodies had been cremated, but the keep's ventilation was inadequate to remove all the smoke from the premises.

Frazour was leaning over a sheaf of papers, in deep concentration. His brother was once again clad all in black leather. He looked as dangerous as he was.

"What have we here?" Sammuel inquired.

"I talked to a number of the vampires to learn the keep's layout," Frazour responded. "Most of what I have been able to deduce came from walking through the structure myself. Yorik was a shrewd manipulator. He would have built hidden entrances and exits into his stronghold. When he came back from conquering another army, I would imagine he did not march his whole force through the front gate. I want to be aware of them all and close any entries we are not covering."

"You are concerned we will be attacked soon?" Sammuel said.

"There are too few of us to properly defend this monstrosity," Frazour admitted. "Our women are powerful, but limited in what they can do in a battle. Afton can only flame out two vampires at a time and has yet to be able to use the restraint circle in an offensive manner. Emma is even more limited, only having the ability to attack one vampire at a time with physical contact. They would do more damage in a short period of time with a sword. Lastly, Miranda's power cannot be used within the keep."

Everything his blood brother said was correct. There were reasons for concerned. Sammuel joined his brother looking at what he had drawn of the keep's design. It appeared to be an accurate reproduction of the building's interior.

"What are you looking for?" Sammuel asked. "The exit outside the harem is not advantageous for the enemy to enter. Its passageway is very narrow. I barely made it through myself."

"If I were Yorik," Frazour said, "I would have subterranean rooms to store weapons, hold prisoners, and provide an easier escape route. The land surrounding the structure is sloped. Yorik would want to have his army enter and exit on a flat surface. There has to be an entry hidden somewhere in the meadow below. I have been unable to find one in the keep, so far. This place is like a maze; the hidden entrance could be anywhere. We should be concentrating on the keep's defense, not feeding the small number of worthless vampires left behind."

"What do you think happened here?" Sammuel asked

"I believe whoever was responsible for the massacre killed most of the drones left behind, rather than trying to earn their loyalty," Frazour answered. "He did not stay, since the majority of his force is elsewhere, perhaps the Bertram Hive. They left the humans here alive, so I suspect they will return. The question is when."

"Have you shared your concerns with Lorenz and Afton?" Sammuel inquired.

"No," Frazour replied. "I cannot prove anything I have shared with you. However, it makes no sense how this keep was left behind. A true victor would have stayed and solidified his right to the hive."

Sammuel was not sure what to believe. His primary concern was Miranda and Patrice's safety. Somehow they needed to either evacuate Yorik's keep or fortify their defenses. He did not like the odds against them if they stayed.

CHAPTER 22

Something was off. Sammuel could not put his finger on exactly what caused his anxiety. A week passed in the Venture Hive with no incidents. The vampires were slowly changing their feeding habits. Only three of them had to be destroyed after not adhering to the rules Lorenz set in place.

He did not like the women being separated from them. If attacked, the harem was located too far away to quickly assemble them for a unified defense. Afton must have had the same concern, since she changed the schedules, keeping the mates together during the hours the sun did not brighten the sky. Half of their force was present in the harem, while the others were in the great hall.

Emma was permanently in the harem because of all the water present. Sammuel missed his discussions with Frazour. That particular blood brother was the most experienced warrior among them, but keeping him in the harem with Emma would not aid them in the initial attack, should one come to pass.

Frazour still had not found the entry to the subterranean portion of the keep. They were both confident one existed. Sammuel looked down wondering if an army gathered below. For a week during daylight hours, he and Frazour scouted the meadow looking for any signs of an army venturing through the area the night before. They had found nothing.

Sammuel glanced in Miranda's direction. She was sitting with Afton near the fireplace enjoying a private conversation. The two women were becoming closer as they spent more time together. Although he wanted to be the center of her universe, he realized she needed more than he could provide in the way of companionship. Miranda had starved her whole existence for friendships.

The smoke in the hall had finally dissipated and the nightly fire was built to warm the room for the evening hours. In his peripheral vision, Sammuel spotted a vampire he believed he had not seen before. Internal warning alarms sounded in his mind.

Not wanting to alert his target, Sammuel casually walked across the room to join Lorenz. Neither Miranda or Afton looked in his direction, questioning his movement. Lorenz looked up and smiled. His blood brother looked good with the healthy tan being a fire elemental afforded him.

He pulled out the map Frazour had been working on for over a week. It was their practice to search the keep daily and update the layout. Lorenz had returned from his inspection thirty minutes ago.

"Examine the map as you always do, but look over my left shoulder," Sammuel communicated telepathically. *"There is a vampire among the group in a clean gray robe I do not recognize. I need you to validate he is not among the vampires we have been working with."*

Sammuel could see Lorenz's reaction reflected in his eyes, but not in any other way. His blood brother looked down at the map and then in the direction of the vampire in question. Their target stood out compared to the other vampires in the great hall. When he turned his head to look at his soul mate, Frazour knew he was communicating to Afton.

"Drake, Jace, and Frazour, I need you to return to the main hall," Lorenz communicated through the telepathic channel he shared with his blood brothers. *"We have a vampire here who is a new arrival. I want us all assembled here before we find out how he entered and determine if he is alone. Come in, but only far enough where wo you remain unseen within the shadows. I do not want the vampire alerted to your presence. Sammuel will approach the vampire when you are all in place."*

Sammuel was relieved his mate was with him in the great hall. If there were additional unknown vampires in the keep, he wanted Miranda close to him for her protection. The human females would be safer in the harem, but the elemental women were generally better off in close proximity to their mates.

The two brothers continued to pretend to review the map while the others got into position. They just needed Jace in place and Sammuel would approach the unknown vampire. Afton and Miranda alternated between whispers and laughter. When he reached out to Miranda, he knew she was unaware of what was about to occur.

"Miranda," Sammuel was finally ready to tell his soul mate what was about to transpire. *"There is an unknown vampire in our midst I am about to confront. Stay near Afton."*

Sammuel had no way of communicating with Patrice. She had been with Jace earlier and hoped they were still together when Lorenz contacted the youngest among them.

"I am ready," Jace finally communicated.

"Is Patrice with you?" Sammuel inquired.

"Yes, and she is ready to taste some vampire blood," Jace shared with him. *"She said drinking from Drake is no challenge. Your daughter likes to go in for the kill."*

Sammuel could not help smiling about his bloodthirsty offspring. Patrice did enjoy bringing down vampires and draining them dry. The look on his face did not alert the vampire he approached that anything was wrong.

"The sun will be rising in several hours and you will be able to drink again from the humans," Sammuel said.

He touched the shoulders of the vampires on the outside of the group as he moved toward his target. Although, the unknown creature looked in his direction, he did not seem alarmed by Sammuel's presence. Once in front of his subject, Sammuel grabbed his arm.

"How did you get into the keep? It has been a week since our arrival and this is the first time I have seen you," Sammuel said.

The vampire tried to escape his grasp, but was unsuccessful. His blood brothers joined him and the other vampires backed warily away. They originally headed in the direction of Afton and Miranda, but a sudden eruption of flames from the fireplace made them hurry to the far end of the great hall. Vampires feared fire since it could destroy them. Emma was now with her elemental sisters.

"I was in a chamber feeding off a servant when you arrived," the vampire explained. "When the others came to collect me and the human, I refused to join them. They were too weak to report my not adhering to the commands of a hive leader I do not recognize."

Looks were shared between the brothers. This vampire was too articulate to be one of the vampires that had been left behind after the elimination of the majority of Yorik's followers.

Frazour pulled a knife from one of his leather boots. "Let me ask the question with a little more incentive to provide an answer."

Sammuel pushed the prisoner in Frazour's direction. His brother grabbed the vampire with one hand and held a dagger to his throat with the other. Frazour's captive seemed to enjoy the danger he was in. He mocked Frazour by leaning into his knife, drawing his own blood.

Infuriated, Frazour shoved the vampire to the stone floor and drove the knife a little farther into the vampire's neck. If the creature was bluffing about his indifference about death, Frazour had called him on it. Patrice for good measure, joined them on the ground and started to feed from the vampire's wrist.

"You have one more chance before I sever your head from the rest of your body," Frazour growled. "I figure if I do not get an answer before Patrice is done feeding, that is your wish."

"Maybe Emma can start draining him from his head and I can burn him from his feet and we will meet in the middle," Afton called from where she and the other elementals sat around the fireplace.

"Lorenz," Frazour said, with a smile on his face, "have I mentioned recently how much I like your soul mate?" His blood brother returned his attention back to the creature he had his knife embedded in. "Last chance to keep living."

"You are too late," the vampire replied. "Do your worst. Nothing you do will stop what is about to happen to you."

Patrice released her grip on the creature's wrist and Frazour let his knife slip the rest of the way. The vampire's head rolled away from his body. They got their answer, but not the one Sammuel hoped for. The keep would soon be under attack, and they did not know by whom or where they would be entering.

Miranda could feel a disturbance in her element. The land had been violated in some way. Something unnatural had trespassed into its domain.

"They are coming from underground," Miranda said.

She was certain she translated the feeling correctly. Chills ran up her spine and goose bumps lined her arms. Miranda rubbed her hands up and down her arms, hoping to ward off the foreboding she felt.

"Impossible," Frazour said. "We have checked all around the surrounding area."

"What if they did not enter close to the keep?" Miranda asked. "Afton told me about an underground hive you encountered not far from the Bertram Hive. Why can't something similar be underneath this keep? Yorik had massive armies, I understand. What if he kept the majority of his troops underground?"

"I lived here for weeks before I was able to leave with Lorenz," Afton said. "There was not a whisper of any such army. They would have to be fed."

"Not if they were the first force to enter an enemy's keep," Frazour said. "Those soldiers would be blood-crazed shells that would weaken the defensive army before Yorik and his main forces moved forward. The entry could be miles from here."

Miranda felt violated, as her element reached out. "They are coming now. The ground below has been disturbed. I don't know if they are miles away or right underneath us. The dead vampire may have been too insignificant to disturb the ground's balance and made it through undetected."

She looked at her friend, who stared at the vampires in the corner. They were huddled together as a group. Not one of them stepped forward to voice their support in the upcoming battle. Various emotions crossed Afton's face.

"We have no choice," Afton said. "Once the fighting starts, they cannot be trusted to support us. It is more likely they will switch to the other side and join the attack."

Patrice and Frazour were the first to draw their weapons and with lightning speed started to cut down the vampires they had been trying to domesticate. Jace, Drake, and Sammuel joined the fight. Their prey did not put up any resistance to the attack. It was over before Lorenz could leave Afton's side to join the slaughter.

Miranda could not imagine what Afton was going through. Her dreams had been placed on the first group of vampires in the Venture Hive to transform into the type of beings who lived within Lorenz's settlement. Her soul mate had been right. The Venture Hive was too ambitious as a first location to establish a new colony.

"Do we stay and fight or evacuate this deathtrap?" Sammuel asked. "We can head back to Lorenz's or journey to my fortress."

"We are all here for the first time in centuries," Lorenz said. "I do not want another strong hive on my doorstep. I vote we stay and fight."

Under normal circumstances, Sammuel would have expected Lorenz to support leaving. However, he knew what the Venture Hive meant to Afton. His own decisions now partially reflected Miranda's desires and safety.

"There is no telling the size of the force approaching," Jace said. "Not to mention, we do not know where they will be entering the fortress. It is unclear whether we are dealing with two hundred or two thousand vampires. There are too many unanswered questions."

Frazour shook his head. "It is too soon after Yorik's death to bring together a sizeable army. Between our strength and our elemental women, we should be able to take on whatever is coming at us."

"Are you willing to risk Emma's life on that assumption?" Jace asked. "I am not a fighter, never was. You know I have never run from a battle, but this is insanity. Ask yourselves: What are you fighting for, and what do you have to lose."

From her growing sense of dread, Miranda had to agree with Jace. They were too important to the future of the Nightshade universe to lose any of them in a fight they were not prepared to win. Emma and Afton were both wearing dresses, not their usual battle gear.

What should we do, Sammuel? Miranda reached out to her soul mate. She was in no condition to make a decision. He had the experience to make the best decision for them both.

"We stand united or we get out of here fast," Sammuel finally said. "If we evacuate, we have to take the humans from the harem. They cannot be left behind. It is a miracle they still lived."

"Majority rules," Lorenz said. "Raise your hand if we stay."

Not a single hand was raised, not even Afton's. Jace's argument had swayed the group. It was time to leave the Venture Hive. Miranda continued to feel the growing tension in her body caused by her element. They needed to leave, and quickly.

"We will depart through the harem's exit," Afton said. "Our best chance is to get to Lorenz's settlement. The vampires there will support us if we are followed."

They headed toward the exit from the great hall that led to the harem when a force of vampires came running down the passageway. They were out of time. The men and Patrice drew their weapons, backing up to give each other room to take on their adversaries.

Miranda turned to run farther into the hall, when another group of vampires entered from the keep's north wing. There must be at least two entrances from the underground hive into the keep. She prayed there was not a third.

"They are coming in behind us as well," Miranda called out.

Sammuel was beside her before she finished her sentence. His blade was stained with corrosive vampire blood. She stood behind him as he took on several approaching vampires. His movements were fluid and graceful, as he continued to fight off the aggressors. Miranda tried to come up with a way her elemental gift could be used to help fight the horde, but came up with nothing.

Several of the vampires coming toward her left burst into flames. Afton continued to light them up, but there were so many of them. Emma's power required physical contact with the enemy, something that was impossible for the time being. The men and Patrice continued to cut down vampires, but more took their place. When they brought down a vampire, it seemed like three took the place of the fallen creature.

Jace had been right. Even if they had reacted quickly when she started to feel strange, the force was too great. The circle they created in taking on the vampires was getting smaller, as more of the enemy pushed forward.

A blade came out of the crowd of vampires and sliced into Sammuel's arm. Miranda let out a muted cry. Her soul mate did not lose his stride in taking on the vampires. Miranda watched as blood started seeping through his shirt. The wound would heal quickly, but how many more injuries would Sammuel be able to withstand before he finally bled out?

CHAPTER 23

Miranda gasped as Sammuel withstood the fifth strike that drew blood. He knew she psychically felt each successful blow. Although his body healed rapidly, based on sheer number, they were up against a superior force. His brothers were not doing much better. He did not want to think of Patrice being sliced and eventually being brought to her knees. For the time being, they were all still standing.

The three elemental women were inside what was left of the small circle they had used to protect them. Afton was still flaming vampires, but the frequency of her strikes was lessening as she weakened.

More vampires entered the hall, waiting for their turn to take on the false masters of the Venture Hive. Their standing in the vampire community had once been an asset, but now made them a target. What prestige a group of vampires would achieve if they took down the princes and the elementals they mated with. Yorik's daughter would have been prize enough.

Their telepathic conversations had waned as the battle continued. All of their power was directed toward the fight. Sammuel did not know how much longer they would be able to hold off the massive army before the first of them fell. It was doubtful any of them would be spared.

He had failed to protect his mate. Sammuel was also going to lose the daughter he had given immortality three thousand years ago. All would be lost today. His death and those of the ones he loved was certain. There was nothing he could do to forestall the inevitable.

A bolt of lightning brought down the three vampires before him. A barrage of more bolts quickly followed, vaporizing the vampires where they stood. Afton glowed with power and fire jolted from her fingers, taking down a half dozen vampires with each flame that shot from her hand.

Piles of ash lay where the vampire army had stood just moments before. As more vampires entered, they were quickly met with bolts of electricity and Afton's fiery elemental gift. They slowly expanded their protective circle, each looking around in wonder.

Sammuel was at a loss. Afton had never been able to produce lightning before. It was not part of her elemental sphere. He imagined only an air elemental would be able to produce such power.

It was then that he finally realized the energy did not come from someone within his group, but outside their dimension. The Creator had returned to aid them before each of his children was struck down. Lorenz had told him what kind of elemental The Creator's mate was, but not what their father had been. Emma and The Creator's woman had been claimed by the water element.

The air crackled above him and a gateway opened. The Creator and his mate entered their realm through the portal. The Creator's dark auburn hair was blown by the wind surrounding him. Energy rolled off his body, too potent to be contained. Sammuel joined his brothers, on his knees before the most powerful being in creation. Miranda knelt beside him.

"I am displeased by the condition and situation in which I find my children," The Creator said. "You have all been blessed with a gift, yet you risk it to help the mortals to whom you are far superior. Three of you have already claimed your soul mates and started your transformation into another existence. It is time for the six of you to join me and leave the Nightshade universe behind. Drake and Jace will follow once they have done the same."

"No," Afton said. "I have already been bullied by one father, I will not be told what to do by another. When we join you, it will be our decision, not a dictate. Although, I thank you for your assistance today, we will not be joining you until we are all ready. I made a terrible miscalculation, but I learn from my mistakes. There is still so much good we can do in this realm."

"Child, you speak nonsense," said The Creator's blond soul mate Aurora. The powerful elemental turned to address her sister of water. "Emma, you are a powerful being, yet you were helpless just now. Come and I will teach you what real power is all about. Our water element is a wondrous miracle to behold."

"There are still two more soul mates to find and claim," Emma said. "If one of them is Portia, I want to be here to support her. She loves Jace, but is afraid to give up what she is. Her cat kept her alive all these years, which is why she could not reveal herself to you, Jace."

The truth of Emma's words struck Jace. His blood brother's focus had been on Portia's betrayal, not the reason behind it. Hope blossomed, reflected on his face.

"I need my brothers and their mates," Jace admitted. "My mate cannot even face me in her human form. You know me well enough to know I can be patient with animals, but not with humans. I will need their advice and companionship to deal with the human side of my mate."

"A soul mate must come willingly," The Creator said. "There is only one for each of you. If you fail to get Portia to join with you, Jace, you will be lost to us. I see the wisdom in keeping your brothers in this plane of existence for the time being. You are so dear to me, my boy."

"Creator," Sammuel spoke up. "Thank you for the miracle that is Miranda. I must ask of my daughter. My brothers are of your blood and have the ability to evolve into elementals once we find our mates. Patrice is a generation beyond, created by me to save what little I had left of my human existence."

"I know of your daughter and what you did," The Creator said. "There is one for her, but he does not exist in this dimension."

Before Sammuel could ask The Creator another question, a portal opened and their father and his mate entered it and were gone. The air was static with electricity, the only evidence a gateway had existed. He stared in disbelief at the empty hall before him. All that remained was the ash of what had been an entire vampire army.

He could feel Miranda's unease as soon as the portal closed. It temporarily refocused his attention on his daughter's fate. His mate continued to stare where The Creator had disappeared.

"That Being created you?" Miranda asked in disbelief. "We will evolve into something similar to him?"

Sammuel took Miranda into his arms. "We will never be as powerful as he is—"

"Or as arrogant," Afton interrupted to say. "I am tired of being bullied by beings more powerful than I am. Although, this time he is right about the situation I put you all in. I am sorry, it will not happen again. For now, we need to focus on Jace and Patrice."

Miranda looked at his daughter and asked, "Are you all right?"

"Another dimension?" Patrice repeated The Creator's word. The magnitude of what that meant was reflected in her voice.

Drake took Patrice into his arms. "Join the party, love," Drake said. "My soul mate lives in a parallel world in a woman's womb. We will find yours together. None of us will abandon you. There are six of us that share the same blood and we will not leave you behind."

"We have a cat to tame and I need all the help I can get. Afterwards, your soul mate will be our only focus," Jace said. "Besides, we are not without resources to find your mate, little sister."

Sammuel was touched by the support of his blood brothers. He knew they would never forsake Patrice, just as he would never fail to support any of them. Miranda took his hand and squeezed it in a show of support.

"We should return to Lorenz's settlement and rest before we return to Sammuel's fortress," Afton said. "Besides, Shirl should be arriving there soon and we can share with Patrice what crystal telepaths can do with inter-dimensional travel. However, I have one request of Miranda before we leave."

"Anything," Miranda said.

"When we have left and are a fair distance away, I want you to level this place," Afton requested. "We cannot afford any master vampire re-claiming the Venture Hive and be able to house an army the size my father was able to support."

"It will take a tremendous amount of energy to bring down this keep," Miranda said. "Once we reach your settlement, Sammuel and I will need time alone together to restore my strength."

Afton smiled, seeing right through his soul mate's lie. "That will not be a problem. I believe we all need time alone with our loved ones before we head back to Sammuel's and assist Jace in convincing a very stubborn feline to join us."

Miranda stood upon the same hill they had first viewed the Venture Hive keep a little over a week ago. Not knowing the extent of the underground hive, Sammuel wanted them a good distance away before she brought down the structure. They expected a chain reaction related when the catacombs collapsed.

She was not altogether sure what it would take to bring down a large keep, but she figured the land was already distressed by the invasion of its soil. Miranda envisioned the collapse of its walls and ceilings, just as she had earlier when bringing down the subterranean portion of the farm's lab.

Afton and Lorenz had begun the journey back to their settlement, taking the humans with them. It was decided the humans did not need to witness the power Miranda was able to command. They would remain ignorant of the fact that she alone would bring down the Venture Hive's stronghold. Jace, Drake, and Patrice were safe in a day shelter.

The ground shook and the keep began to crumble before their eyes. The shaking started gradually, but increased in intensity as more sections of the keep fell. Portions of land around the structure also collapsed indicating where underground tunnels lay. The magnitude of the subterranean section of the hive was far vaster than they ever expected. Tens of thousands of vampires could have been housed in an area that size. Afton had made the right call when she asked the hive to be destroyed.

"Do you think some of the vampires who may have been underground survived?" Miranda asked. She questioned the anxiety that began to plague her.

There was no telling if all the enemy force was above ground when The Creator struck. Miranda was too concerned about Sammuel and had not been concentrating on what her element could have told her. She wished she had paid attention to her surroundings after the battle was over.

"It is impossible to determine how many vampires were part of the force set against us or who the master controlling the army was," Frazour admitted. "We will have to be vigilant in how we move forward."

"It is fortunate Afton requested the Venture Hive be destroyed," Emma commented. "This place now represents one less threat against us. One of Yorik's lieutenants was placed in charge of the Bertram Hive, he may have led the army The Creator partially destroyed."

"For now it is all conjecture," Sammuel said. "We can all use a short reprieve from battling blood lusting vampires. I can think of at least one way to occupy my time."

Miranda could feel the lust emanating from Sammuel's being. He was right, they needed to focus on other things and restore themselves. She could feel the fire within her grow, she literally ached to be with her soul mate.

"I'm exhausted," Miranda said. She knew her voice indicated she was anything but fatigued. There was a playfulness in her delivery she had not expected. In fact, she felt great physically. "Sammuel and I need to exchange energy before I can go on. Emma and Frazour should continue on their way while my needs are met."

Frazour started laughing. "We will catch up to Lorenz and Afton. Sammuel, you need to see to your soul mate before she collapses from the effort it took to bring down the keep."

Their two travel companions started on their way and were out of sight when Sammuel finally brought Miranda into his arms. "You are such an amazing liar. When you destroyed the keep, your element actually filled you with energy. I could barely keep up with draining your excess power."

"I know," Miranda admitted, "but we don't need a bed to make love and I need you so badly I can barely stand."

She leaned closer to him and brought her lips to his. Miranda did not want to contain her desire any longer. She had to burn off her excess energy and could not think of no better way to do it. He deepened the kiss, but Miranda wanted more.

They quickly shed their clothing and Sammuel lay on his back. This time she would ride him. Miranda straddled his hips and brought him into her body slowly at first. She could kiss and cuddle with him when she was spent. Right now, Miranda wanted him so deeply inside her she could feel him touch her core. Her need was too great to continue at the slow pace she originally set. There would be other opportunities to savor what she felt. For now, she wanted to release her passion.

She rode him fast and hard, setting a pace that no human would be able to withstand. There were advantages to being an elemental. Miranda drove herself to the brink, barely able to breathe. She wanted to reach that point where he would breathe for her and control her heart rate, the point they were once again one.

Finally, Miranda reached the point she sought, only to climax within an instant of reaching that perfect state. She cried out as the tremors of the orgasm overtook her. Sammuel's cries harmonized with her own.

Sammuel withdrew from her and he brought her down to lie beside him on the softest grass she had ever encountered. She ran her fingers over the silky, thick grass. Under her touch, it grew softer, yet thicker.

"The grass was not originally like this," Sammuel said. He must have noticed her obsession with the lawn. "When we made love it became so thick it was almost like lying on a mattress. Those flowers were also not there before, either."

Miranda turned to see a small bed of tulips, daffodils, lilies, and irises. They were a multitude of different colors. It was a beautiful sight. Her element had rewarded her with a perfect spot to love her mate.

"I do not want to leave this spot and desire to make love to you again," Sammuel said, "but I want to make it to Lorenz's before the sun sets. We should be there when Patrice arrives to welcome her and have already picked out the perfect set of rooms for her. The Creator gave me hope today that Patrice has a future other than spending the rest of her days as a vampire."

How could she not love a man who cared so deeply for his child? She assumed that one day she would be able to bear him an elemental child. They would produce a family he would not be able to lose.

CHAPTER 24

They had been at Lorenz's settlement for a week and there had been no sign of Shirl. Jace had been driving them crazy, anxious to find and confront Portia. The women were asked countless questions about his mate. They had spent hours with Portia while she was in her human form. Frazour also tried to fill in any missing gaps in regards to the shifter's past. Sammuel could not help but wonder how Callum was going to take all of this.

Jace hung around for Patrice's benefit. Patrice wanted to talk to the crystal telepath about the worlds outside the Nightshade dimension. Somewhere out there, Patrice's soul mate lived. Her mate was a mortal being and capable of dying, so time was critical.

Miranda had done everything in her power to distract Sammuel from worrying about his daughter. She had become insatiable, incessantly demanding they make love. They continually strived for that moment when they were one, complete. His once timid soul mate had become a sex goddess.

Once again they were in the main hall, awaiting Shirl's return. He was relieved when a portal finally opened and a small army of telepathic beings entered their universe. To his surprise the last to enter was Beatrice. Miranda screamed with joy and ran to her younger sister.

He barely recognized the young girl. Her skin was tan, her hair had lightened with exposure to the sun, she had gained weight, and she had a huge smile plastered across her face. Beatrice was truly happy and talking a mile a minute.

Cassie Jarlyn came up to them and embraced Miranda. "I thought you would enjoy seeing your sister. When we met, she said you demanded we be friends, so I better be her friend. Your sister is a real firecracker. She has adapted very well in the community. A family who lost their daughter has adopted her."

Miranda's friend spoke so quickly, Sammuel had problems understanding her. His soul mate on the other hand had no issues comprehending what Cassie said. She was laughing so hard, tears rolled down her cheeks — tears of happiness for her sister, as well as, hearing of her sister's antics in the parallel dimension. Beatrice was free and able to get into all sorts of harmless trouble.

The crystal telepath stood next to a short woman with light auburn hair. He would have barely noticed her had Drake not been on his knees embracing her midsection. This must be the Alexandra, Drake continually talked about.

He needed to introduce Patrice to Shirl and discuss what The Creator had told them. Sammuel believed the crystal telepath was the key to his daughter's future happiness. Miranda, Cassie, and Beatrice were in the midst of a discussion, so he did not bother to inform his mate he was leaving her side.

Patrice stood outside the group, staring at Shirl. She knew exactly who Shirl was and what she was capable of. He had met the woman before and felt comfortable introducing her to his daughter without delay.

Sammuel came up to his daughter and embraced her. "Are you ready to meet the woman who can navigate inter-dimensional portals with her mind? The man standing next to her, guarding her like a rare gem, is her soul mate, Starc."

"He reminds me of Frazour." Patrice laughed. "Well, at least that expression on his face. Starc's dark blond hair, height, and build do not resemble your blood brother's dark, powerful, terrifying presence."

On the rare occasions they were together, Patrice always had an odd fascination with his blood brother. The wild nature of Patrice recognized Frazour's dark side. Sammuel could only hope her soul mate would reflect his daughter's once lighter personality. It had been so long since he had seen it.

"Come on," Sammuel said, taking his daughter's hand. Together they approached the tall blond woman. "Shirl, this is my daughter, Patrice. I turned her into a vampire three thousand years ago. The

Creator told us her soul mate is in another dimension. With him, she will be able to transform into an elemental."

Shirl looked stunned. He was not sure if it was because of the time period he had mentioned, the fact his daughter was a vampire, or that there was a man in the vast expanse of infinite dimensions that needed to be found.

"It is nice to meet you, Patrice," Starc said. "Obviously, my mate needs a moment to gather her thoughts."

Telepathic soul mates' psychic bonds did not seem too different from their elemental soul mates in relation to the bond between them. Although, they were not immortals, they were able to unlock the next evolutionary level of their telepathic abilities.

"Wow, three thousand years," Shirl said. "Alex, what was happening on earth around 984BC?"

The woman with the light auburn hair turned. "What? "Um, I'm not sure. The early Iron Age, I think. King David may have been King of the Israelites. You know, of David and Goliath fame."

Sammuel was shocked Shirl had not reacted to the fact his daughter was a vampire. He guessed it really should not be unexpected as his was a world populated by vampires. Shirl had been able to stand up to Drake, which was quite an accomplishment.

"Can you really navigate the portal?" Patrice asked.

Shirl gave his daughter a genuine smile. "Yes, I can. Do you have any information about which dimension your soul mate can be found?"

"Unfortunately, no," his daughter responded.

Sammuel hoped when Jace and Portia mated, The Creator would reappear and he could ask that simple question. It was an impossible task to find one man among countless dimensions. He wished he could ease Patrice's disappointment.

"Sorry about eavesdropping," Alex interjected, "but Star knows who Patrice's soul mate is."

Now it was Sammuel's turn to be speechless. How could a child in the womb have that information? Although, he should not be too surprised, Drake and Star recognized their link as soon as Drake touched Alexandra.

"Who is he and where does he live?" Patrice said. He had never heard such hope and excitement in her voice before.

"Well, that's the part that is hard to explain," Alexandra said. "Star does not talk to me. She sends me feelings, which I translate into words."

"I do not understand how she would know who my soul mate is," Patrice said.

"Let me try to explain," Drake said. "Star is a rare empathic telepath with powerful abilities. She sensed who I was when I first touched her mother. Being around us before and after we mate, Star has been able to pick up a frequency we emit. It is similar to how Shirl navigates the portal. Star sensed that particular tone in a male Alexandra has encountered, but was unaware a female counterpart was possible."

"Do you know who this man is?" Sammuel asked. He had never heard of such a power, but so many things had come to light once he met his soul mate and the people from the Troyk universe.

"No," Alexandra replied. "I did not even know she was an empathic telepath. Do you know what that is?" Alex turned and asked her mate, who had been standing behind her the whole time.

"There are legends about such people," Tarsea said. "I have never met one or at least anyone who would admit to having such power. We need to keep this information between us and not share it, for Star's protection. My daughter, who has not even been born yet, faces numerous dangers. I do not like it. We will discuss this when we return home, Alexandra."

Drake stood and confronted his mate's father. "I have an agreement with Benko Jarlyn. Do not attempt to interfere with me and my soul mate."

Shirl placed herself between the two men. A courageous woman. "Let us focus on one problem at a time. Is there any way to find out who Star has identified as Patrice's mate? Did you pick up any strange vibes when you were near other men?"

Alexandra looked at Tarsea and swallowed hard. "I only have eyes for you, Tarsea, but there is no harm in looking. Right? When I see another man, it's natural to think, 'oh he's cute' or 'what a body'. Yes, I pick things up from Star, but I can't decipher what she's feeling. It could be her empathic power. Now that I know he's out there, it will be easier to narrow down who it might be. Since becoming aware of Star, I have only been in the Troyk universe, the penal colony, and the Nightshade dimension. So, he is in one of those worlds."

"Thank you," Patrice said.

His daughter stepped forward to hug Alexandra, but her soul mate's glare stopped her cold. Sammuel could not fault Tarsea for wanting to protect Alexandra from any perceived threat. If Sammuel had been in the same position, he would have reacted the same way had any vampire approached a human Miranda.

These people had brought his mate joy and his daughter hope. There was little else he would have wished for. He thought of Tanya. If she had held on a little longer, there would have been hope for her as well. Sammuel wished his daughter would concentrate on what she had to look forward to and not start thinking about all Tanya had lost.

Miranda stretched out next to Sammuel. Their lovemaking becoming more intense each time they were together, and that period of perfect connection lasted a little longer. Today was a near perfect day, something she never before believed possible.

Sammuel had made her wish a reality, with the help from a crystal telepath from another dimension. Beatrice had found a home where she was safe, loved, and taken care of. Now that same woman held the ability to bring Patrice and her mate together, once he was identified.

"You asked me once what I wanted and you made it a reality," Miranda said. "What do you want?"

Sammuel placed his thumb under her chin and lifted her face so she could see him. "I have everything I could ever desire right here; and today I learned Patrice will have a future. There is nothing more I could wish for."

"Perhaps another child, one day?" Miranda asked. "One who will not be in danger of dying in a raid, but a powerful elemental in his or her own right."

"If that comes to pass, I will welcome our child into my heart," Sammuel said. "But do not mistake my answer as a failure on either of our parts if it does not happen. I imagine a child between two immortal beings is a rarity. How else would the population be controlled?"

In just over a moon's cycle, Miranda's life had changed dramatically. She had a man she loved, a group of friends, and a new home she could not wait to see again. Sammuel had promised to show her the ocean when they returned to Stone Meadow. Her future was now as vast as the ocean she longed to see.

The End

*Enjoy the first chapter of the book that introduced
the Nightshade Universe.*

THE CRYSTAL TELEPATH

WORLDS APART SERIES: BOOK TWO

CHAPTER 1

SEDONA, ARIZONA

She exited the car, so weak she could barely close the door. The remnants of the second migraine this week had left her feeling lethargic. Shirl Tomlinson knew she had to power through, regardless of how dreadful she was feeling. Her best friend, Alexandra Mann, had been missing for almost a week. As she walked to the front of the Sedona Police Department headquarters, she was oblivious to the beauty of the surrounding area. Several people exiting the building made way for Shirl as she entered. She barely noticed their presence or the way the men perused her body. She was too sick to care.

For a relatively small town, the place was extremely busy. Barely able to stand, she staggered toward the front desk. She had to dodge a number of officers; otherwise, she would have ended up flat on her face on the marble floor. The man who stood behind the counter saw her distress and made his way around the restricted area to aid her. The artificial light was so bright, she had to squint her eyes as she watched him approach.

"Miss Tomlinson, are you all right?" the concerned officer asked. Shirl wished she could remember the young officer's name. He was wearing a name badge, but her vision was blurry and she could not make out the letters. She just wanted to crawl into the corner and fall into a deep, painless sleep.

"I am recovering from a migraine and I am not feeling quite right," she said. One severe headache after another had tapped her strength. She did not know how much more she was going to be able to take. Having only minimal health insurance coverage, her options were limited in her quest to find what was wrong with her. Every doctor she saw scratched their heads, baffled by the escalation at the severity and frequency of the headaches she had been suffering the past two years.

"I'll get Commander Lewis. He will give you an update on our efforts to find your friend." The officer took a couple of steps and then asked over his shoulder, "Can I get you any water?"

Shirl shook her head. She had taken medication before she left the hotel room. Everyone in the Sedona Police Department knew her by now. She arrived on Monday, as soon as she was able to drive. Alex had been missing since last Friday. For three full days, the police station had been her home away from home.

She sat on the bench, clasping the crystals that hung around her neck. As each day ended with no sign of Alex, Shirl got more frantic, fearing she would never see her friend again. What would she do without Alex in her life? They had grown up together in a Phoenix orphanage. Whenever anything went wrong, she always ran to Alex for help. Although Alex was two years younger, Alex was always the responsible one.

Commander Lewis appeared and sat next to Shirl. He was a good looking man, probably in his late thirties. The man was also tall. Generally, she had to look up at him when they talked, she liked that. For some odd reason, she did not trust men she had to look down upon. She knew that was stupid, but that was how she felt.

Lewis was the second highest ranking police officer in the department, under the chief of police. Shirl could see from the expression on his face, he did not have good news to share. At least they hadn't found a body. The last two nights Shirl had woken in a cold sweat, dreaming she'd been taken to the morgue to identify Alex's corpse.

"I don't know what to tell you, Miss Tomlinson. There have been no sightings of your friend. We know she checked into her hotel Friday afternoon and was not seen again. Her car was found in a parking lot near Boynton Canyon. We believe she went hiking, but there are no signs of foul play. We have had men up and down that canyon looking for Alexandra. There was a part of the trail that looked like someone was dragged for ten feet or so, but there is no evidence she fell. Why don't you head home? I'll call you if we discover anything."

Shirl felt tears falling down her cheeks and reached into her purse for a tissue. "I can't leave here without Alex or knowing what happened to her." People did not just disappear off the face of the Earth. Sedona seemed an unlikely place for human trafficking. A new age cult, perhaps, but Alex wasn't the type.

"Can I at least take you to dinner? You look terrible." Shirl had to smile at Commander Lewis's comment. Men usually fawned over her. It was nice to have a man be honest with her about her appearance. He was a no nonsense guy, saying what was on his mind.

She didn't feel threatened by him. Commander Lewis was the type of man to drag his wife along, eliminating any type of impropriety. It would be nice to get her mind off Alex, even for one meal. "That would be nice. I can't remember the last time I ate." She had a couple of power bars in her car, but hadn't been able to stomach the idea of eating them.

"Why don't I pick you up tonight in your hotel lobby after I get off, around seven." The seasoned police officer knew this meet-up location would be non-threatening compared to meeting her at her hotel room. "My wife Carol will meet us at the restaurant." Yup, she called that one right!

"I guess at this point, I should at least ask your first name," Shirl said. "It would be weird calling your wife Carol while calling you Commander Lewis."

"Frank, my first name is Frank."

Commander Lewis patted her hand and returned to work. She watched as he crossed into the restricted area behind the front desk. A large clock displayed three o'clock. She had four hours to kill before he would pick her up. There was no sense staying on the hard bench. She could get an update at dinner tonight. Besides, they had her cell phone number if they found Alex in the meantime.

Shirl walked to her car and sat behind the wheel for a while, not sure where she wanted to go. The medication had kicked in and she felt a little better.

She started toward Boynton Canyon. Shirl rarely went hiking with Alex. She didn't like the dust that covered her on the few occasions she went. Alex didn't make a big deal out of having to go alone.

Generally, their friend Candy was along and she would hike with Alex. Candy had grown up in the orphanage with them. It was hard not calling her to join Shirl in Sedona while she waited for news of Alex. Candy was a high school coach and her team had just returned from a tournament. She hadn't even told Candy that Alex was missing. Shirl didn't want to worry her friend in case Alex reappeared. That possibility continued to slip away.

When she arrived, the parking lot was relatively empty. Alex's disappearance had been all over the local newspapers. People were shying away from this particular trail, afraid a wild animal had attacked her friend. There was no evidence to support the claim, but that did not stop the rumor mill from spreading that story.

Boynton Canyon was beautiful with its deep red rocks. Shirl had always been fascinated by this place. It was one of the four vortexes Sedona was famous for. The energy emitted by the vortexes always renewed her.

These sites were believed to be multiple dimensional pathways emitting spiraling spiritual energy. Shirl soaked up any article on the subject as well as anything dealing with mystical powers.

One of the few items she had from her birth mother was an amethyst crystal that started her fascination with crystals and healing stones. She wore four to five crystals a day, depending on her mood. Her mother's amethyst was the only crystal she wore constantly. It seemed to balance her in some odd way. Shirl felt less alone, like having family close by. She knew it was stupid, but maybe one day it would lead her to some discovery of who she was meant to be.

Curiosity about the section of the trail with the drag mark Commander Lewis mentioned got the better of Shirl. Grabbing a power bar, she started toward the trailhead. She'd walk the path Alex had taken when she disappeared. If she got too dusty, she'd take a shower before Frank picked her up for dinner.

She walked slowly, conserving what strength she had. Between nibbling on the nutrition bar, the medication, and the vortex's energy, she felt vitality coursing through her body. As she walked the trail, she held onto her crystals, trying to channel Alex. She was not expecting anything to happen, then her mother's amethyst started to glow.

Shirl held the crystal in front of her and stared at it in wonder. As much as she knew about crystals, she had never read anything about them glowing. She felt a slight pull and stopped.

The air ahead shimmered and she felt the continued emission of energy. Slowly, she approached the anomaly. She could see the trail on the other side of the air displacement.

Shirl looked down and noticed the dirt and foliage along the path looked as if something had been dragged along it. It ended right in front of what she could only think was an event horizon. Alex must have been pulled through the point of no return. The gravitational pull would have been so great, Alex would not have been able to escape from it.

Taking a deep breath, Shirl walked into the unknown.

Inside a black void, she felt as if falling. Twisting and turning, she had no control. Deafening, high-pitched sound pierced her ears. Her crystal glowed brighter.

Terror taking hold, she attempted to grab her crystal necklace. After her second attempt at regaining use of her flailing arms, she secured the amethyst in her hand.

Just short of all-out panic, she started to think about home. It worked for Dorothy in Oz, allowing her and Toto to return to Kansas.

She crashed against the ground, out of the portal's grasp. Shirl slowly climbed to her feet and realized she was no longer in Sedona. It must have been a portal to another dimension. That could be the only explanation why she was no longer on the trail surrounded by red rocks and dirt.

She stood on a mountain path, overlooking a city built of pale stone. The community was abloom with purple flowering trees and plants. The violet sky must be a result of the colored pollen emitted.

Shirl was surprised her mind was reacting rationally, although she was still a little dazed. Her normal reaction would have been to panic. Instead, she took in her surroundings and making scientific assumptions. She could not remember the last time she had thought so clearly. There was no pain or pressure impacting her brain.

Alexandra was somewhere in this city, she was certain of it. Shirl was not sure how she was going to find her or what type of people she would encounter. But she had to start looking.

She started down the mountain pass, paying close attention to her steps. The trail was steeper than the one in Boynton Canyon. Her sandals were comfortable, but not equipped to traverse the rocky path. She was also a little wobbly from the rough ride within the portal and had eaten no food to speak of for days.

Sweat trickled down her neck. She brushed at the liquid and her hand came back covered in blood. Shirl felt the same trickle on the other side of her neck. She was bleeding from both ears.

Another step. Bright red streamed from her nose. Her shirt collar was soaked with blood. A strong wave of nausea washed over her. She grabbed a tree branch along the trail.

Leaning on the tree did not abate the nausea. She fell to her knees and retched along the side of the trail. With little food and nothing to drink, it was closer to dry heaves.

Voices and footsteps were coming closer. Eyes popping open, she glanced through a red haze. Not only was she bleeding from her ears and nose, blood vessels must have broken in her eyes.

Shirl could hear the two men address her, but could not comprehend what they said. Her ears were buzzing and she could barely concentrate through the nausea that still overwhelmed her. One of the men knelt next to her as she felt herself fall into unconsciousness.

Enjoy the first chapter of the YA Sci-fi adventure

'SELECTED'

ZARATAN TRILOGY: BOOK ONE

THE INVASION

CHAPTER 1

Barrow, Alaska was gone in a blink of an eye. The small town
north of the Arctic Circle had disappeared. Although there
was no rubble or nuclear fallout, the United States pointed
their finger at the Russians. When the same thing happened
to an isolated settlement in Siberia, both governments looked to the
heavens.

With the world in turmoil, everything in Kara Howard's life
turned upside down. She had thought her parents invincible. For
the first time in her life, she saw fear in their eyes. They became
engrossed in their respective jobs as a means to replace abject fear
with a more familiar anxiety. When home together, the family was
glued to the television, expecting all their questions to be answered.
Cable and network news filled their programming by reporting
the same stories, but with slightly different slants to keep their
viewership.

She and her brother, Kyle, attended school as usual, but their class-
rooms were half full. Parents were removing their children to spend
what little time they had left together. Classes were combined since
many of the teachers did not report to work. Everyone tried to create
a sense of normalcy in a world on the brink of unknown destruction.
They failed miserably.

When a third city was destroyed in China, a satellite captured a
beam of light coming from deep space. Its origin was unknown, but
it was proof Earth was being invaded by aliens. People around Kara

were so wrapped up in their own uncertain fates, they did not mourn the Chinese citizens who no longer existed.

A week had come and gone since the attack on Barrow. As far as she knew, the aliens had not contacted any government. Kara joined her father on the couch, his gaze never leaving the television screen. Father and daughter would spend another night sitting together, while he surfed every news channel in search of some explanation for the alien's actions.

He wrapped his arm around Kara. "How are you holding up, baby?" She was the youngest and fourteen, but her father still used the endearment. There was comfort in the name and the way he said it.

"I'm scared, Daddy. Why haven't they told us what they want?" Kara thought it was silly to keep a brave front at this point. The world was panicking, so why shouldn't she?

"I wish I knew."

It must have cost her father a lot to admit not being able to answer her question. She had always gone to him for explanations when she could not find answers on her own. Her father had always been the one she ran to and confided in. There was nothing her father did not know until this point. Regardless, he was still her hero.

They sat in silence as, channel after channel, none of the news anchors could answer her simple question. Heads of state addressed their nations with no concrete explanation given. Radio signals were broadcast into space so the aggressors would know we were aware of their presence and what they had done.

Her mother returned home from work each evening, then locked herself in her bedroom and cried. Kara could not understand how she functioned at work only to return to her family an emotional wreck. Shouldn't she make more of an effort to support her family, rather than the strangers at work? Her father often tried to lure her out of their room, but all he ended up doing was starting an argument. As far as Kara was concerned, her mother should have stayed at work.

Kyle, unable to handle the friction at home, stayed out with his friends most of the time. She had no idea what they did when they were together and Kara figured she didn't want to know. What good were rules and regulations at this point?

On the tenth day, a message was broadcast to the citizens of Earth. Kara was home watching television when the message came through. She had stopped attending school. It seemed senseless to show up for class when only a handful of students and teachers were present. Her parents didn't seem to care either way.

The aliens had hijacked the world's communication networks to share their message with Earth's population. A man with a slight violet tint to his skin appeared. In the background were symbols Kara did not recognize. The set looked odd, like they may be three dimensional, but her flat television did not adequately display the alien cyphers.

One of the images resembled a bolt of lightning on a purple background. The other contained various stripes crossing what appeared to be a planet or a moon. Earth's technology did not seem to adequately handle the telecast. The being stared into the camera and Kara leaned forward in her chair to get closer to the screen.

He appeared to be human, except for his light purple skin. The alien had light brown hair and the camera was too far away to make out the color of his eyes. Even his ears appeared normal.

When he first spoke, all she heard was gibberish; and Kara felt stupid that she had expected him to speak English. A translation finally came through in a tinny monotone, a computer obviously translating his words to the innumerable languages of the Earth's diverse population.

Kara was alone when she learned her possible fate. The visitors wanted human children between the ages of twelve and fifteen. Sixteen-year-old Kyle was safe.

In two days, every child who met the age requirement was required to report to their schools. Children who were home schooled were to attend their local public school. For every child not in attendance, the city they lived in would be destroyed. The aliens had chosen isolated towns to demonstrate their power. This time, they would destroy a city regardless of its population.

She lived in a suburb of Chicago. Just one absent child would dictate the fate of the whole city and the aliens had already proven what they were capable of doing.

Kara's stomach roiled with the news. She ran to the bathroom and threw up the lunch she had eaten an hour earlier. Her hands shook as she turned on the water to brush her teeth. The child that stared back at her from the mirror was white as a ghost.

She fell to the bathroom rug. Curled up like a baby, she cried until she had no tears left. It was hours later when her father finally found her.

Kara awoke the next morning to a deserted house. It was possibly her last day on Earth and she had been abandoned. Tired of feeling sorry for herself, Kara decided to spend the day at her favorite place.

She pulled her bicycle from the garage and peddled to the beach. Rather than taking the steep driveway down to the water, Kara parked her bike in the south parking lot and walked down to the beach. It was a cold and windy day, so she was surprised she was not the only person to seek refuge on the shores of Lake Michigan. The sand was crowded with families spending what little time they had left with their young teenagers.

A feeling of isolation engulfed Kara. She took off her shoes and walked along the shoreline. The water was frigid, but that did not hinder the feeling of peace spreading through her soul. It was why she came here. The beach always made her feel better. Kara wondered, *'If I am one of the selected, will the distant planet have a similar place?'*

She looked up, gazing at the bright sun. There was not a cloud in the sky. No large spaceship was hovering over Chicago like in *Independence Day*. Although she searched the heavens, there was no evidence of the alien presence everyone knew was lurking overhead.

The waves roared to shore. Even Lake Michigan echoed the turmoil of the world's population. Kara sat just past where the water broke onto the flat sandy beach. She closed her eyes and let the sound embrace her. Kara was making a memory. Wherever fate led her, she could always return here in her mind.

"Kara?" A familiar voice broke her concentration.

She turned to see Matt Sparks standing beside her. Normally, she would have been thrilled to see the boy she had a crush on for as long as she could remember. Today, he was just a reminder of all she had to lose.

Matt lived two doors down. He was the blond haired, blue eyed boy of every girl's dream. He was tall and lean, and not too skinny like a lot of boys his age. Kara went to the JV football games to support her neighbor, who was the team's quarterback.

"Hi, Matt," Kara said.

He sat beside her. Together they watched the waves rhythmically pound the sand before their feet. She wondered what was going through Matt's mind. He was fifteen and shared her uncertain fate.

"Are you nervous about tomorrow?" Matt asked. His voice had an unusual tremor to it.

Perhaps he was seeking comfort. Kara knew his parents were going through a bitter divorce. The Sparks' public verbal sparring matches were legendary on the block. Matt was a pawn in his parents' legal battle. He was alone today, like she was.

The odds were she would never see him again. Why not be honest? "I am scared to death I will be chosen. I've been ordinary my whole life. Knowing my luck, tomorrow I will be extra-ordinary."

Matt laughed, a glorious sound. She made another memory. He had the perfect smile and her heart skipped a beat. Matt was not hers to lose, but she felt the loss just the same.

"Special K," Matt said, "wherever you are or whatever you do, it will be special." She loved the name he dubbed her when she was five. "Our parents really suck!"

It was her turn to laugh and she did so until tears ran down her face. The Fates had gifted her with a perfect day after all. She leaned back on her elbows and tilted her head back, her long brown hair pooling onto the sandy beach. The sun's warmth beat on her face, further enhancing her uplifted mood.

"A part of me *wants* to be selected," Matt admitted. "The Earth is so limiting now we know space travel is possible. We will always live in fear of them returning. There has been no discussion about sharing technology. They are here to take, not give."

Kara turned her head to look at Matt. She had not thought of the benefits of being taken, only the disadvantages. Would life on Earth for those left behind go back to normal when the aliens departed?

"I haven't looked at it that way," Kara said. "My thoughts were limited to being forced to leave my friends and family. They destroyed three towns and murdered thousands of people."

"Whose side do you want to be on, Kara?" Matt asked. "How many millions have died in our wars, were victims of genocide, or died from starvation? The way I look at it, they could have shown their strength choosing to destroy Mexico City, Tokyo, or Mumbai."

Kara sighed and fell back on the sand. The sun heated the pulverized shells, their warmth felt great against her back. This discussion was getting too serious. She wanted to laugh with Matt, not dwell on their bleak reality.

He lay next to her. How she wished he would take her hand. Their fates would be sealed tomorrow. Would she ever lie on the shores of Lake Michigan again?

ABOUT THE AUTHOR

When Evelyn Lederman retired from her career as an insurance exec-utive, she cheerfully anticipated the freedom to finally spend as much time reading as she'd always wanted. The twist in her story came when as-yet unwritten characters started cropping up in her thoughts, asking her to tell their stories. Now, she spends her days in Florida on the beach… with her laptop.

She writes adult paranormal romance The Worlds Apart and Nightshade Saga series. In addition, Evelyn also has the first of her Young Adult series, 'Selected', also published. It is the first book in the Zaratan Trilogy series.

Contact her at evelynlauthor@gmail.com and visit her website at www.evelynlederman.com

TITLES BY EVELYN LEDERMAN

Worlds Apart Series

The Chameleon Soul Mate: Book One
The Crystal Telepath: Book Two
The Warrior Woman: Book Three
The Mind Control Telepath: Book Four

Nightshade Saga

Nightshade: Book One
Feral Nightshade: Book Two
Lethal Nightshade: Book Three

Zaratan Trilogy (Young Adult)

Selected

Magic, New Mexico Kindle World Novella

A Touch of Patience

Visit **www.evelynlederman.com/books**
for a list of print and eBook vendors.

www.ingramcontent.com/pod-product-compliance
Lightning Source LLC
Chambersburg PA
CBHW071508170626
46811CB00007B/2771